Once Upon a Princess

CLARE LYDON
HARPER BLISS

OTHER CLARE LYDON BOOKS
The London Romance Series
The All I Want Series
Twice in a Lifetime
Nothing To Lose
The Long Weekend

OTHER HARPER BLISS BOOKS
The Pink Bean Series
The French Kissing Series
In the Distance There Is Light
The Road to You
Far from the World We Know
Seasons of Love
Release the Stars
Once in a Lifetime
At the Water's Edge

Copyright © 2018 by Clare Lydon & Harper Bliss
Cover design by Caroline Manchoulas
Published by Ladylit Publishing – a division of Q.P.S. Projects Limited - Hong Kong
ISBN-13 978-988-78014-5-0
All rights reserved. Unauthorised duplication is prohibited. This is a work of fiction. Any resemblance of characters to actual persons, living or dead, is purely coincidental.
All rights reserved.
No part of this book may be reproduced in any form or by any electronic or mechanical means, including information storage and retrieval systems, without written permission from the author, except for the use of brief quotations in a book review.

To Meghan and Harry.

CHAPTER 1

Olivia Charlton clenched her left fist, a headache beginning to wrap itself around her brain. She could still hear the whir of camera lenses, the shouts of the photographers asking them to turn around, but she didn't look back. They'd posed for 20 minutes and taken questions, and that was as much as the press were getting today. Her smile was broad and her head held high, her hand wrapped around that of Jemima Bradbury, now her fiancée.

It was early May, and the sky was blue and cloudless.

Unlike her mood, where storm clouds were brewing.

It was only when she was through the thick, black wooden gate and into the courtyard of the estate that she dropped Jemima's hand and relaxed her shoulders, blowing out a frustrated sigh.

She still couldn't believe her parents had made her hold a press conference to announce her engagement at such short notice — less than 24 hours. It wasn't their style, which led her to believe they were worried she was going to bolt. They weren't wrong.

When she glanced up, Jemima was flexing her hand, a soft

smile on her face. "Jeez, you nearly broke a bone, you were holding my hand so tight. Anyone would think you didn't want to marry me." She punctuated her statement with a single raised eyebrow. "And what was that answer about the proposal? You could have at least made up a good story, given the press what they wanted. This is a happy occasion, in case you've forgotten."

Jemima cocked her head, her long, blonde hair cascading around her tanned shoulders. She was wearing a specially tailored white skirt and matching top with black trim, and her feet were encased in a pair of pristine white Manolo Blahniks.

"What's the point of a made-up story, Jem?" Olivia raked her fingers through her long conker-brown hair, her shoulders tightening all over again. "You really want to marry me? When you know damn well we don't love each other?"

Call Olivia old-fashioned but she'd always thought that, when she got engaged, she'd be in love with her future bride. It was something her mother couldn't understand, something she kept telling her youngest daughter wasn't important in their circle. "Love comes quite far down life's must-haves, Olivia. I thought, by the age of 33, you would know that."

A soft breeze wafted over her as she stared up at the back of the red-brick Surrey estate, her home for the past three years since she'd come back.

Or her prison, as she often thought.

Jemima laughed, a pained expression settling on her face. "I've tried the love thing, and it didn't work out. It often doesn't." She paused. "It didn't work out for you and Ellie, did it?"

Hearing her ex-girlfriend's name was still like a punch to the gut.

Jemima went on. "And you're not such a bad catch from where I'm standing. You're a princess. Getting the opportunity to marry a royal is one I don't intend to turn down." She sighed and reached out to take her fiancée's hand.

Olivia jumped as they connected. Jemima's palm was sweaty.

"We could be good together, you know that. We've got history." Jemima fluttered her long lashes Olivia's way, in a practised move.

"I'm not sure that's enough." Yet here they were, engaged. She and Jemima had gone out in their early 20s until Olivia had decided on a career in the army rather than one as a socialite. Sure, they still mixed in the same circles and they'd had an ill-advised one-night stand a year ago that Olivia still winced about, but now, her old flame was being thrust into her life once more by royal decree. The trouble was, everyone — including Jemima — was far happier about it than Olivia was.

"The press might be fooled because we make a great-looking couple and that's what they want." Olivia locked her gaze with Jemima's. "But don't you want something more? Do you really want to settle for me?" She wanted Jemima to think hard about what she was getting into, because she had more choice than Olivia. Whereas, in the back of her mind, Olivia had always known an arranged marriage was likely to happen, having seen her sister go through it.

Jemima let out a strangled laugh. "Marrying Princess Olivia, fourth in line to the throne is hardly settling. And we could rub along together just fine. It's not like we hate each other, is it?"

It wasn't, Olivia had to agree. Despite being exes, they'd always got on. She went to kick a stone in the courtyard, but then realised she was wearing 4-inch heels and not her trainers: today, she was a professional princess, not a soldier. She wanted to stuff her hands in her pockets and stalk around the courtyard, but it wasn't so effective in a poppy-red dress and full make-up.

"Think about it, this isn't such a terrible plan," Jemima said, splaying her manicured hands. "Don't you want to settle down, and wouldn't you rather do it with someone who knows your world, understands it and looks good on your arm? Wouldn't that make life just a tiny bit easier?"

Olivia licked her lips, knowing Jemima had a point. But the nagging doubt was still in the back of her mind, and she couldn't let it go. She'd tasted love once with Ellie and she wanted it again.

When she got married, she wanted it to be for real, for life, forever.

And none of those things belonged in the same sentence as Jemima Bradbury.

∾

Her mother's private secretary, Malcolm, came out of the ornately carved door and bowed his bald head before speaking. "The Queen will see you now."

He didn't say another word, but his narrowed gaze told Olivia all she needed: do not cause the Queen any unnecessary trouble because it will be me who has to clear it up.

Olivia gave him a sweet smile as she walked past.

She'd never liked Malcolm.

Her mother — Queen Cordelia to give her full title — was fiddling with her phone when she walked in; her father — Prince Hugo — was reading today's *Times* in his favourite armchair. It was golden, tattered and creaked at every opportunity, but he refused to let Mother re-upholster it and so far, she'd agreed. It was a small victory in the life of her father, one he clung to.

When Olivia cleared her throat, he put the paper down.

The Queen glanced up, then folded her arms across her chest: this was going to be just as hard as Olivia had feared.

She motioned to the soft blue couches in front of the fireplace, and her mother followed. They sat opposite each other. Olivia flexed her toes in her high heels. She'd kept the same clothes on, because she knew her mother would be fully made up and ready for battle. She hadn't been wrong: the Queen was dressed in a figure-hugging grey trouser suit and matching heels, her appearance as sharp as her attitude.

"So, did you watch it?"

Her mother nodded. "We did." She paused, crossing one leg over the other. "You could have smiled more, looked a bit happier." She squinted as the afternoon sunshine hit her face through the leaded palace windows and put a hand up to shield herself. "You looked like you were announcing a funeral, not a wedding."

"Your mother's right." Her father came over to sit next to his wife in his usual black suit and striped tie, his pallor grey. "You didn't look like you wanted to be there."

"Because I *didn't* want to be there, you know that!" Olivia threw both hands in the air: her parents could send her from zero to 100 in seconds. How could they be so calm when they knew this wasn't what she wanted? They'd had the conversation only three nights ago, and they knew where she stood.

"And you know that questions are being asked and you're of a certain age." Her mother's face was icy. "Your sister knew it and got married without a murmur. We're not even making you marry a man—"

"—Big of you." Olivia scowled.

"—It is, actually. You're going to be the first lesbian princess to marry, and Jemima is a good fit for that. If you must marry a woman, it has to be the right kind of woman. This is not just about you, Olivia, this is about being a member of the royal family — you need to settle down. And ever since Ellie, you don't seem to want to try."

Why was everyone bringing up Ellie today? Ellie was in the past, married to another, and Olivia wanted to focus on her future. That may or may not feature love, but she wanted to at least give it a try. To do that, she had to calm down, play it cool. Appealing to her father was her best bet.

"I just wasn't fully prepared for that press conference today — you only told me about it last night. And it felt like we were lying, like they could see through the charade."

Olivia knew it was time she faced up to her royal responsibilities — the clock was ticking — but she hadn't thought it would leave her feeling so... empty. Bereft.

"Nonsense — the press see what they want to see," the Queen replied, clasping her hands on her knees and fixing her daughter with her stare. "Everyone knows you and Jemima have a history, and you look perfect together. Tomorrow's papers will be awash with your pretty, smiling faces. Well, Jemima's at any rate."

"She's really not that bad a compromise, Olivia," her father said, before looking away.

Olivia ground her teeth together: he'd compromised and look where that had got him.

If there was one marriage Olivia didn't want to emulate, it was her parents'.

She wanted a love match, a love that burned bright every day.

She stood and walked to the fireplace, her heels clicking on the polished wooden floors. She stared at the photo of Alexandra holding her as a baby, a proud older sister at the age of six. Alex had done her duty and married Miles, and now they had two children of their own.

Olivia had no desire to emulate their marriage, either.

She turned to her parents, gathering all her courage into a ball and taking a deep breath. "I just need a few weeks to sort my head out. This has thrown me. I know what you want, and I know we agreed, but saying it out loud felt... wrong. Dishonest."

"Welcome to royalty," her father replied, straight-faced.

Olivia shook her head. "I'd like to go away and stay at the Cornish house. Just to clear my head and sort out what I'm really thinking."

"The engagement's been announced now; it's a bit late to run off." Her mother's face was stoic. The Queen didn't do touchy-feely, and she certainly didn't understand her daughter.

"I just need some space, Mother." Olivia pursed her lips. Surely her mother could see that, even if she didn't agree.

"Besides, there aren't any staff at the Cornish house at the moment; we've had to cut costs, show willing," the Queen added. "And what about bodyguards?"

"I don't need staff and I don't need bodyguards — I'm not a teenager anymore," Olivia said. "Plus, it means I can really have some alone time, sort myself out." She paused. "Just two weeks, that's all I'm asking. Then I promise to come home and go through with whatever we agree on."

Now it was the Queen's turn to purse her lips, casting her gaze to the floor, then to her husband.

"I suppose you think we should let her go, seeing as Olivia's always had you wrapped around her little finger."

Her father shrugged. "She's only asking for two weeks, and if that's all she needs to work things out, I say she can go." He looked over at his youngest daughter. "Just don't create a scene, don't let on to people you're there, otherwise the press might suspect something's up. Be discreet, no wild nights or getting drunk in the village pub."

Olivia shook her head, relief flowing through her.

They were letting her go.

"I'm a bit old for that." She couldn't remember the last time she'd been anywhere vaguely near a wild night. "I'll get some glasses and even cut my hair and dye it so I won't be recognised. Nobody will expect a short-haired princess."

"Just don't cut it off too short. Not like when you were in

the army. You looked like a man." The Queen wrinkled her nose.

"I looked like a woman with short hair, Mother; stop being so homophobic."

The Queen stood, pulling herself up to her full five feet ten. She'd always been a towering presence in Olivia's life. "We're letting you go, don't push it. Just make sure you're back here so you can start to approve wedding arrangements in a few weeks." Her voice was clipped, not to be messed with. "I've asked Malcolm to start looking at possible venues and to get guest lists organised." She gave Olivia a stony look. "And remember I want long hair in the wedding photos, so not too short."

"The wedding's three months away."

"Not. Too. Short."

"And no wild parties or I'm sending bodyguards," her father added.

Olivia took a deep breath and pulled back her shoulders. "I promise I'll be good."

CHAPTER 2

Rosie craned her neck and stared into the distance, over the empty tracks. She glanced at her watch. It shouldn't surprise her that the train was late again. She took a deep breath. It wasn't as though the cafe was full of customers waiting for her. She tried to relax her shoulders and have a little moment of mindfulness. You could take mindfulness classes in Otter Bay these days — and yoga, of course. Neither were Rosie's cup of tea.

A hoot sounded in the distance. Her sister wouldn't be arriving too late then. She was glad she no longer had to pretend, if only to herself, that she was practicing mindfulness. Although she could do with a minute or two of clearing her head.

The train approached with a loud rumble, clearing Rosie's brain of any thoughts momentarily. Ah. So, loud noise disturbing the weekday quiet of the Cornish countryside was all Rosie needed to free her mind from thoughts — not some silly mindfulness practice.

Rosie tried to catch a glimpse of Paige through the windows

rolling past, but she couldn't see her. The train screeched to a halt and it took another few seconds before the doors opened.

The first passengers disembarked. Rosie kept a keen eye on them. Knowing Paige, she'd be the last to get off the train. Unless visiting Bristol University had got her so excited, she couldn't wait to repeat all the things she'd already told Rosie on the phone.

Rosie cast her glance down and took her eye off the trickle of people leaving the train only for a split second, when something hit her side.

"I'm so very sorry," a woman said.

"Watch where you're going," Rosie said automatically.

The woman was wearing the exact Paul Smith jacket Rosie had seen in a magazine left by a customer in the cafe just that morning — otherwise she would never have recognised such a fashionable item. Her eyes had watered when she'd seen the price.

"I'm terribly sorry," the woman said again and briefly caught Rosie's gaze before hurrying off.

Just another rich Londoner pushing up the price of everything in Cornwall. Rosie watched the woman scurry off, as though she was late for a very pressing appointment. Maybe she was on her way to a mindfulness class.

Rosie hadn't seen that much of her face, yet the woman looked vaguely familiar.

"Hey." Paige appeared by Rosie's side.

Rosie had been so distracted by the stranger barrelling into her, she hadn't seen Paige get off the train.

"Thanks for picking me up," Paige said. "Saves me a ride on the bus and about an hour of my time."

"No problem." Rosie briefly touched her much younger sister's shoulder. "Taxi Rosie is always available for you."

"Can I have that in writing, please?" Paige said.

They walked to Rosie's battered, old Toyota. She'd got it

second-hand for a few hundred quid from Raymond, the local garage owner, who'd put in extra time to fix it up for her free of charge.

"I'd like to add a clause," Rosie said as they reached the car. "Taxi Rosie is always available to you as long as this luxury vehicle holds up." She shot Paige a smile.

"It better be good for a few more months then." Paige grinned back. "At least until I leave for uni."

They got in. It was good to at least have a laugh at the state of their finances. A split second of relief was better than none.

"Tell me all about Bristol again," Rosie said as she started driving. They had to rely on conversation to break the silence — the car radio had given up the ghost almost a year ago.

As Paige raved about Bristol University and summed up all the reasons she would love to go there, pound signs added up in Rosie's brain. But she'd had the opportunity to go to university — at least for the two years she'd been able to attend — and she'd do anything for Paige to have the same experience, without having to take on a crushing student loan. Even though things were very different now.

If she really wanted Paige to go to uni, maybe Mark & Maude's, the cafe her parents had started a couple of decades ago, had no other prospect than a For Sale sign in the window.

∽

Rosie got the funny feeling in her stomach that she always did when she opened her online banking. The dread in the pit of her stomach that made her want to throw up a little. She longed for the day when she could check the state of her bank account carefree — she was always aware of the exact amount in it, and the number of bills that needed to be paid from said amount.

The profit she'd made on the sale of her parents' house after their untimely death had long run out. She'd used it to cover the arrears in the monthly mortgage payments on the cafe.

On any given month, nothing much was left over in the account after paying rent for the tiny flat she and Paige shared — a considerable downsize from the place they'd lived in next door to the cafe before their landlord had jacked up the rent once again. Rosie couldn't blame him for wanting to turn a higher profit with short-term holiday rentals. If only her cafe could benefit as much from the influx of tourists as well.

But Mark & Maude's was old school, closed before dinner time, and not generically trendy in the way well-off Londoners preferred their eating establishments. And they didn't serve any alcohol. Maybe they should change that. How hard could it be to get a license to sell alcohol? Selling adult beverages had certainly done wonders for other cafes in the village.

Rosie glared at her laptop screen, as if it was the screen's fault that her bank balance was so low. She leaned back in her chair, chastising herself for even opening her online banking. It wasn't as if looking at the numbers would change anything. But she'd hoped the desperation of the situation would spark a magic idea in her brain.

She logged off. No magic spark came. She undid her ponytail and shook her hair loose. She was long overdue a visit to the hairdresser.

Footsteps approached and Paige walked into the living room. *"Bonsoir ma soeur,"* she said in French with the heaviest accent possible. Paige had the same dreams that Rosie had at her age. She wanted to travel the world and learn some other languages in the process. Studying French at uni was the start. "What's for dinner?"

"Whatever you're making," Rosie said. "It's your turn, remember?"

Paige sank into a chair. "Emergency pizza from the freezer it is then."

"At least save your unhealthy eating habits until you're at uni, will you?" Rosie slapped down the lid of her laptop. The bank's website was still open and she didn't want Paige to ask her any money-related questions.

"What will you be eating when I'm away?" Paige cocked her head. "Don't tell me pizza from the freezer won't tempt you then?"

Rosie had a hard time thinking so far ahead — and an equally hard time imagining Paige not living with her anymore. Come September, would she be lonely as well as jobless?

"Quinoa and avocado toast with almonds and chia seeds every day," Rosie joked. She remembered the first time a customer at the cafe had asked if they served quinoa.

"It's not really a Cornish delicacy," Rosie had replied, and pointed at the items they did serve on the menu.

The bell rang and Paige jumped up. "I'll get it," she said.

Rosie stretched her arms above her head while she tried to guess who it was.

"Brace yourself," Paige whispered when she walked back into the living room. "Your ex is here."

"Amy." Rosie groaned. "What does she want?"

Hands on her hips, Paige looked at her as though Rosie had just asked the most stupid question in the world.

"Knock, knock." Amy's voice came from the hallway.

Rosie wanted to shoot her sister a look demanding why on earth she had let Amy in, but Amy was already standing in front of her, so there wasn't much point.

"Hi," Paige said to Amy. "I'll leave you to it." She disappeared into the kitchen. Maybe she would take the time to figure out an alternative menu for dinner.

Amy walked over to Rosie and kissed her on the cheek. She kept her hand on Rosie's upper arm a little longer than was necessary — at least according to Rosie.

"What's up, Rosebud?" Amy asked while she gave Rosie a

once-over. "Although I really like your hair when it's down like that, you look a little glum."

Of course Amy wouldn't for a second consider that it was her turning up unannounced — again — that made Rosie look unhappy.

"You know," Rosie said. "A bit stressed."

Amy shook her head. "You can't go on like this much longer," she said. "And you do have options. You know that."

It was easy for Amy to say. Her parents actually knew how to profit from the new quinoa-eating, novelty-gin-drinking, mindfulness-practicing holiday crowd. They basically owned the local economy and their brand-new cafe was direct competition for Mark & Maude's.

"I don't need your help," Rosie said, shifting her position in the chair. She didn't much feel like inviting Amy to sit, lest she give her the impression she was welcome to stay for a chat — or that she wanted her help.

"Don't be so stubborn. You're only twenty-eight. You have your whole life ahead of you. There are so many things you could do if only you didn't cling to your precious cafe so much." Amy had always been a straight talker. "You could get a job managing one of our cafes just like that." She snapped her fingers. "Think about it, Rosie. A steady salary. No staff to pay. There's something to be said for that kind of security." She lowered her voice. "Especially with a younger sister going to uni."

"Stop meddling with my life. It's none of your business." Rosie tried to hide the agitation in her voice. Amy might be right on some level, but Rosie certainly wasn't going to admit that to her face.

"I care about you." Amy took a step closer again. "You know that."

Rosie was just able to keep from rolling her eyes. She'd

heard that line so many times before. It didn't work on her anymore.

"What are you even doing here, Amy?" Rosie couldn't mask the irritation in her tone this time.

"We're still friends, aren't we?"

Rosie sighed. Not as far as she was concerned. She didn't need friends like Amy. "Paige and I were about to have dinner. It's not really a good time for a friendly chat."

Amy glanced at her in silence for a moment. "Message received loud and clear." She turned around and headed for the door.

Fat chance of that. Rosie followed Amy into the hallway, looking forward to the moment she would slam the door shut behind her.

CHAPTER 3

Her mother hadn't been joking when she said the house had been empty for a while. When Olivia stepped over the threshold, she'd coughed and screwed up her face, before throwing all the windows open — well, the ones she could get open. The aroma of dust, mould and something she couldn't quite pin down — fish, stale oil? — was still lingering hours later, but she hoped her efforts to clean and air the house had gone some way to changing things.

Her sister would have demanded staff to do this; being next in line to the throne, Alexandra thought such things below a royal. Olivia's favourite response to that was to stick her tongue out and give her sister two fingers — it never failed to outrage her, which never failed to make Olivia grin. Having spent eight years in the army and completed two tours of Afghanistan, Olivia wasn't shy about real life, she even quite liked it. So getting the house back in order, restarting the boiler, and descaling the kettle with some vinegar she found under the sink so she could have a cup of coffee that wasn't full of bits — these things didn't faze her.

Now, she stood at the open back door, its once-white frame

in need of a sand-down and repaint. She clutched a mug of instant coffee in her hand, and stared out at the overgrown back garden where the lawn could do with mowing, the shrubs cutting back and the tennis court stood abandoned, weeds no doubt sprouting at the base of the sagging net. That net had always seemed so high when she was a kid, with Alexandra throwing tennis balls at her head. She'd always loved it here; it had always been a great leveller.

Olivia had unpacked the package her housekeeper, Anna, had given her — eggs, milk, cheese, bread, tea bags, coffee, biscuits — but she'd have to go shopping tomorrow. Down to the village, whilst trying to stay incognito. She was pretty sure her shorter, naturally wavy and now dark copper-dyed hair, teamed with her black-rimmed glasses, would do the trick. She normally used hair straighteners as her mother repeatedly told her it looked more classic, but she quite liked the natural look. Maybe she'd keep it when she got back to London. If being a royal meant Olivia had to marry Jemima, she could at least have a hairstyle she wanted, surely? A small victory, like her father's battered armchair.

It was only then Olivia remembered she'd be paying with a credit card that had her name on it. She hadn't thought that one through, had she? She wasn't the party girl she once was, and she wasn't in the pages of *Hello!* or *OK!* magazines half as much as her sister, but still. Olivia Charlton was a recognisable name. She'd have to get the palace to send her fake credit card, the one where she was called Charlie Smith — and in the meantime hope she had enough cash to pay for what she needed.

She smiled as she thought about her alter ego, Charlie Smith. Olivia had a lot of time for Charlie.

An army nickname that had stuck. Freed from the shackles of being in the same country as her family, of what it meant to be a royal, Charlie was the truest version Olivia had ever been of herself. When she'd been with her squadron, an integral part of a team, Olivia — or rather, Charlie — had felt the greatest sense of purpose she'd ever felt in her life. On duty, with her uniform on and important work to do, she was just another soldier, just another woman defending her country, and how she'd loved that. It was what she'd hauled her arse through Sandhurst for, what she'd trained for years to do.

But those days had come to an abrupt end three years ago, when her mother had "put an end to her playtime" as she called it, informing her that now she was 30, it was time to take up her royal duties and be a more active part of royal life. And so Charlie Smith had died, along with her relationship with Ellie, which hadn't been able to withstand the force that was royalty.

Olivia took a slug of her coffee. She didn't think about Ellie much anymore — she couldn't afford to — but she knew she'd had a glimpse of another world with her, a glimpse of real life. Now that her life as a professional royal was laid out for her, she doubted she'd ever have that again. She certainly couldn't imagine Jemima being happy about staying here without staff, about having to make her own coffee, about it being *instant*. Jemima would have thrown a hissy fit. Instant coffee was for plebs, and she wasn't one of those.

Olivia's phone beeping in her pocket interrupted her thoughts, and she put her mug down on the counter and checked the screen. She wasn't surprised when she saw who the text was from.

'You're in Cornwall? Without staff??? You just got engaged! I don't know what you're playing at, but Mummy's not happy, and Jemima was in tears at the club last night. Send her a text at least!'

Olivia rolled her eyes and picked up her coffee again. She'd learned long ago the best way to deal with her sister was to ignore her.

And the only reason Jemima was in tears was probably

because she'd had too many vodka martinis and the bar had run out of Grey Goose.

∼

"That'll be £22.96 please." The woman behind the counter smiled at her, and Olivia handed over £30. She'd found another stash of cash in the house, so she wasn't feeling quite as hard-up as she had been last night; plus, her private secretary was getting her credit card couriered to the house today.

She'd wondered if card payments had made it to this part of Cornwall, but they even had contactless. That hadn't been the case in a lot of shops the last time she'd visited, over five years ago. She thanked the woman, gave her back 10p to buy a reusable carrier bag for her shopping, and strolled out of the village shop, pulling her baseball cap down over her face, which was already adorned with sunglasses.

Twenty minutes out of the house, and so far, nobody had recognised her.

Only another 13 days to keep it up.

This morning the weather wasn't quite sure what it was doing — sunshine or white clouds — but Olivia was already feeling freer, more alive than she had in months. Being away from her family and away from London always did that. Being able to walk down the street without fear of paparazzi or anybody telling her parents where she was and what she was doing was something that was rare in her life. It was something most people took for granted, but to her, it was special, as well as always being far too fleeting.

She walked down the main road of the village, only wide enough for two cars in places, peering into the shop windows. A kitchen shop, sure to be popular with tourists; a surf shop, which she made a note to go back to another day; an old-fashioned butcher with a white counter and two men at the end of it, cleavers in hand — she never saw that in London anymore.

As she was peering in the window of a women's boutique, her stomach rumbled, and she thought of all the shopping in her bag. She'd bought bacon and eggs; she should go back to the house and cook them. But she was quite enjoying being out and about, around other people.

The ring of the boutique's door got her attention, and an older woman with a shock of silver hair smiled at her, pointing at the window display.

"It'd look lovely on you — suit your complexion." She was referring to a beige blouse with red and yellow flowers embroidered down the front. Olivia gave her what she hoped was a civil look. Was the woman mad? That blouse wouldn't look good on anyone, but Olivia was used to thinking that when it came to women's fashion.

"Just looking." She had to get away before the woman engaged her in conversation. She had a feeling she might be there for hours.

The next shop front was a cafe — Mark & Maude's. As if on cue, her stomach rumbled again. Olivia made a snap decision and bustled in, took the seat away from the window and shrugged off her slate-grey jacket, putting her shopping at her feet. She swapped her glasses swiftly, but decided to leave her cap on, just in case. She wasn't quite brave enough to discard it yet.

The cafe had looked cute but tired from the outside, and the inside was the same. The tables and chairs were mismatched and the walls could use a lick of paint, but Olivia appreciated the unique counter, the front adorned with hundreds of retro Coke bottle tops, and the chrome serviette dispensers and 50s sugar shakers on the tables. Whoever Mark or Maude were, they had a love of retro.

A banging on the window caught her attention and when

she looked up, the woman from the boutique was signalling to her through the cafe window. Her hand gestures were either telling Olivia to come back later, or that she wanted Olivia's number.

Jesus.

Olivia gave the woman a pained smile, and then heard laughter approaching.

"Did you make the mistake of looking in Connie's window?"

She glanced up to see a woman around her age grinning at her, her lips glistening with freshly applied gloss. She was dressed simply in a pair of jeans, a fitted black top and some white Converse, and her dark blonde hair was tied back in a ponytail. Where did she know her from? Olivia wracked her brain, and then it came to her — the woman from the train station, the one she'd run into.

She pushed that thought aside, and nodded. "I did — is she this persistent with all her customers?"

Her server let out a cackling laugh that bounced off the cafe's walls. "Every single one. It's a unique sales technique exclusive to Connie."

"She's still in business, so it must work."

"Somehow, it does." The woman stared at her further, narrowing her piercing blue eyes. "You look familiar — have we met before?"

Olivia shook her head. "I don't think so — I'm just visiting from London." She put out her hand. "Ol—Charlie." She coughed to cover up her mistake.

"Rosie," came the reply. Rosie studied her a little more. "You do look familiar." She flicked her biro on the order pad she was holding. "It'll come to me, gimme a minute." A quirk of her eyebrow. "Are you just here for the weekend?"

Olivia shook her head. "A while longer — down from

London, just thought I'd get away for a couple of weeks. Got a few things to sort out."

"You staying local?"

Olivia squirmed in her seat, her foot kicking her bag of shopping. "Yeah, some friends gave me keys to their place."

"Nice to have friends in high places," Rosie said, before pointing at the menu. "Do you know what you want yet? We haven't succumbed to doing smashed avocado which I know you love in London, but we can do you a slap-up full English or even eggs benedict if you like."

"I can live without smashed avocado. When did food prep become so violent?"

Rosie let out another cackle, and Olivia was strangely pleased she was responsible. When Rosie smiled, it lit up her whole face.

"I'll have whatever you recommend. Full English?"

"Perfect choice. All the ingredients are locally sourced, and our cook, Gina, even makes her own ketchup."

"Far more impressive than squashing an avocado into a bit of toast."

"You know what, you're right," Rosie replied. "I like you, Miss London. Tea or coffee?"

"Pot of tea, thanks." Olivia paused. "Is this your place?"

Rosie nodded, a cloud crossing her features before she restored her smile. "It is. It was my parents', and now it's mine."

"I like it a lot." She sensed Rosie needed the compliment. "The counter is especially impressive."

Rosie beamed. "You think? That was me. I've always wanted to go to the US, but never managed it. So I decided to bring some Americana to Otter Bay."

"You've done a great job."

"We'll see," she said, tapping her notepad some more. She stopped, tilted her head, then looked back at Olivia. "That jacket — is it Paul Smith?"

A tingle of embarrassment spread through her. Way to blend in, Olivia. "Yeah, it was a present to myself."

Rosie looked at her again now. "You weren't at the train station yesterday, were you?"

She winced. "I was." *Rumbled.*

"Thought so." Rosie's smile stiffened. "Anyway, full English and a pot of tea coming up." She gave Olivia a final penetrating stare, then turned and walked out of view.

Olivia breathed out as a tingle of something shot through her, heat flaring within.

She wasn't quite sure what had just happened.

What she did know was, staying incognito might be harder than she'd first thought.

CHAPTER 4

Rosie leaned against the counter and glanced at the only customer in her cafe. Charlie had taken off her glasses and put them next to her plate while she hunched over her phone. They obviously weren't reading glasses then. That was the extent of her knowledge about this stranger who had waltzed into Mark & Maude's for the first time three days ago. Strangers represented a big part of the cafe's business, of course, but Rosie found it hard to take her eyes off this particular one. There was something in the way she held herself and in how, every few minutes, she looked up from her phone and stared in Rosie's direction.

Charlie hadn't glanced up in a while. Rosie assumed that whatever she was reading on her phone must be extremely interesting because it had held her attention for much longer than before. Rosie hoped that meant Charlie would give her a good long look next time she cut her gaze in the direction of the counter.

Rosie suppressed a sigh. Did she really not have anything better to do than entertain thoughts like this? Like come up with a cunning plan to pay for Paige's university fees, and have an equally bright idea to help Gina pass her citizenship test.

But no, at the moment, it seemed she had to keep her attention on her only customer, bracing herself for when their eyes would meet again. Charlie was responsible for a small uptick in turnover after all, what with her having shown up for breakfast every day this week.

Ah, there it was. Charlie put her phone down and ran a hand through her short, curly hair. Rosie tried to keep an eye on her whilst at the same time trying not to come across as though she had been spying on Charlie.

Charlie sent her a smile along with a lingering look this time. Rosie smiled back and sprang to attention. She would much rather be summoned by a customer by means of a smile than a dismissive hand wave or, as preferred by a certain kind of people from out of town, a haughty "Waitress!"

Rosie walked over to Charlie's table. "Can I get you anything else?"

"Goodness no." Charlie rubbed her belly, drawing Rosie's glance to it. She looked as though she had one of those annoyingly flat stomachs, even though the woman surely didn't appear to count calories — especially not when eating at the cafe. "You've overfed me once again."

"I do apologise," Rosie said. "Even though it is kind of our unique selling point."

Charlie chuckled. "Well, you did say you wanted to bring some Americana to Otter Bay and you're definitely on point with your portion sizes."

"Thank you." Rosie nodded. "I'm so glad to have met someone who really gets what this place is about." She noticed Charlie's plate wasn't entirely empty.

Charlie must have seen her looking. "It was delicious, by the way," she said. "Please send my compliments to the chef."

Chef. Rosie never really thought of Gina as a chef. Did cafes even have chefs? She didn't think so. "Will do."

"I'm serious," Charlie continued. "There's a reason why I've been coming here for breakfast three days in a row."

Rosie nodded in appreciation. Most people didn't come to Mark & Maude's for the snazzy decor. If it weren't for Gina's magic touch with food, the cafe would probably have been on the edge of going bust much sooner.

"And here I was thinking it was the charming, personable service," Rosie half-joked.

"There's that, of course." Charlie had left a generous tip the previous two times she'd stopped by.

"How about a coffee on the house?" Rosie asked.

Charlie regarded her from under her long, dark lashes. "That would be lovely, although I do have a request to make." She narrowed her eyes. "Only if the owner joins me."

Rosie's lips spread into a smile. "Let me see if that would be possible." She cast a dramatic glance about the otherwise empty cafe. "I wouldn't want to neglect my other clientele."

"Naturally." Charlie played along.

"Looks like the owner has some free time on her hands."

"Lucky me," Charlie said.

Before Rosie turned around to prepare the coffees, she gave Charlie a quick wink.

∼

"My compliments to the maker of this coffee," Charlie said. "The standards in this cafe are impeccably high."

"If there's one thing you can't compromise on, in life as well as in business, it's the quality of the coffee." Rosie sat opposite Charlie, who hadn't put her glasses back on.

"I only have instant back at the house where I'm staying, so this is a real treat," Charlie said.

Rosie let her jaw fall open in an exaggerated fashion. "The blasphemy."

Charlie cast her glance down. "I know," she said, her tone demure.

Rosie spotted someone looking in the cafe window and even though Mark & Maude's could really do with the business, at that moment, she hoped they wouldn't come in. She was having too much fun with Charlie. Thankfully, the front door remained closed.

"You'll just have to stop by here every day then." Rosie tried locking her gaze on Charlie for longer than a split second.

"Invitation accepted." Charlie stared back at her, then looked away. "I'll pay for my beverages, of course."

Rosie waved her off. "I'm just glad for the conversation. Even though we get many of your kind here, I don't make a habit of having coffee with them."

Charlie raised an eyebrow. "*My* kind?"

"No disrespect meant. I love your kind." Rosie hoped the flush she felt creeping up the back of her neck wouldn't make it to her cheeks. What was she rambling on about?

Charlie grinned at her and defused the tension by taking another sip from her coffee.

"You don't seem to need those glasses much," Rosie said, changing the subject. To her dismay, she realised that her comment about Charlie's 'kind' could be taken in more ways than one. Instigating innuendo about Charlie's sexual orientation hadn't been Rosie's intention at all. She could only guess at how Charlie had interpreted it.

"They're new. I'm still getting used to them," Charlie said. "Have you lived here all your life?"

Rosie nodded. "Born and bred in Otter Bay."

Charlie smiled at her. "What a dream."

"Yeah right," Rosie said. Then the front door opened and Aunt Hilary walked in. Rosie looked at her watch. A few regulars would soon come in for lunch and she and her aunt usually worked the lunch service together.

"Hello, Rosie." Hilary walked up to Rosie to give her a quick hug.

"Aunt Hilary, this is Charlie, our newest, most loyal customer."

"Delighted to meet you." Aunt Hilary extended her hand and Rosie witnessed how Charlie shook it in a firm grasp. No limp-wristed handshakes for this posh Londoner.

"And you," Charlie said. "I was just telling Rosie how delicious the food and coffee are here."

With that, Rosie's private chat with Charlie had ended. She looked at her watch again. Charlie would leave the cafe soon and then it would be almost twenty-four hours before Rosie could offer her another coffee on the house. Rosie's days had a tendency to fly by, but after this chat with Charlie, tomorrow still seemed so far away.

She focussed her attention on the conversation between her aunt and Charlie again, ignoring the silly thought that had just flashed through her brain.

Charlie was just someone passing through — here today, gone tomorrow. And although Rosie's gaydar — which didn't get a lot of practice and was anything but finely tuned — was on alert, she shouldn't be looking forward too much to seeing Charlie tomorrow.

CHAPTER 5

Olivia reached the top of the climb from the secluded cove and strode along the sandy path cut into the cliffs — only wide enough for a single person — taking deep breaths of coastal air as she walked, tasting the salt. The sun wasn't out yet, but there was still warmth to the early summer air, the white clouds a blank canvas overhead. Sunshine or not, though, being outside never got old — since she'd come back to royal duties in the capital, she'd spent far too much time indoors. She was headed east on the coastal path today, with the promise of a pub on the beach at the halfway point, where she planned a well-earned drink before the two-hour walk back.

Today felt even more daring, because she'd left her phone back at the house on purpose. If her mother knew, she'd kill her. Heck, if Malcolm knew, he'd kill her, too. A prominent member of the royal family wasn't allowed to just go wandering along clifftops, where the slightest gust of wind could plunge her into the sea — but what they didn't know wouldn't hurt them. Plus, with Charlie's jeans, baseball cap and sunglasses, nobody was ever going to recognise her. She'd bought a bottle of water in the supermarket earlier and had attempted a slight West Country twang. She wasn't altogether sure she'd pulled it off. Olivia's best friend from her army days had relations in this part of the world and had tried to teach her how to say certain phrases, but accents weren't her strong point.

She had a banana and a chocolate bar in her backpack, but her stomach hadn't rumbled yet — and that was all thanks to Rosie, Gina and their delicious breakfasts. They were so filling; she hadn't eaten lunch any day this week, and occasionally had skipped dinner, too. Not only was Rosie's food amazing, the service wasn't bad, either.

Olivia didn't know what it was, but there was something about Rosie she was drawn to. Sure, she was attractive, there was no getting away from that — her hair the colour of dappled sunshine, her electric blue eyes that lingered on Olivia for just a few beats longer than they should. Plus, she had curves in all the right places, and her arms were pleasingly defined from hours of working in her cafe.

However, on top of those physical attributes, Rosie radiated a positivity and a resilience beyond her years — when she was close by, Olivia found it hard to drag her gaze away. She was sure Rosie had caught her looking a few times, but she was trying to be covert about it. The thing was, Rosie couldn't be more than 30, yet she was running her own business and just getting on with life. Olivia knew many 30 year olds, and none of them were doing that — at least, not any she was friends with now.

Even now, just thinking about her, Olivia's pulse ticked up a few beats and her blood raced that little bit faster. She stumbled on the rocky path and almost tripped and fell but saved herself at the last minute. She took a moment to steady herself. Okay, perhaps she shouldn't think about Rosie until she was on more level ground.

Was Rosie a lesbian, too? There were no obvious signs, but

then again, Olivia didn't want to stereotype — she'd met many women in the army whom she'd sworn were lesbians, only for them to then introduce her to their husbands. Where Rosie was concerned, it was just an inkling she had. Or perhaps it was wishful thinking?

However, even as she thought that, she shook her head. What did it matter if Rosie was gay or not? It didn't matter at all. Olivia was just passing through, so nothing could happen. Plus, she was engaged to be married — at least that was the story her family were telling the world — even though she and Jemima weren't in a relationship in any way at all. Jemima was history, but history just kept on repeating, that was the problem in Olivia's life. Just ask Alexandra. If nothing changed, Olivia would be forced to live her own version of Groundhog Day forever.

Rosie, however, wasn't part of her history, and that was the other thing Olivia liked about her. Rosie was a clean slate, she was unknown — and Olivia's only thought whenever she saw her was how much she'd like to change that, and fast.

She kicked the ground as the sandy path began to slope, meandering down to the beach, the rocky terrain green with moss to her right, the rocks and ocean beyond stretching out to her left, grey and white with mellow waves, as if the sea was dozing. She wasn't going to let her predicament get her down today. Rather, she was going to enjoy the rest of the afternoon, safe in the knowledge that nobody knew who she was or where she was.

When she arrived at the pub 20 minutes later, the lunchtime crowd were clearing out, so she took her white wine spritzer onto the massive pine deck built on the sand. She pushed her sunglasses firmly onto her face, angling her head as the sun finally peeked out from behind the clouds. The deck had around 30 tables on it, and the local seagulls weren't being shy about swooping in to help themselves to the remains of lunch. Seeing as some of the creatures were almost as big as her sister's cat, Olivia was glad she wasn't eating.

She'd only been sitting there two minutes when she heard a throat being cleared nearby. When she turned her head, there was Rosie.

Olivia immediately stood up to greet her, then had no idea what to do with her arms. That was the other thing that happened in Rosie's presence: a fine sheen of nervousness broke out all over her skin, momentarily making her lose all control of her limbs and senses. It both unnerved her and thrilled her all at the same time. It hadn't happened since Ellie.

"Long time no see," Olivia said, finally managing to get some words out.

Rosie checked the phone she was holding in her left hand. "What's it been? Three hours?"

"Maybe three and a half."

Rosie gave her a look. "Sounds like you've been counting."

To cover the blush she could feel rising in her cheeks, Olivia held out her hand and motioned for Rosie to sit down.

She did so, putting her phone on the table, quickly followed by her drink.

"What are you on?" Olivia pointed at the reddish-brown liquid in a half-pint glass with a stem.

"Cider. Local Cornish speciality." Rosie nodded at her drink. "Not quite your white wine spritzer." She grinned. "Next time, I'll buy you one."

Olivia smiled: there was going to be a next time. "I'd like that," she said.

Freed from the confines of the cafe, Rosie looked different somehow — more defined, sharper, relaxed. As if when Olivia stared at her, Rosie had been auto-enhanced. On this deck, Rosie was no longer 'Rosie the cafe owner'; she was simply Rosie. If there had been any barriers between them — cafe owner and customer — they were now completely down.

Rosie snagged her sunglasses from her handbag and put them on, before leaning back with a sigh. "It's so lovely to get a shot of vitamin D, especially after today." She swept a hand through her thick locks and Olivia followed it, taking in her smooth fingers, her short nails. Perhaps her thinking wasn't quite so wishful.

"What's happened since I left? I thought you'd still be at the cafe."

Rosie shook her head. "I was. Then my ex showed up and there are only so many times I can tell her I'm not interested." There was a pregnant pause as Rosie realised what she'd said, but she avoided eye contact, ploughing on. "So, when my sister Paige showed up after school and said she'd help Hilary finish up, I thought I'd take the chance to grab a bit of fresh air, you know?"

Olivia nodded: she knew only too well. She also knew she was sucking in her cheeks to try to keep herself from smiling too broadly at the fact that Rosie had confirmed her ex was a woman. Olivia's inkling had proved correct: Rosie liked women. Olivia's heart boomed, but she kept it together.

"What about you?"

Olivia took a sip of her wine as a stalling tactic. She'd love to tell Rosie her woes, how she was being forced into a marriage she didn't want with a woman she didn't love; how Rosie was the most intriguing woman she'd met in a very long time.

But she couldn't.

So she didn't.

"Just making the most of my time here." Olivia took in a lungful of the salt-whipped air and gazed out across the golden sands to the waiting sea. Now the sun was out, the water was a layer of greens and blues, its foam leaving a lace pattern on the sands as it ambled in and out. "I just love being by the sea, it makes me feel calm." That was true — being near Rosie was having the same effect, too.

"Far less hectic than London I'm sure."

Olivia thought of her mother, Jemima, her father. And then she closed her eyes. Not today.

"Way calmer," she agreed. "It also reminds me of happy childhood memories of being by the sea with my parents up in Scotland — I think that was the first time I realised as a kid that travelling outside your normal situation makes you a different person, which is what gave me the travel bug. Although the air in Scotland is different to here — so clean, it makes you feel healthier just being alive. And Scotland makes Otter Bay look hectic. Up there, there are only a few sheep and cows to contend with."

"No seagulls the size of a horse?" Rosie said, as three of them swept onto a nearby table, swiping a chip from a toddler's hand. The boy promptly burst into tears.

"None of them." Olivia paused. "It's also lovely being here and getting away from family and relationship pressures. I've got an ex wanting more from me than I want to give at the moment, and it's not making life easy. She's persistent, and the kicker is my family are in her corner."

At Olivia's admission, Rosie lifted her gaze to meet Olivia's and something shifted low in Olivia's belly. A rumble of something long forgotten. A feeling, a longing, a want. Her neck muscles stiffened as emotion trampled through her like a thoroughbred whose reins she was trying to keep hold of. It felt like something had shifted, but that was stupid. Because, even if Rosie had no intention of going back to her ex, Olivia's situation was very different.

"At least your family like your ex," Rosie said, before shaking her head. "I mean, Amy's not terrible, but she's just a bit too much sometimes. And she needs to get the message. I've tried subtlety, but everyone in the village just thinks we'll end up together, seeing as we're the only two lesbians who live here." Rosie gave a resigned smile. "That's the trouble living in a small town — the choices aren't dazzling, and Otter Bay is not a favourite lesbian holiday destination."

"It is from where I'm sitting," Olivia replied, a sudden confidence flooding her. "And for what it's worth, if you're on the market, the lesbians don't know what they're missing."

Once the words were out, Olivia didn't know where to look, or even where they'd come from. When had she turned into such a smooth talker? After a few beats, she risked a look at Rosie, but, far from looking put out, Olivia only spied warmth in her eyes.

"Thank you," Rosie replied, leaning forward and putting a hand on Olivia's arm. "Whether you meant it or not, I needed that today."

Rosie's touch sent Olivia's pulse into orbit. She was glad Rosie's ex had come in today, because the domino effect had led Rosie to this pub and to her. "Let's just say this lesbian is glad she ran into you." She held Rosie's gaze. "You've brightened my first week here to no end, and I hope you stick around for the next."

Rosie gave her a crooked smile. "I'm not going anywhere."

Olivia held up her drink. "Then here's to us and week two."

CHAPTER 6

Rosie unlocked the door and their tortoiseshell cat, Cher, greeted her enthusiastically as always, after which she broke into a high-pitched offended-sounding meow, as though she hadn't eaten in days.

"Have you fed Cher?" Rosie yelled. Their flat was so small, Paige would be able to hear her from whichever room she was in.

Rosie walked into the living room and found Paige tucked under a blanket in the sofa.

"When have I ever come home from school and not fed the cat?" Paige sounded almost as offended as Cher's meow earlier. The cat kept pushing herself against Rosie's shins. "Would I even be sitting on this sofa, looking this relaxed, if I had not fed the cat?" Paige shook her head. "She would never allow it." She tapped her hands on the blanket and called for Cher to come sit in her lap. The cat obeyed. She had the uncanny ability of displaying very dog-like behaviour.

Their Aunt Hilary had given them Cher five years ago, when she was still a kitten and Paige had been going through a phase of desperately wanting a puppy. It was hard to deny her sister, who had already lost so much at such a young age, and the cat had been the perfect compromise.

"Sorry." Rosie dropped her bag on a chair and sat on the sofa. "How was your day?"

Cher had turned her meows into some heavy purring and pushed her furry head into Paige's hand. "Same as always," Paige shrugged. "Boring teachers and annoying boys."

Rosie chuckled and glanced at her sister and the cat in her lap. How could it be that this girl would be going off to university soon? The past eight years, Rosie had often had to be more like a mother to Paige than an older sister. Paige was only ten when their parents had died so suddenly. She and her sister had ended up close but, nevertheless, Rosie'd had to deal with the inevitable hormonal tantrums that came with living with a teenager.

But Paige was no longer a girl. She'd had to grow up much faster than most of the kids her age and it showed. It made perfect sense she'd be leaving for uni come September. If Rosie found the money to pay for it, which she had to do sooner rather than later.

"How was your day?" Paige asked. Cher looked up and glanced at Rosie as though she too wanted to know the answer to that question.

"It was quite busy, actually." She remembered Charlie sitting at what had become her regular table away from the window. Rosie had been run off her feet for the better part of Charlie's stay and hadn't been able to chat with her, even though she'd been looking forward to it. "There's this new customer. A woman," Rosie said.

Paige arched up her eyebrows. Cher no longer seemed interested in the conversation. "Someone from London who's staying in the area for a few weeks. She's come to the cafe every day this week. She's rather… nice."

"Nice?" Paige sat up a bit. "What does that mean?"

"You know, much more polite and courteous than most. Very sure of herself. Witty." Rosie had long forgiven Charlie for rudely bumping into her at the train station when she first arrived. She might be a rich Londoner who wore fancy jackets but she didn't behave like one.

"I know other women who are very sure of themselves. One in particular," Paige said. She nodded her head in the direction of the flowers that stood in a vase on the table.

Rosie sighed. "That's not self-assuredness," she said. "That's just plain old desperation."

"At least Amy's predictable and consistent. And, judging by the amount of flowers she sends you, she has many, many feelings for you," Paige said, a smirk on her face.

"Those feelings stopped being mutual when her parents opened their new cafe."

"Come on, Rosie. That was just business. You can't blame Amy for that."

"I guess not." Rosie shook her head. "There are other issues with Amy. For starters, she clearly lacks imagination if she thinks sending me flowers every week is going to change my mind about her." She huffed out some air. "We're just not right for each other, and that's without running competing local businesses." Rosie reached over and petted Cher on the head. She needed to feel something soft and soothing. "She's just as pushy as her parents."

"You'll just have to wait for another woman of your inclination to pass through Otter Bay." Paige smiled at her.

Like Charlie, Rosie thought, a flutter rising in her belly. She shook the thought from her mind and refocussed her attention on her sister.

"Summer's coming, and with it the lesbians will flock, as they do every year," Rosie joked. She should be so lucky.

The bell rang. Rosie momentarily stiffened. She hoped it wasn't Amy. Cher raised her head at the intrusive noise. Rosie got up to open the door and found Aunt Hilary standing in the doorway.

Relief washed over Rosie. Not only because it wasn't Amy turning up unannounced again, but also because Aunt Hilary would be bringing food.

"Dinner's here," Aunt Hilary said as she beamed Rosie a wide smile.

At the sound of the door opening, Cher had jumped out of Paige's lap and circled around them in the hallway, eternally hopeful of getting more food.

"Let me take that from you." Rosie kissed her aunt on the cheek and took the hefty Tupperware container from her. So often she wondered what she would have done without Aunt Hilary.

Aunt Hilary had tried to persuade her not to come back to Otter Bay after her parents' death, but instead finish her last year of university. But not being near Paige after losing their mum and dad had been inconceivable to Rosie. And how was she expected to study after her whole world had been shattered?

Aunt Hilary picked up Cher and, as usual, told her she was the prettiest cat not just in Cornwall, but in the whole wide world.

Paige started setting the table and ten minutes later the three of them were eating Aunt Hilary's delicious sausage and bean casserole.

"If Gina fails her citizenship test again, you should take her place," Rosie said. "Your food is so scrumptious and comforting."

Aunt Hilary waved her off. "I'm a bit over the hill for working in a kitchen, dear." Then she looked Rosie in the eye. "I'm sure Gina will pass. She's a brilliant woman. How can she possibly fail?"

"It's the written test she keeps failing. She's good with all the rest because she is, indeed, brilliant. I'd hate to lose her over a stupid test like that. She's taken it four times already. And she even has family in the UK." Rosie all but threw her hands in the air in desperation.

"That's just ridiculous," Aunt Hilary said. She looked at Rosie again. "Is that what's been worrying you? I've seen you look better." She put down her fork. "Or is it the time of year?"

Rosie tried to make eyes at Hilary and have her stop this line of conversation in front of Paige.

"Eight years next week," Paige said, reminding Rosie, once again, that she wasn't a little girl anymore.

Aunt Hilary nodded slowly. "If only Maude and Mark could see you now." There was a slight wobble in her voice. "They would be so proud of the two of you."

Aunt Hilary didn't know the extent of trouble the cafe was in — and had no clue of the cost of a university education these days.

"Should we do something?" Paige asked, sounding much more mature than her eighteen years. "To commemorate?"

When Rosie thought of herself as an eighteen-year-old, she remembered a much more carefree person than her sister. Life had handed them both a tough deal, and the past decade had been a real struggle, but at least Rosie had been twenty when she'd heard the news of the crash, Paige had only been ten.

Rosie might not have graduated from university, but she was damned proud of the kind of eighteen-year-old her sister had turned out to be. It could have gone in so many directions. But Rosie had come back to take care of her sister and keep their parents' cafe going. She'd done a damn good job of raising Paige and, despite the cafe's current cash flow problem, she could at least hand herself that one.

"We could do something," Aunt Hilary said, as she did every year. Losing her sister and her brother-in-law had been equally hard on her and she'd never been one to mark the occasion.

She'd bestowed plenty of warmth on Rosie and Paige when they needed a more adult shoulder to cry on, mainly in the shape of home-made casseroles and dealing with the avalanche of administration that comes with the sudden death of two family members, but she wasn't one to display too many emotions, not even in front of her nieces — her saying she was proud of them was not an everyday occurrence.

"It's not because it's the anniversary that we have to do something special to remember them," Rosie said. "I think about them every day. I go to the cemetery at least once a week." Actually, Rosie hadn't gone yet this week and she suddenly remembered that she'd missed the previous week's walk there as well.

Then Cher jumped on the table and all three of them reacted instantly by shooing her off.

"That cat has such bad manners," Aunt Hilary said.

"Paige spoils her too much," Rosie said matter-of-factly. It was nothing but the truth. She was also glad that Cher's appearance on the table had steered the conversation away from the subject of the anniversary of her parents' death.

Cher sat on the rug licking a paw, looking all innocent.

"If only I could take her with me to uni," Paige said.

"What? And leave me *all* alone?" Rosie said, putting on a faux-pathetic tone.

"I'll be here for you." Aunt Hilary briefly put a hand on Rosie's shoulder.

Rosie shot her aunt a smile. She wondered if, with Paige leaving in a few months' time, it might be time for her to leave as well. Sell the cafe and simply leave Otter Bay behind. Apart from Aunt Hilary, she had no family here. She could travel to Southeast Asia where backpackers could survive on a few pounds per day — at least she'd read that on one of the travel blogs she followed when she felt like dreaming up a different life. She and Amy were over, so love was hardly keeping her in this village either — if whatever they'd had between them had even been love.

Rosie glanced at the spot on her arm where Aunt Hilary had just touched her. She'd stay for her aunt, of course. And for Cher. And to give Paige a home to come back to during breaks.

"You'd better treat Cher like the princess she is," Paige said. "She'll have a hard time enough as it is getting over me no longer being here."

Her and me both, Rosie thought.

CHAPTER 7

Jemima's texts were becoming more frequent and more terse; every time Olivia read one, she wanted to crush her phone.

Apparently, people were starting to wonder where she'd disappeared to. Olivia wished she had her horse with her — a ride would do wonders for her stress levels.

She knew Jemima would find it hard to believe that Olivia would announce her engagement to the world and then run out on it, but Olivia wasn't the woman she'd been when they'd gone out in their early 20s. Then, she'd been christened the Party Princess by the tabloids, and when she was 22, marrying Jemima Bradbury wouldn't have been such a terrible proposition. After all, she had the looks, which was all Olivia had cared about. However, over a decade later, things had changed, but even Olivia knew wriggling out of a royal romance the press were already speculating over wouldn't be so easy. The likely guests and possible locations were already being debated daily.

She'd been on the Cornish coast for two weeks — her allotted time — but her father had approved seven more days, much to her mother's chagrin. According to a text from her sister, Grandma had waded in on Olivia's behalf, for which she was thankful. Her grandmother, just like her father, always had her back.

Now she had an extra seven days, she was determined to make the most of them. Namely, she was going to eat in Rosie's cafe every day, and if she was lucky, time her visits to coincide with Rosie's breaks so they could sit and chat. Because in her time here, seeing Rosie and eating her delicious food had quickly become the highlight of Olivia's day.

Somehow, in Rosie's presence, she relaxed and could be herself — or at least, Charlie. She chatted freely, glossing over the finer details of her life, happy to listen to Rosie's news. She'd met Rosie's Aunt Hilary, her sister Paige and she was warmed by their connection, the easy bond they all shared. Rosie's parents were no longer here, and she hadn't probed for details, sensing it was a sensitive subject. But she knew now that the cafe was named after them, and she knew their daughter was a woman she wanted to be around. Rosie was everything Jemima was not: funny, plucky, real. And also, as luck would have it, gay. With every passing day Olivia was dreading leaving this reality and heading back to her royal bubble.

This was brought home to her this morning as she strolled along the Cornish clifftops again, the sea a shimmering carpet of blue to her left. The salty air tickled her nose, the sun drenched her back and as she cast a glance up the incline, she saw a mass of gravestones lined up to her right; neat rows of local history, all with a prime sea view. She bit her lip and took a deep breath; cemeteries always had a pull for her, reading the story of other people's lives. But since Afghanistan and the many friends she'd lost there, they held extra meaning. She'd avoided going in so far, but today, her feet took her there.

The first stone she came across was for a woman named Eleanor, who'd only made it to 23, hardly any age. The next belonged to Arthur Brown, who'd lived till 54, dying in 1926. It was only when she cast her gaze along the row that she noticed a familiar figure sat on the side of a raised white marble stone, arranging flowers on the well-kept plot.

Rosie.

It was clearly a private moment, so Olivia approached with caution, stuffing her hands in the pockets of her skinny jeans. When she was in earshot, she went to say something; however, clearly sensing someone nearby, Rosie turned before she got any words out.

Seeing her, she dropped the yellow rose she was holding and stood, brushing down the front of her red trousers, straightening her sky-blue T-shirt that showcased her full breasts perfectly.

Olivia blinked, pushed that thought aside and gave Rosie a smile. "Sorry, I was just having a look around the place — I didn't mean to interrupt."

Rosie sniffed and wiped her eyes. "You didn't." She shook her head slowly, letting her eyelids flicker shut. "It's just... this is my parents' grave. And today is the eighth anniversary of their death." She sighed. "This time of year is always hard I guess." She blew out a long breath and rubbed her hands together. "But I was just saying goodbye, so." She indicated back towards the sea. "Walk with me?"

Olivia nodded. "Love to." She waited for Rosie to fall into step beside her, and they walked without talking for a few moments.

"I'm really sorry about your parents." She'd seen first-hand what grief could do to people; eight years was no time at all. "How did it happen, if it's not too intrusive of me to ask?"

Rosie's mouth twitched, but she shook her head. "No, it's okay." She paused. "They died in a plane crash. They were coming back from Venice, celebrating their silver wedding. It was a special place for them — they went on honeymoon there, too."

She gave a tiny shrug, and Olivia had an urge to take her in her arms, to tell her everything would be all right. She'd only known her two weeks, but somehow, making sure Rosie was all right had worked its way into her list of top priorities. The world had been unfair to Rosie, that much was clear, and Olivia wanted to make sure that from here on in, Rosie had a smooth ride.

"Most of the time I think I'm pretty sorted about it, but sometimes, it overwhelms me." She put her hands in her pockets, mimicking Olivia's stance. "Normally not on the anniversary, but sometimes in the cafe when someone orders a Cornish pasty, which our chef makes to my mum's exact recipe." She smiled, turning back to the grave. "Actually, Gina's are probably better," she whispered, "but I can't let Mum know. I already go to their grave with all my other worries, she doesn't need to know that."

Olivia furrowed her brow. "I'll have to try one." She'd avoided pastry items so far, but that was a recommendation she couldn't refuse.

Rosie brushed her arm as she replied. "You must."

At her touch, something fluttered against Olivia's ribcage. She hunched her shoulders, sinking her hands deeper into her pockets, warmth tip-toeing down her spine.

They were back on the coastal path now. Daisies lined the route and the waves crashed on the rocks below. Olivia knew from walking this path every day this week that in five minutes they'd be looking down on a golden sandy cove, known only to locals. The tourist crowds preferred the bigger stretches of sand with working loos and ice creams within easy reach.

"Your other worries?" Olivia said. "I thought living here meant you had no worries, a simpler life." She swept her hand through the air. "Look at it: it's one of the most idyllic places in the world."

Rosie scoffed as she kicked a stone and they watched it scuttle off the clifftop, falling to certain death.

"Don't believe everything you see." She ran a hand through her smudged blonde hair, her forearm flexing as she did. "Where do you want me to start? My chef might be deported, and I might have to sell the cafe soon because it's just not a viable business anymore. And if that happens, that's the last bit of their legacy gone. Mark & Maude's has been in Otter Bay since before I was born."

They came to a gnarled wooden bench just before the path that led down to the cove, and Olivia pointed at it. "Wanna sit?"

"Sure." Once there, Rosie threw up her hands and gave her a determined grin. "You know what, don't listen to me — life's not all bad, I'm just having a rotten day."

"Understandably." Olivia might not like her family much right now, but at least they were still around to annoy her.

"Yeah, but I'm getting melancholy on my day off, and you're on holiday, you don't need me being a moaning Minnie. I've got my health, I've got Paige and Hilary, and I've got a bucketful of happy memories of Mum and Dad — and not everyone can say that, can they?"

Olivia swallowed down hard: no, they certainly couldn't. "For what it's worth, I think you're doing wonderfully."

"You're only saying that's because otherwise you would have starved for the past two weeks."

She had her there. "I admit, your food is fabulous, but the company's not bad, either."

Rosie eyed her, a blush invading her cheeks. She looked adorable. "I've enjoyed you coming in, too," she said, her gaze flicking to the ground, then back up to meet Olivia's gaze.

Olivia swallowed hard as something shifted inside.

"And I love how enthusiastic you are about my hometown. Makes me appreciate it that little bit more."

Olivia dragged her eyes from Rosie, and across the sea in front of them. "You're lucky to live here. I travel all over with my work, but sometimes I forget that the best places are on our doorstep."

"What is it you do? You never said."

Olivia cleared her throat, avoiding eye contact. "PR, marketing — very dull, big family business. I used to be in the army, so I've been to places a little off the tourist map, too."

Rosie gave her a wistful smile. "I had plans to travel, too, after uni — but then life threw me a curveball. But one day, I'll make it happen." She paused. "For now, let me live vicariously through you. Where have you been?"

Olivia's mind flicked through her internal photo album of the places she'd travelled. "All over — Africa, Asia, Australia, America. I loved Venice, too, but Rome is my all-time favourite city."

Rosie turned her body to her. "Wow, you really have been all over the world. I've only ever been to France and Spain. I'm officially jealous."

"You're not scared of flying since what happened to your parents?"

Rosie's shake of the head was definite. "If anything, it's made me want to travel more, seize life. My parents loved to travel, and they'd want me to do the same. Paige is off to university this year, so I won't have as many ties anymore. The only trouble is, I don't have the money to do it." She paused. "But, like I said, one day I'll have enough money and time to do it properly. Or maybe I'll meet a rich woman who'll sweep me off my feet and make it happen. I'd be okay with either one."

Olivia squashed down an impulse to volunteer her services on the spot, but it wasn't easy. Rosie's smile was something she'd give in to any time, any day.

Rosie gave a sigh, then jumped to her feet, clapping her hands. "Enough sitting around here. Do you have plans today?"

Olivia stood up, splaying her hands. "Absolutely none."

"You wanna spend it on the beach with me?"

"I'd love to." She resisted telling Rosie there's nothing she'd love more. She didn't want to over-egg the pudding.

"Correct answer." Rosie took her hand, nodding at the slope leading down to the sandy cove to their right. "Race you. Last one down there buys dinner later." She dropped Olivia's hand, gave her a piercing smile that lit up her whole face, and took off, her white Converse kicking up sand as they went.

Olivia hesitated, then broke into a sprint, running after Rosie, the wind whistling past her ears, a grin splitting her face.

Ahead, Rosie had already disappeared over the top of the slope and began to scream as she ran down the hill, arms above her head, her laughter puncturing the air. As gravity took over and Olivia found herself being swept towards the beach, she began to do the same, pure exhilaration coursing through her veins. Sunshine kissed her face as the grassy slopes either side of her rolled by, and at the bottom, Rosie had her arms outstretched on either side of her, as if she were flying.

Olivia mimicked the action as she came in to land. She couldn't remember the last time she'd run down a hill with carefree abandon like this. It was wild, freeing, and everything her mother would hate, which made it taste even sweeter.

Her breath caught in her chest. She neared the bottom where the path became sandier and her foot caught on something hard. She stumbled, sailing through the air and crashing into Rosie. They both let out a shriek as momentum sent them tumbling to the sand, Olivia landing with a dull thud on top of her.

Time stood still as Olivia soaked in the delicious pressure of their bodies moulded together, her pulse ticking upwards at

Olympic pace. For a brief moment, the sea receded and the sun dialled down, and it was just the two of them, together as one.

But then reality swept back in as Rosie let out a groan underneath her.

Olivia pushed herself off, staring down, panic oozing through her. "Are you okay?" She reached out but didn't know where to put her hand, leaving it hovering over Rosie's shoulder. "Are you hurt?"

Rosie unscrewed her face and cracked open an eye. She clutched her ribs, a smile creeping onto her face. "I'll live, no thanks to you."

Olivia smiled and sat up, before helping Rosie to do the same. When she put a hand on the base of Rosie's spine it connected with bare skin where her T-shirt had ridden up. They both stilled, gazes locking together.

Olivia didn't move her hand and Rosie didn't break her stare.

Olivia held her breath; in that moment, she knew it wasn't just her who'd been thinking about this. It wasn't just her whose life had, over the past two weeks, tentatively peeked around the corner for another option.

Rosie's heated stare, focussed only on her, told her she had, too.

That thought sent Olivia into equal measures of rapture and panic.

Eventually, after several long moments, Rosie cleared her throat. "I know I said I wanted to be swept off my feet, but this is taking it a little far, don't you think?"

CHAPTER 8

As they walked to the pub, Rosie wondered what would have happened if she hadn't made that joke. She glanced at Charlie from the corner of her eye. She walked with a different gait to anyone she knew — spine straight and chin up. She'd probably been taught to walk like that in the army.

"Welcome to the Dog & Duck," Rosie said, and held the door open for Charlie.

She walked in behind her and glanced around. It wasn't too busy — yet. They should be able to have a quiet drink. At least until the crowd arrived for the pub's weekly karaoke night. But as far as pubs went in Otter Bay, the one owned by Amy's parents was the only option.

"What can I get you?" Rosie asked after they'd found a table.

Charlie looked at her with sparkling green eyes. "Surprise me with a local brew."

Rosie nodded. "Very well."

She headed to the bar and said hello to the bartender, Dave, who smirked at her. Oh great, it was starting already.

Rosie placed her order and didn't give Dave any information on who she was with. She and Amy might have spent an inordinate amount of time perched on a stool at this very bar when they were still together, but that didn't mean Rosie owed him any explanations.

Dave put two glasses of Cornish cider in front of her. "I wish I could give them to you on the house," he said. "For good luck and all." He winked at her.

He knew well and good Rosie would never accept a free drink from this particular house. She paid for the drinks and headed back to the table.

"What have we here?" Charlie studied the liquid in the glass.

"Local cider," Rosie said. "The same one I was drinking at the beach pub earlier this week. I hope you like it."

"Let's see. That tumble down the hill has left me quite thirsty."

Rosie watched Charlie bring her lips to the edge of the glass and take a tiny sip. The corners of her mouth drew down.

"Yum," Charlie said.

Rosie chuckled. "Maybe it's a bit more of an acquired taste than I remember."

"I'm sure the second sip will be better, what with the taste acquisition process steadily progressing." She drank again and made a visible effort to smile right after.

"I can get you something else," Rosie said. "This is supposed to be an enjoyable evening."

"It is." Charlie briefly looked her in the eye. "Honestly." Charlie averted her gaze and Rosie followed it. "Pub games," Charlie almost-shouted. "They've definitely gone out of fashion in London."

"Wanna play?" Rosie arched up her eyebrows.

Charlie nodded and got up. She came back with one of the boxes of skittles.

"This seems to be the most popular game in town." Charlie sank her front teeth into her bottom lip. "You'll have to teach me."

Rosie tilted her head. "You've never played skittles?"

"As I said, pub games are terribly out of fashion where I'm from."

Rosie nodded. "And you being such an on-trend bird…"

"Exactly." Charlie's eyes narrowed as she smiled.

Rosie moved the cider glasses aside and set up the game.

"It's tiny bowling," Charlie exclaimed.

Rosie chuckled. "Exactly." She wondered, not for the first time, if Charlie was even from this planet.

Rosie explained how the game worked, showing Charlie how to wind the string around the ball and how to launch it at the pins. They played a few rounds, all of which Rosie won.

"You should start a petition to get games like this back into London pubs," Rosie said. "So many of you come down here for the weekend, only to make fools of yourselves at skittles."

"Truth be told, I'm more a wine bar kind of girl," Charlie said.

"I'd gathered as much." Rosie pointed at the game. "One more round?"

Charlie looked around. "How about a game of pool instead? I'd like to beat you at something today."

"Oh, the game is on." Rosie jumped to her feet.

"Yes, it is." Charlie followed her to the pool table. She seemed more confident about this and opened the game, pocketing a ball straight away. "Impressed yet?" She stood there grinning with the cue in her hands.

"A tiny bit more than I've been thus far this evening." Rosie's hands itched for her turn to come around.

Rosie almost missed Charlie's next ball going in because her gaze had drifted to the outline of Charlie's behind in her jeans as she leaned half her body over the pool table.

Charlie turned around and looked at her triumphantly. "I guess I'm better with balls than with tiny bowling pins."

Rosie didn't reply. She was still processing how good

Charlie looked in skinny jeans — she looked nothing like the woman in the Paul Smith jacket who had bumped into her at the station two weeks ago.

Charlie missed the next shot.

Rosie was up. She pushed the thought of well-fitting jeans from her head and focussed on the task at hand. She scanned the position of the balls on the table. If she could concentrate, which was not a given in these circumstances, she could have a good run. Or maybe she should just let Charlie win, what with her having lost at skittles already. But Rosie couldn't do it. And Charlie had grinned at her with a bit too much confidence in her pool skills just a minute ago.

Rosie pocketed the next four balls. After she missed the fifth by a hair, displaying her skills regardless, she took a step back and waited in silence. If she could remain focussed, this game was hers for the taking.

"It's definitely on then." Charlie looked at her over the rim of her glasses. "You're a worthy contender."

Rosie refused to let her gaze wander while Charlie manoeuvred around the pool table. She kept her attention on the table alone.

"How about we make this a little more interesting?" Charlie asked. She came to stand right in front of Rosie. "I saw on the blackboard they're having karaoke here later. The loser has to sing a song for the winner." She plastered a huge grin on her face.

Poor Charlie. She had no idea that Rosie had won trophies for playing pool at uni. Granted, she was a bit rusty. But that earlier four-ball streak was just her warm up.

"Deal." Rosie extended her hand. Charlie shook it. Her hand lingered a fraction too long, and the prolonged touch of skin was about to lessen Rosie's focus again. She withdrew her hand. "You're up, Miss London."

"Just for your information, pool is still widely played in the capital," Charlie said before she turned around and studied the table.

Rosie watched as she effortlessly sank the next three balls.

"Just keeping things exciting," Charlie said after missing the next ball.

"I thank you for the opportunity to kick your arse," Rosie said. She wasn't this cocky when she played pool at university. Then again, she'd rarely played against women like Charlie. It wasn't just her behind that looked good in those skinny jeans. Rosie also felt quite flustered by the intensity of Charlie's gaze when she talked to her, and the promise of an impressive shoulder line underneath her jumper.

"Are you still playing or are we spending the night here while you line up your next shot?" Charlie asked, a smile on her lips.

"I'm trying to focus," Rosie said.

"Hm," was all Charlie said. She walked to the other end of the table and leaned on her cue.

Rosie could swear that Charlie stood sideways like that, one hand on the cue, the other resting on a rear jeans pocket, on purpose. To distract her.

She narrowed her gaze, shifted her focus, and potted her next ball straight into the pocket. Only three more shots and she'd be crowned the winner. And Charlie would have to sing her a song. She'd get a full three minutes to ogle Charlie while she was on stage — but only if she paid attention to the game now.

Rosie hunched over the table and got ready to sink the blue ball. Just as she had started to draw back the cue, the door of the pub opened, and Amy walked in.

Rosie couldn't stop the momentum of the cue and it hit the white ball from the wrong angle. She didn't pocket the blue ball. The white ball hit the black instead which, agonisingly slowly, rolled to the opposite side, where it tumbled into the pocket.

"Bloody hell," Rosie said. It hadn't even been Charlie distracting her.

Charlie waved a fist in the air. "Looks like you owe me a song." She sent Rosie a crooked grin. "I can't begin to tell you how much I'm looking forward to that."

~

They had polished off a dinner of fish and chips and another few drinks — cider for Rosie, white wine for Charlie — when Amy wandered across to their table.

"Evening, ladies." Luckily, she didn't lean in to kiss Rosie on the cheek. "I'm in charge of karaoke tonight. Can I put your names down?"

"Rosie owes me a song, so you can definitely put her down," Charlie said.

"Does she now?" Amy brought a hand to her side. She looked at Rosie, then focussed her gaze on Charlie. She scowled. "Do I know you from somewhere? You look familiar."

Charlie pushed her glasses up her nose. "I don't think so. I just have one of those faces." She turned away from Amy.

"I could have sworn I did." Amy let it go and turned to Rosie. "So, I'm putting your name on the list. Okay?"

Rosie nodded reluctantly. Charlie had won fair and square. "Just give me some time to, um, limber up my vocal chords." She grabbed hold of her glass.

With a sly grin, Amy walked off.

"Not someone you're very fond of?" Charlie asked.

Rosie looked into her glass. No matter how much she drank, her vocal chords would never be limber enough, nor would she be able to gather enough nerve to get up on that stage in front of Charlie *and* Amy. Besides, she'd had more than enough cider already. "She's my ex." Rosie leaned over the table. "Whose family is also doing their very best to put my cafe out of business." She took another sip of her drink. It was helping her to get these words out. Charlie looked sympathetic enough.

"The one you were telling me about?" Charlie's eyes grew wide.

"Yup. And I can't seem to escape her. She's everywhere. My life would be so much better if Amy stopped turning up."

"The only other lesbian in the village, eh." Charlie sent Rosie a smile.

The screeching feedback of the mic interrupted their conversation. Then Amy's voice beamed out of the pub's ultra-modern sound system.

"The time has come, folks," Amy said. It was way beneath her to apologise for the annoying microphone noise. "For some good old Otter Bay karaoke."

About three people on the side of the stage clapped.

"I'm your compere Amy. Most of you know me already, of course."

A few more people cheered. The way Amy was talking, you'd think she was introducing herself at Wembley Stadium instead of the pub in Otter Bay.

"As tradition has it, I'll kick off tonight's proceedings." She chuckled into the microphone. At times like these, Rosie wondered what she'd ever seen in Amy.

Amy nodded at Dave behind the bar, who was in charge of the music. The first notes of *I Will Always Love You* started playing.

Rosie wished she could curl up in a ball and hide under the table.

When she glanced at the stage, she saw Amy looking straight at her as she launched into the song. Rosie closed her eyes and took a deep breath, trying to pretend this wasn't happening.

When she opened her eyes again, Amy had reached the chorus, and Charlie's hand rested on Rosie's forearm. "Another one of those, perhaps?" She picked up Rosie's empty glass.

Rosie nodded because she had no idea how else she was going to make it through this evening.

CHAPTER 9

Olivia stood at the bar, repeating her assumed name over and over in her head.

Charlie. Charlie. Charlie.

Her brain was smudged from the cider and wine, and a couple of times tonight, she'd nearly said the wrong thing. Given away facts about who she really was. And if that happened, all hell would break loose. She couldn't imagine Rosie being so relaxed around her if she knew who she really was. And tonight, she was revelling in how relaxed they were in each other's company. Although Rosie's ex turning up had shifted the mood completely.

She paid for the drinks and the bartender gave her a once over. "How's it going over there?" he asked.

His stare was unwavering, and Olivia was thrown. "It's going… fine." Was that the right answer?

"That's good," he replied, gripping a Peroni pump, his knuckles white. "Rosie's very well loved around here, just so you know."

Olivia's eyes widened. Shit, she was getting *the talk* from one of the bar staff?

"I understand why," she replied. "Thanks for the drinks." She pocketed the change and crossed back to their table, her annoyance only fuelled as she saw Amy belting out the final bars of Whitney Houston's classic direct to Rosie. It seemed like the whole pub was trying to tell her something tonight, but she wasn't deterred so easily. Something had changed with her and Rosie today, and her alter ego, Charlie Smith, wasn't a woman to ignore that.

As she sat down, the pub clapped politely for Amy, and Olivia saw the next song flash up on the large karaoke screen: *Royals* by Lorde.

She winced, the pub felt crowded, the room too small. She hated this song for obvious reasons, but that had never stopped her friends singing it to her on a regular basis. Jemima had even sung it the last time they'd been at a karaoke bar together, a couple of years back. Had she been singing it ironically even back then?

"Looks like I'm up," Rosie said, giving her a wink.

Wait, Rosie was singing this? Could this evening get any more surreal?

Olivia watched her get up on stage, saw Amy take the opportunity to whisper something in her ear, to which Rosie shook her head, giving her a look as dirty as the martinis Olivia favoured back home.

Olivia narrowed her eyes: she'd only met her tonight, and already she was not an Amy fan.

Rosie tapped the microphone before she spoke. "This one's for a newcomer to the village — I guess it's payback time," she said, before launching into the opening verse.

Sure, Olivia hated the song, but hell, Rosie had been holding back: she could really sing. Had honest-to-goodness, shivers-down-her-spine silky vocals. When she hit the chorus, even Olivia couldn't help a smile crossing her face as Rosie's husky voice nailed the lyrics, layering them with honey. By the time the song was over, she was transfixed. Rosie was a natural on stage.

When she sauntered back over to their table, Olivia gulped, taking in her sapphire stare, the curve of her hip, the sweep of her tongue on her lower lip.

Everything about Rosie was in technicolour tonight.

She stood, clapping slowly. "Hidden talents, Ms Perkins. That was just incredible — you should be on stage with a voice like that. I know some people…" She stopped, staring at her wine.

No, she didn't.

Charlie Smith didn't know any people.

Charlie Smith was an ex-soldier working in PR and marketing.

She heard her father's voice in her head: "No getting drunk at the village pub, Olivia."

But luckily, Rosie wasn't paying attention. Instead, she gave Olivia a tight smile, before picking up her cider and downing half of it in three practised moves.

Olivia widened her eyes. "Thirsty?"

Rosie shook her head. "Blame my ex," she said, giving a shudder as she took another swig. "My hands need something else to do rather than get tight around Amy's neck, which some people in here might object to."

Olivia wasn't one of them.

Her stomach flip-flopped as she thought about all the things she could happily find to keep Rosie's hands occupied.

And then she picked up her drink and took another swig.

Her father knew her so well.

Women and booze were always her undoing, weren't they?

She jerked her head towards the pool table. "Shall we have another game to keep your hands occupied? No songs up for grabs, just loser buys the next round."

Rosie grinned, her gaze raking the full length of Olivia's body. "You're on," she replied.

∽

Half an hour and another drink later, their pool prowess had taken a nosedive off a low cliff: they were both now officially drunk and officially terrible.

"I always thought playing pool got better as you drank?" Olivia furrowed her brow.

Rosie regarded her with glassy eyes and a satisfied smirk. "Maybe we should start playing strip pool, to sharpen our focus, up our game."

Desire pressed into Olivia's core and she cleared her throat and tried to think of something other than Rosie with her top off, breasts out. It wasn't easy. "If you start undressing, I think that would have the opposite effect on my focus." Then she closed her eyes, feeling her cheeks burn.

Charlie Smith was nowhere near as smooth as Olivia Charlton. Exhibit A: Charlie Smith got drunk on cheap wine and blurted out stuff without thinking.

Damn it.

Only, when she opened her eyes, Rosie was grinning at her with smouldering intent. Or was it drunk intent? Olivia couldn't be sure.

"It might not improve our focus, but it'd certainly liven up the night, don't you think?"

Something moved in Olivia low in her body. Way low down. She took a deep breath and pressed her feet into the ground.

They stood staring at each other, a heat creeping up Olivia's back, when Amy's spiky voice broke the moment, like taking a sledgehammer to ice. *Thwack.*

"All right ladies, who's winning this one? Are you playing

for the honour to sing again?" Amy stood between them, her back to Olivia, hands thrust into the pockets of her dark jeans. Up this close, Olivia could see a few grey hairs gathering on the back of her head; she'd have to start dying her hair soon, as Olivia guessed Amy wouldn't be the sort to go grey gracefully. Grace didn't seem high up on her list of virtues.

"No, we're just playing for fun this time," Rosie said, her voice harder than it had been a few seconds ago. "And you're kinda in the way."

Amy turned, giving Olivia a once-over. "And I wouldn't want to get in the way of such a beautiful moment between you and Princess Olivia-lookalike here," she said, reaching out and clutching Olivia's chin, studying her face. "That's who you remind me of, it came to me when I was singing. You *really* do look like her, if it weren't for the shorter, darker hair and glasses. I don't think princesses are allowed to have short hair, against fairy-tale laws." She let go of Olivia's face.

Rosie steamed in, grabbing Amy's arm and spinning her around. "Hey! Enough with pawing our guests. Just because this is your pub, you don't get to do whatever you like. I've told you that before."

"It's okay," Olivia said, trying to smooth things over, even though it was far from okay. If she didn't have her father's words ringing in her ears, she would have kicked Amy's arse by now. Grabbing her by the chin? Not a cool move. "I'm sure Amy didn't mean anything by it, did you, Amy?"

As Amy spun back around to face her, Olivia fought down the urge to grab her chin, too.

Be the bigger person, don't stoop to her level.

"That's for me to know and you to find out," she replied. Her surety reminded Olivia of her sister: she had a feeling not many people had ever said no to Amy in her life. Perhaps Rosie was the exception to the rule, and that was clearly driving Amy mad.

"You have to agree, though," Amy continued, gesturing to Rosie with her hand. "Stick a brown wig on her and a posh dress, and she'd be the spitting image of the lesbian princess. The only thing is, I doubt a princess would be playing pool in the Dog & Duck, would she?" She nudged Olivia with her elbow. "You should have sung Rosie's song, that would have been funnier." She grinned at her own joke.

Not for the first time, Olivia wondered how Rosie had ended up with Amy. She was a good-looking woman, sure, but the problems started when she opened her mouth.

Maybe she should introduce Amy to Jemima.

"On the contrary, I don't think anybody would have been able to sing that song any better than Rosie." Olivia shot her pool partner a warm smile, which she was sure would wind Amy up.

Sure enough, while Rosie beamed at Olivia's comment, Amy all but growled.

"She's got an amazing voice — but I'm sure you know that, seeing as you used to go out." Olivia paused, leaning on her cue, pulling herself up to passport height, a pleasing few inches taller than Amy. "I know it flowed through me like honey."

Amy's eyes flickered as she said the last line, and she stood up as tall as she could, squaring up to Olivia, getting right in her grill. "You think you're clever, do you?"

"Amy, don't—" Rosie said.

But Amy wasn't listening. "—coming down here from London with your posh accent, your arrogant ways. Buying our homes, hitting on our women. Well you should know, money doesn't buy everything. It doesn't buy class, which you clearly don't have."

Olivia let out a strangled laugh. "And you do? Still pining after your ex when she's clearly done with you? Singing that song tonight?"

"Enough you two!" Rosie shouted.

But she was too late.

"You want to do this posh girl? Because we can so do this." Amy's face was inches from hers, her cheeks alive with cider splotch. "You wanna take this outside?" When she said the last line, some of Amy's saliva landed on Olivia's top lip.

Keep your cool, keep your cool.

"I don't think you want to take this outside, trust me on that." A flare of anger blazed through Olivia and she glanced at Rosie, shaking her head. "It's okay," she told her over Amy's shoulder.

"It's not okay—" Rosie began.

"—Why, are you chicken shit?" Amy asked, placing her palms on Olivia's chest and pushing her backwards. "Are you scared, posh girl? Because round these parts, we fight for what's ours, we don't just buy it."

She finished speaking, narrowed her eyes and swung a punch upwards, aiming for Olivia's right cheek.

But Olivia had seen it coming.

Rosie's shout pierced the air as Olivia swayed backwards, keeping her balance with ease, and grabbing Amy's balled fist in her hand.

With one swift move, she had hold of Amy's arm, turned her around, twisted her arm up behind her back and pushed her down face first onto the green baize, the pool balls clicking and scattering at the intrusion.

Olivia's blood coursed through her veins and she closed her eyes as Amy let out a surprised gasp as she landed on the table with a low thud.

The whole evening stilled, and Olivia winced, lowering her head so her mouth was level with Amy's right ear. "I asked you nicely, but you didn't listen. You do not want to get in a fight with me. And you especially do not want to upset Rosie, because that upsets me."

She drew herself up, let go of Amy's arm, and turned to

Rosie, hesitancy creasing her words. "I'm sorry, but she left me no choice." Olivia blew out a breath, holding her right arm, shaking as Amy stood up.

"I'm going outside to get some air." Olivia ran towards the pub door, gasping for breath, her whole body shaking. She yanked the door open and fell into the summer evening.

What she'd said was true, Amy had left her no choice — she hadn't retaliated with violence, she'd just tried to stop it. Still, it didn't mean she wasn't cross with herself for taking the bait and losing control.

She couldn't afford to draw attention to herself, but she'd risked it all to defend Rosie.

Because in two short weeks, Rosie was already under her skin.

CHAPTER 10

In her mind's eye, Rosie kept seeing Amy with her face pressed into the pool table. It sure beat the sight and sound of Amy belting out a love song for Rosie's benefit. What was Amy even thinking doing that?

"Are you all right?" Rosie asked. They'd left the pub and had started walking in the direction of Rosie's home. "I'm so sorry about Amy. She's not really over the break-up yet, but she shouldn't have taken it out on you."

"I'm fine," Charlie said, squaring her shoulders.

"As you might have noticed, Amy can be very persistent," Rosie said on a sigh.

"You don't say." Charlie inhaled deeply. "But I shouldn't have stooped to her level."

"Are you kidding?" Rosie glanced at Charlie, first from the corner of her eye, then turning herself fully towards her. "You're my hero now." Rosie couldn't suppress a smile. Was she still drunk? The fight had sobered her up somewhat, yet she felt a little giddy.

Charlie chuckled. "Let's not go overboard."

"Clearly, Amy didn't know who she was dealing with." Rosie bumped her shoulder lightly into Charlie's.

"That's an army training for you. I'm so glad all the gruelling hours of boot camp finally paid off and I got to be your hero." She slid her arm through Rosie's.

Rosie had walked home from the Dog & Duck a little tipsy many a night, but never with an ex-army officer on her arm — let alone someone who had stood up for her like that.

"How long were you in the army for?" Rosie asked.

"Eight years." Was that a hint of wistfulness in Charlie's tone? "Until my parents made me join the family business."

"From the army to PR," Rosie said. "That's quite the career switch." She'd spent most of the evening talking about herself. It was about time she found out a little more about Charlie.

Charlie shrugged.

"Would you have liked to stay in the army?" Rosie held onto Charlie's arm a little tighter.

"Let's just say I wouldn't have minded."

They came to the end of the street. It was the end of May and it was a lovely spring evening. Rosie would have happily walked around the streets of Otter Bay with Charlie on her arm for a good while longer.

"Shall I walk you home?" Rosie asked.

"We must be much closer to yours," Charlie was quick to say, her arm stiffening against Rosie's body. "How about I walk you home instead? I was in the army, remember. I can get myself home safely." She beamed Rosie a smile.

"I can get myself home safely as well. This is Otter Bay." Rosie smiled back.

"And everyone here looks out for you," Charlie said.

They were still standing on the corner of the street. Obviously, Charlie didn't want Rosie to walk her home — either she didn't want Rosie to see where she was staying or she didn't want to feel obliged to invite Rosie in.

"It's a small village. It must be very different from living in London." Rosie started walking in the direction of her home again. Charlie followed, their arms still linked.

Charlie threw her head back. "You can see the stars here. That's certainly very different."

Rosie looked up at the sky. Clouds drifted by and, in between, she saw a few stars shining down on them. She hadn't looked at the stars in a long time. It reminded her too much of her parents. They used to sit her down outside after dark and point out the stars and constellations. Rosie didn't want to talk about her parents again, so she looked down and didn't say anything for a while.

"It must be hard living in the same village as your ex," Charlie said once they'd turned the corner into the next street.

They'd almost reached Rosie's home, but Rosie wanted this walk to last a good while longer. Charlie didn't know where she lived, so they could go another spin around the block if she felt like it.

"It's not too bad. I'm used to it," Rosie said.

"Maybe it's a bit like being in the army. That's basically like living in a small village." Charlie fell into step with Rosie's slower pace. "I loved someone," Charlie continued. "A fellow officer. It didn't work out." She glanced sideways at Rosie. "Although, and I mean no offence, my ex seems much more… civil than yours."

"None taken." Rosie could hardly excuse Amy's behaviour. "Must be that army discipline." She pressed her upper arm against Charlie's. She was wearing a thin overcoat over her jumper and Rosie could feel the hard outline of her biceps. "Is that the ex you mentioned the other day? The one your family's so fond of?"

Charlie shook her head. "The two couldn't be more different," was all she said, her voice terse.

Rosie took the hint and didn't inquire further.

"That's a lot of exes." Rosie joked. Maybe she was tipsier than she thought.

Charlie shrouded herself in silence.

Rosie must be saying all the wrong things, yet she didn't seem to be able to stop herself. She knew so little about Charlie. Maybe if she changed the subject, she'd be willing to divulge a little more about herself. "Must be fun working in the family business, what with being able to take a few weeks off like this." Rosie made her voice sound light. "What is it that you do exactly?"

"It's so dull, I wouldn't want to bore you with the details." Charlie sounded chirpy again. She sighed. "God, I love it here." She inhaled deeply, then exhaled slowly. "This is the life, Rosie."

"What, being accosted by my ex every evening? I don't think so." Rosie slowed down even more. "Or, if you mean having a dashing army officer come to my rescue instead, then yes, I do tend to agree."

They came to a full stop. Rosie could see the door of her home a few yards away. There was no one else in the street. She briefly glanced up at the stars. With Charlie by her side, she could do that now.

Charlie slipped her arm from Rosie's and faced her. She fidgeted with the hem of her coat sleeve. "I'm so glad I met you," she said.

"Me too," Rosie whispered. She locked her gaze on Charlie's. Her green eyes glistened in the light of the street lamp beside them. "When and why are you leaving again?" she asked.

Charlie painted on a tormented grin. "I'm not sure about either." She reached for Rosie's hands and took them in hers.

The touch of their skin sent a jolt of something warm and long-forgotten up Rosie's spine. For the first time ever, Rosie wished Paige was already at uni so she had the flat to herself and could ask Charlie to come up. But that was out of the question now.

"That's me right there." Rosie nodded in the direction of her front door.

"I'd best get home as well," Charlie said, but didn't let go of Rosie's hands.

"I'll see you in the cafe tomorrow?" Rosie asked.

"Try to keep me away." Charlie smiled a real smile now. She tipped forward a fraction.

That warm sensation travelling up Rosie's spine earlier was quickly transforming into an expanse of heat spreading over her entire body. She hoped Charlie didn't feel how her hands were going clammy.

Rosie slanted her upper body in Charlie's direction as well. Then Charlie planted a soft but quick kiss on Rosie's cheek and withdrew.

"I had a lovely time today." She sent Rosie another smile, retracted her hands from Rosie's grip, and went on her way.

Rosie watched her go. She kept her eyes on Charlie's back — upright gait, pert backside — while she headed for the front door. She waited to put the key in the lock until Charlie had rounded the corner.

Just before she did, Charlie turned around and waved.

For tonight, it was enough.

∼

Before heading inside, Rosie looked at the stars one more time. She didn't seem to remember any of the things her parents had taught her about them. Perhaps because it had been so long ago — Rosie hadn't been ten and Paige hadn't even been born — or, perhaps, because, after their death, it had been too painful to remember.

She went upstairs and found Paige asleep in front of the television. She switched off the TV and covered her sister with a blanket. Cher was snoozing at Paige's feet.

While she looked at her sister's sleeping face, Rosie regretted having wished her away for the night. Come September, she'd probably be wishing Paige had never left. It wasn't as if Charlie would still be in Otter Bay to keep her company.

Nevertheless, the thought of Charlie made her break out into goose bumps. She touched her fingertips to the spot where Charlie's lips had landed on her cheek.

They'd spent the better part of the day together — and what a day it had been — yet Rosie was none the wiser about Charlie. Every question she had asked was met with an evasive reply. All she really knew, because she'd witnessed it with her own eyes, was that Charlie could hold her own in a fight.

Rosie, on the contrary, had confided in Charlie quite a bit. What ever happened to quid pro quo? But it wasn't as if they'd been on a date. They'd run into each other — again — and spent an enjoyable day together. Charlie didn't owe Rosie anything.

Rosie's fingertips still grazed the imprint of Charlie's lips on her cheek. If Rosie'd had her way, she would have kissed Charlie on the lips. Christ, she really liked her. But Charlie was just passing through. Soon enough, she'd leave Otter Bay and it would just be Rosie again. And she would resume running into Amy, who might or might not pipe down after her run-in with Charlie. Rosie hoped for the former but feared the latter once Charlie was gone. Amy would probably seize the opportunity to exploit her vulnerability.

Rosie cast one last glance at Paige and switched off the living room light. She headed to her bedroom, which was really not the kind of room to invite a sophisticated woman like Charlie into, and pondered how sick she was of losing everything and everyone that mattered to her. First her parents. Soon Paige would be leaving. If she was honest about it, she was also on the verge of losing the cafe, the last tangible memory of her parents. And then Charlie swooped in, made her feel all warm and fuzzy inside, only to have to leave as quickly as she had arrived.

What kind of life was that for a twenty-eight-year-old? Something would have to change.

Rosie sank down on her bed. If only she could ask her parents for advice as to where she had gone wrong, because right then, it felt like nothing was going right in her life. Except for that peck on her cheek ten minutes ago. That had felt more than right.

Rosie stared at the picture of her parents on her bedside table. It had been taken only a few months before the crash. Her dad grinned, as usual. Her mum peered into the lens, trying a smile, and although she was the warmest woman Rosie had ever known — and the best mother she could have wished for — her gentle and good-hearted nature was impossible to capture in a photo.

Sometimes Rosie wondered if things like your parents dying well before their time happened for a reason. It would have been nice to cling to that kind of belief after it had happened, when she'd been so devastated. But Rosie had long since concluded that there was no deeper meaning to her parents dying. It was a tragic accident. All the passengers on the plane had died. So many people's lives had been ripped to shreds, not just hers and Paige's and Aunt Hilary's.

She was glad she had told Charlie about her parents, even though Charlie had been less than forthcoming in return. And she was equally glad that they'd shared that kiss on the cheek.

If Rosie had learned one thing from her parents' death, it was to enjoy a moment like that. Not many of them came around when you lived in Otter Bay.

CHAPTER 11

Olivia's brain rattled in her skull, in desperate need of refreshment. She stood at the kitchen sink and filled her third tumbler of water, slugging it down as if she hadn't drunk for days. It was shaping up to be a scorcher of a day in Cornwall, and she was determined to keep busy, determined not to dwell too much on the confusing nature of yesterday. Because, if she thought about it for too long, she felt like her head might explode.

However, every time she tried to herd her thoughts away, they just kept drifting back to Rosie.

Good god, Rosie. She was a woman who knew her own mind, and she went after what she wanted.

Plus, she wore a shirt well, and that smile? Her smile lit up every room she walked into. Olivia could sit and stare at that smile all day.

Plus, she was capable. So fucking capable. She would have made a damn good army officer. Plus, she'd look hot in a uniform. But that was beside the point.

Rosie'd had so much responsibility put on her at such a young age, and yet she'd coped admirably. What would Olivia have done in her place? She had no idea, because life had always been handed to her: do this, go here, say this. She'd never had to make her own way in the world, no matter how hard she'd tried.

She'd done as much as she could: coming out as gay, joining the army and making herself useful. However, as she'd got older, she'd realised she'd have to bow to royal duties eventually. With nothing else on the horizon, and even her father willing her to get engaged, Jemima had been the perfect, willing ruse.

That is, until Olivia had to stand up and declare it to the world. Thinking she could do something and *doing it* were two completely different things. The press conference had spooked her, and she'd been kicking herself ever since. This was real life, this wasn't a game.

Rosie would never have stood for it. Olivia liked her guts, she liked her energy; hell, she liked her.

And therein lay the problem.

She really liked her.

And she couldn't like her, because she was engaged to be married.

Her phone pinged; even that sound jarred.

She might need some headache pills. Did she have any headache pills? The good ones with codeine, not just the normal strength? She opened and closed a few cupboards in the kitchen, but no luck. She opened the drawer next to the cutlery and found a pair of scissors, Sellotape, birthday candles and matches. It didn't matter where she went, every kitchen drawer seemed to contain these items.

She swiped on the text message, dread seeping through her.

'When the hell are you coming home? Giles is hosting his dinner this weekend and we said we'd go weeks ago. I can let you have a couple of weeks, but even you must agree this is stretching it a little.'

Olivia winced, rubbing her temples as her headache kicked up a gear. The trouble was, she agreed with Jemima. She didn't want to be a bitch, but that was how she was coming across. She'd agreed to the marriage after all, she owed Jemima something.

However, she couldn't get away from the fact that six weeks ago, they hadn't even been dating — and now they were engaged to be married. Whenever she'd imagined her wedding, she'd never imagined it to be arranged, a business deal. But that was what it boiled down to, and she hated it.

She grimaced, filled another glass with water, and skulled it. When did her life get so damn complicated? When she bowed down to her mother and her tirade on royal duty, that's when.

Her mother had texted this week to say she was sending some grounds staff to sort out the garden, but Olivia had told her not to bother. She was trying to keep a low profile in the village, and if locals turned up to work, the chances of her doing so would decrease drastically.

So far, she'd managed to fly below the radar, but last night had come close to blowing her cover. Rosie could only be fobbed off so many times with vague answers, and Amy, unbeknown to her, had come uncomfortably close to the truth. She was thankful their pool-table spat seemed to have gone unnoticed, but maybe it wasn't such an uncommon occurrence in the Dog & Duck. Maybe Amy antagonised customers on a regular basis. Olivia wouldn't put it past her.

She still couldn't wrap her brain around her and Rosie.

But as well as skating close to the edge, yesterday had given Olivia a glimpse of how easy life could be, how simple it was when you really thought about it.

Spending time with people you felt comfortable with, having drinks and dinner, sitting chatting on the beach. She didn't quite know how it had happened, but she and Rosie just seemed to fit — and that was a very scary thought.

In so many ways, she reminded her of Ellie. Gorgeous, funny, ballsy. Ellie was the first woman Olivia had ever loved, and also the first one she'd truly lost. All the others had drifted into her life. But Ellie had slammed into her, left a dent, and then when the whole royalty deal proved too much, backed away. She hadn't been prepared to live her life in a straitjacket, and she didn't think Olivia should either.

Of course, she'd been right, but Olivia realised too late, and by that time, Ellie was gone.

If anything did happen with Rosie, would the outcome be the same? Would Olivia demand a different deal? Would her mother let her? She was getting a bit ahead of herself. They hadn't even kissed yet. She'd thought about it last night, but instead kissed Rosie's cheek at the last minute.

The rumble in her body low down told her she badly wanted to kiss Rosie, but it wouldn't make life any simpler, would it?

Her phone ringing interrupted her thoughts, and she blinked, then held up the screen. She still needed headache pills.

The call was from her cousin, Sebastian. Gay and closeted, Sebastian was an Earl; his wife Helena, also gay, was a countess. Olivia never wanted to go down that road.

"How's it going, little cousin?" Sebastian was three days older than Olivia, hence she was always the little cousin.

"It's going great." Olivia opened a final drawer and spied a packet of ibuprofen. She checked the date: two months over. They'd have to do.

"Liar," Sebastian said with a chuckle. "How long you planning on hiding down there?"

"I'm not hiding."

"You're so hiding. Not that I blame you. But listen, I was at the palace the other day and your mother was not happy. You'll be pleased to know Grandma was there fighting your corner, telling your mother exactly what she thought of your upcoming sham of a marriage."

A sham. That described it exactly. Olivia's head still throbbed. "Gotta love Grandma."

"Who doesn't?" Sebastian paused. "But back to your mother — she made a point of telling me all the things you were doing that she didn't approve of, like I could do something about it. Like we had some weird gay code."

"We kinda do, but still." Olivia took the pills and washed them down with water.

"If I was you I'd give your parents a call. Try to smooth things over. It doesn't help that Jemima isn't being all that discreet, if you know what I mean. She's telling her tales of woe to anyone who'll listen."

So much for Jemima understanding her way of life. "Anyone who'll blab to the press?"

Sebastian paused. "I don't think so, but it's only a matter of time. You know what some of these reporters are like."

It would be too much to ask Jemima to keep a low profile. Olivia sighed. She couldn't control Jemima, she never could — and that might be the one aspect of their match-up her mother had overlooked. Jemima had always been something of a loose cannon.

"What are you doing down there? Isn't it a bit boring?" Sebastian asked. "Are you living on cream teas and pasties?"

Olivia thought of the delicious pasties at Rosie's cafe and her stomach rumbled.

"Not quite."

"I thought you'd be back by now."

Olivia paused. Should she tell Sebastian, her most-trusted cousin and the only one who truly understood? As if proving her point, she didn't have to.

"You sly dog." Sebastian broke the silence. "You've met

someone down there, haven't you? Oh my god, if your mother only knew—"

"—but she's not going to, though, is she?"

"Not from me!" Sebastian sounded pleased with his detective work. "But tell me more."

Olivia blew out a breath, warmth spreading through her at the thought of Rosie. "I have met someone, but nothing's happened and it can't go anywhere, can it? She runs the local cafe, she's gorgeous, independent, fierce — all the things I love. She's not interested in fame or wealth. And she wants to go travelling, which, as you know, is why I joined the army."

"So, what's the problem?"

Olivia stared at the phone. Sometimes, Sebastian could be very dim. "Apart from my upcoming wedding?"

"Yes, yes, apart from that. You know you could keep her as a mistress if you did start something. Come to me for the lowdown on getting the balance right."

Olivia's stomach lurched. "I'm not really the mistress-keeping type — and I know for sure Rosie isn't mistress material, either." She paused. "But the thing is, she's just so... real, you know? And she likes me for me. But of course, the other problem is she thinks I work in PR and I'm an ex-solider. So I'm not being totally me. And I'm betting if she finds out the truth, she might run a mile."

"You don't know until you tell her. She might surprise you."

Would she? Olivia imagined telling Rosie she was fourth in line to the throne, but then sirens blared in her brain and she quashed that particular scenario pronto. "Maybe. She's so gutsy, but she's got issues, too. I want to help, but I'm not sure how. She needs money to keep her cafe afloat, and I want to just write her a cheque."

She filled Sebastian in on the situation at Mark & Maude's.

"If she's everything you say she is, she won't take kindly to you coming along and throwing money at her. She's too proud.

Plus, it sounds like that's what her ex tries to do. Also, it might blow your cover."

Of course, everything he said was true. Maybe he wasn't so dim after all.

"If you really want to help and get into her good books, you'll have to do something she can run with. Something that will make a difference to her. Help her out with a problem, give her your time, show her you care. Any fool can throw money at a problem, but not everyone can solve things in the moment."

Of course — why hadn't she thought of that? She should help Rosie out — and she knew exactly how. "Sebastian, I don't say this often, but you're a bloody genius."

He spluttered. "I am?"

"You are, but don't spread it around."

He laughed at that. "And Olivia?"

"Yes?"

He paused. "I don't know if this is my place to say, but… don't be too long down there."

The hairs on the back of her neck all lifted at once. "Why?"

"It's Jemima." Another long pause. "When I said she wasn't being discreet, it's not just telling people you've buggered off." A big intake of breath. "Look, I was in the club at the weekend and not to put it too bluntly, Jemima had her tongue down another woman's throat."

Nausea rose in her. What the fuck was she playing at? "Someone we know?" Olivia stopped — of course it was someone they knew. "Let me guess, Tabitha Middleton."

There was a lengthy pause before he replied. "Yes, Tabitha."

Olivia almost laughed it was so comical. Tabitha, whom Jemima had sworn she was done with.

She should have been madder, but instead she just felt sad. They were living separate lives at the moment, after all.

"Did I do the right thing?" She could almost hear Sebastian's audible wince.

She sighed. "You did, big cousin. Don't worry. I'll sort Jemima and I'll get in touch with Mother. Today is going to be a day of deeply uncomfortable conversations, isn't it?"

"Rather you than me," he replied. "See you soon — call in when you're home, I miss you."

"I will." She ended the call and opened the back door, standing in the door frame, soaking up the lunchtime sun.

Fuck Jemima and fuck it all.

She was here, and she was going to help Rosie, even if nothing happened. At least she'd leave here knowing she'd made a difference, and that was what mattered. Her mother and her fiancée could wait.

Plus, Rosie would feed her, and right now, that was a more pressing matter.

CHAPTER 12

When her alarm went off, Rosie had been awake for a good long while. She put a hand on her chest, feeling her heartbeat. Her heart was slamming against her ribcage as though it wanted to break free from its confines.

The walk home with Charlie — her hero — had sobered her up, but the signs of a hangover were still very much present.

She touched her finger to the place on her cheek where Charlie had kissed her. *Charlie.* During the bouts of fitful sleep she'd had, Charlie's face had appeared in her dreams several times.

Even though she knew Charlie would be leaving Otter Bay as soon as next week, meeting her had loosened something inside of Rosie. Not only the desire to kiss her on the lips instead of the cheek, but the possibility of change. Of something different. Spending time with Charlie had shifted her perspective and made her realise that she wanted other things besides waking up early every morning and spending her days in a ramshackle cafe.

This thought had dawned on her with the particular clarity that came with the kind of night she'd had. Fitful sleep alternating with long stretches of being awake had left her mulling over her entire life.

Around four in the morning, the conclusion had presented itself loud and clear. Images of her bank balance, memories of her mum and dad, hopes for Paige and, maybe for the first time ever, dreams for herself, had played like a movie in her mind, converging in the decision she was finally ready to make.

Rosie knew what to do. She'd known for a long time, but she'd been waiting for the right sign to cross her path. She laid a finger on her cheek again and gently pressed down.

~

"Look at this place," Rosie said. She swept her arm about in a dramatic fashion, then brought a hand back to her head. The cider she'd indulged in last night might have been local, but it was not being very kind to her this morning. "It's a dump."

"It's not a dump, Rosie," Aunt Hilary said. "Sure, it could do with some sprucing up, but that's not what this place is about."

Rosie stared at the door. Charlie hadn't been in yet. She was probably in bed, sleeping it off. But she had said she would come by today. She glanced at the clock on the wall opposite her — which looked just as worse for wear as the rest of the cafe. It was only midday. Charlie would probably stop by for lunch instead of breakfast today.

Rosie opened the folder she'd brought from home. It only contained one item — a piece of paper she'd picked up a while ago, when things had first taken a turn for the worse. She showed her aunt the For Sale sign she kept inside the folder.

Aunt Hilary shook her head. "Are you sure this is what you want? This place is your life."

"Of course I'm not sure, but I'm definitely sure this place should not stay open the way it is, either. And I can't keep stalling while I'm haemorrhaging money. I need to make a decision." Rosie glanced at Aunt Hilary. She looked tired, her eyes sunken, the grey roots of her hair showing. She imagined she didn't look much better herself.

Rosie had mulled it over in her head a million times, but she already knew all the pros and cons. She'd just been afraid to make the decision, because it would change her life completely.

Perhaps her evening with Charlie had something to do with that. If she no longer had the cafe to worry about, she could go to London at some point in the future to visit her. She pushed the thought from her mind immediately. That was not a valid reason to try and convince Aunt Hilary. It was just... Rosie didn't quite know what it was. Just a feeling she got when she thought about Charlie and her self-assured, sexy ways.

"I do understand," Aunt Hilary said. "But it's a big decision, and, if you don't mind me saying, you look a little exhausted this morning. Maybe it's not the kind of decision to make when you're not feeling one hundred per cent."

"I look tired because I was up half the night coming to this conclusion. The only possible one." She expelled a sigh. "I need the money to pay for Paige's university."

"Paige can get a student loan," Aunt Hilary said.

Rosie shook her head. "Mum and Dad paid for my education. I want to do the same for Paige, so she doesn't have to start her working life in debt."

"If you put that For Sale sign up," Aunt Hilary said, "you do know who's going to be the first to make an offer, don't you?"

"Greg and Linda Davies," Rosie said, "most likely using their lovely daughter as a proxy."

Aunt Hilary narrowed her eyes. "Speaking of the lovely Amy," she said. "I heard there was a little, how shall I put it, altercation between her and the new girl in the pub last night."

Rosie's jaw slackened. She should have known that Aunt Hilary would have heard by now. You couldn't bat an eyelid in this village without everyone knowing about it. If she sold the cafe, Rosie could get out of here, if only for a little while — take a break from Otter Bay's stifling atmosphere.

"Yes, well, you know how annoying Amy can be." Rosie almost said that Amy had it coming, but that wasn't something she would say to her aunt.

"I think you know best of all." Aunt Hilary tilted her head. "Do you really want Mark & Maude's to become part of the Davies conglomerate?"

"Conglomerate?" Rosie chuckled. "I wouldn't go as far as to call owning two B&Bs, one pub, and one cafe slash bar in town that." When Rosie spelled it out like that, it was beginning to sound a lot like a conglomerate.

"You're forgetting the wine bar and if they add another cafe to all of that," Aunt Hilary said. "They'll be one step closer to owning all of Otter Bay."

"That might be so, but it's not a reason for me to hold on to it." Rosie picked at a serviette. She wasn't sure she could hold her own against much more scrutiny. Because not only was her entire life wrapped up in Mark & Maude's, her memories were as well. Her dad in the kitchen, with his indestructible white apron, her mum in the front, having a chat with every single customer — even the ones who didn't much feel like chatting.

"I just wanted you to be aware of it."

Rosie let her gaze swoop over the cafe again. What would Amy's parents do to it if they bought it? They'd probably make it look like a replica of a trendy coffee bar in London — and put quinoa and smashed avocado on the menu.

"Someone else might buy it," Rosie said, trying to inject a sprinkle of hope into her voice, but she couldn't even muster that.

"I wish I could help," Aunt Hilary said. "This place means a lot to me as well."

Rosie took a deep breath. "Maybe we've let our feelings for this place stand in the way of making the right decision. It's been losing money for more than a year. I have no savings. I can't keep on sitting around waiting for something amazing to happen. It's not realistic."

"We might have a great summer," Aunt Hilary said.

"Yeah, like last year." Rosie hung her head. "When it rained almost every weekend."

"Nothing we haven't seen before. And people do love a pasty when it's pouring down outside."

"Yes, but a lot of them prefer to eat it in a fancier-looking place." Rosie craned her neck and tried to look into the kitchen through the open door. She didn't see Gina. When it was quiet — and it often was — she usually went out the back and sat on the bench outside, chatting on her phone to her family in Argentina. "And chances are Gina will have to leave soon."

Aunt Hilary nodded. "Say you do sell it, what will you do?" Aunt Hilary's eyes were narrowed in concern.

Good question. Perhaps it was that particular uncertainty that had kept Rosie from making the ultimate decision for too long. "Definitely not work for the Davies'," she said on a sigh. "I couldn't bear that."

"You should be able to get a good price for this place." Aunt Hilary scanned the cafe, as though making an estimate in her head. "You'll be able to get by for a while, until you find your feet, at least."

"I'd love to go to America," Rosie said. "Drive down the Pacific Coast Highway, like Mum and Dad did before they had me."

"I'd miss you if you went." Aunt Hilary drew up a corner of her mouth. "But I'd understand if you wanted to leave. You were never meant to come back here in the first place. You've done more than your best. You looked after Paige." She cocked her head. "Maybe it *is* time you put yourself first." Aunt Hilary leaned over the table. "And it's not as if Otter Bay is teeming with eligible bachelorettes, is it?"

Did her aunt just wink at her? Rosie grinned to let her aunt know she appreciated the sentiment, but it was a little disconcerting to have *that* kind of conversation with her nonetheless.

Rosie picked up the For Sale sign. "So, what do you say? Shall I put this up?"

"Have you talked to Paige about it?"

"I haven't told her my final decision yet." Rosie had always tried to shield her sister from money woes, but Paige was a bright girl, and she could put two and two together. "I'll talk to her after school."

"How do you think she'll react?"

Rosie pursed her lips. Not long ago, she'd wanted to keep the cafe and stay in Otter Bay, so Paige could have a place to come home to in between terms. "She's going away soon. Her life's going to go from Otter Bay dreariness to Bristol University excitement. She cares about this place, I know that, but her life's about to change so drastically, I think she'll accept my decision."

"Are you sure you want to hang that up before you've talked to her?" Aunt Hilary nodded at the sign.

"I'm afraid that if I don't hang it up this very second, I'll start changing my mind again." Rosie fidgeted with the edges of the For Sale sign.

Aunt Hilary gave a slow nod. "It'll be the end of an era."

A pit the size of a football seemed to sink right down to Rosie's stomach. Saying it and doing it were very different things. She didn't know if she could actually instruct her hands to lift up the sign and stick it in the window. It was such a monumental act of change. But Rosie needed change. This was the only option. And she needed the money.

She considered asking Aunt Hilary to put up the sign for her, but it was important that she did it herself. Like an act of transition. The first step to a new life.

Rosie stood and walked to the window closest to the door.

The sign would be most visible if she hung it next to the menu. She fished a roll of Sellotape out of the back pocket of her jeans. She'd put it there that morning, when she was still feeling extremely determined to do this.

"Here we go," she said, and stuck the sign on the window. Mark & Maude's was now officially for sale. She stared at the sign and, for a split second, contemplated taking it down again. That ball in the pit of her stomach was not getting any smaller. But she'd crossed the first hurdle. It might have been hard, but there were opportunities on the other side of this as well. Rosie tried to focus on those instead of the memories the cafe evoked.

A shadow passed by the window. Someone outside stopped to look at the sign. With the way word travelled in Otter Bay, soon the entire village would know. Rosie tried to make out who it was checking out the For Sale sign, but she couldn't see their face. Whoever it was, she was sure they'd do a good job of spreading the word.

She was about to turn around when the door swung open. The person who'd been eyeing the sign was coming in. The questions would be starting already.

Rosie braced herself and, as she straightened her spine, came face to face with Charlie.

CHAPTER 13

When Olivia walked up to Mark & Maude's, Connie from the next-door boutique was standing in her doorway. When she saw Olivia, pound signs flashed in her eyes and she pointed at the blouse in the window. Olivia gave her a panicked smile and broke into a jog to get into the cafe before Connie snagged her into conversation — but when she got to the doorway, she stopped dead.

Somebody was putting a For Sale sign in the window. A dog-eared, home-made For Sale sign that looked like it'd seen better days.

Mark & Maude's was for sale? Rosie had told her things were bad, but she didn't think they were that bad.

Was she too late to help? Not if she could help it.

She ran a hand through her carefully styled hair — she'd had a shower and given herself a pep talk in the bathroom mirror before she left — and pushed open the door. She found herself looking down into Rosie's unsure, nervous gaze. She clutched a small roll of Sellotape in her right hand.

"What's all this?" Olivia said, pointing at the For Sale sign. "I thought you were going to give yourself more time?"

Rosie let go a sigh. "Sometimes, the answer just presents itself and you know it's the right thing to do."

Olivia wasn't convinced. "But this is your mum and dad's place."

Rosie put a hand on Olivia's forearm and looked into her eyes. "And that's just it — it's their place. Like I was just telling Aunt Hilary, it'll always be theirs, never mine. And it might not happen overnight, but I need to move on, make a new start." She squeezed Olivia's arm. "Pot of tea and a full English?"

Olivia nodded, a slight frown still creasing her face. "The greasier, the better."

As Rosie went to leave, Olivia touched her arm again, glancing around the near-empty cafe. At nearly lunchtime, she could see why Rosie thought it was a lost cause. "Have you got time to have a quick cup of tea with me?" After yesterday and then this, she wanted to see if Rosie was okay.

Rosie's mouth twitched; then she nodded. "Sure. I'll just go tell Gina."

Olivia sat at her usual table, as Hilary drew up beside her, her face drawn. "Do you mind?" She set down a pot of tea and two mugs and indicated the seat opposite.

Olivia nodded and sat up. The family matriarch was asking for an audience; when that happened, she listened. "Please, have a seat."

"I won't stay long," Hilary replied, drumming her fingers on the table before bringing her eyes up to meet Olivia's. "This time of year is always hard. Rosie thought about selling last year, but this time she seems more determined." She paused. "Can you have a word with her? She seems to listen to you. I just don't want her to make a mistake she regrets in the future."

Olivia nodded. "I don't, either." She reached over and patted Hilary's arm. "Leave it with me."

Satisfied, Hilary got up.

Rosie returned, and Hilary gave her a hug, poured them both a mug of tea, then bustled off.

"A lot's gone on since last night," Olivia said — for her and Rosie both. Rosie didn't even know the bombshell that had been dropped on Olivia this morning about the wedding and Jemima's indiscretions — and she couldn't ever know.

A wave of hopelessness washed over Olivia, but she pushed it away.

Rosie gave her a resigned look, casting her gaze around the cafe. "It's hardly jumping, is it? Not exactly a hotbed of cafe life. We're losing money, and I can't keep repeating the same story. But on top of that, Amy's behaviour last night, and meeting you and all the places you've been has made me feel very... small town. Like I need to get out, live a little. I can't hang around here, limping on forever."

Living in such a small town sounded ideal to Olivia, but the grass was always greener. They both wanted a simpler life, but their situations couldn't be more different. The struggling cafe owner and the princess. It sounded like a straight-to-TV rom-com.

"I get it, but you also need to see it from where I'm sitting." Olivia sat forward, taking a sip of her tea. "You make great tea, by the way — a staple of cafe life but not always a given."

Rosie leaned forward, giving Olivia a conspiratorial smile. "Yorkshire Tea. It's our top-secret ingredient."

Olivia grinned. "My mother's favourite, too." She slapped herself — they weren't here to talk about her family.

Rosie sat back. "So, tell me how you see it. Because I see it as tired decor plus no customers equals sell the place."

"But you have it in your power to change that." Olivia cocked her head. "You have a great chef, right?"

"The best."

"But you're not making the most of her." Olivia hoped she wasn't overstepping the mark here, but she wanted to help.

"I'm not?" Rosie's tone was cool.

"No. I agree you need to give this place a facelift — not that hard, some bold colours, some new crockery and cutlery, new branding."

"Branding?" Rosie rolled her eyes. "Now you're sounding *very* London."

Olivia gave her a grin. "Maybe you need a bit of London to survive, seeing as the tourists pouring in this summer will be from there." She paused. "Anyway, facelift, and then here's my grand plan: a new summer menu and," she paused for added effect, "evening opening with a small but brilliant menu. A few candles on the tables, and you can charge more for the food. Plus, Gina will be happier not just cooking fry-ups and pasties." She winced. "Even though the pasties are delicious."

Rosie folded her arms across her chest, regarding Olivia sceptically. "Are you Gordon Ramsay in disguise, giving me a restaurant makeover?"

Olivia spluttered. "I hope I've got a smaller chin than him."

Rosie let out a bark of laughter. "You're way less obnoxious, too." She paused. "But seriously, why are you so hell-bent on helping me? What's in it for you?"

Olivia shrank back, wincing at her tone.

Rosie reached over and put a hand to her arm. "That came out way harsher than I meant." She squeezed. "Sorry."

What was in it for her? Nothing. She just wanted to help Rosie because… Why? She wasn't sure. Maybe because she'd helped Olivia put some perspective on her crazy life? Reminded her there was another way to live, and that despite what all Olivia's family and friends thought, their way was not the only way.

Olivia steadied herself before replying. "I just want to help you." She shook her head. "I feel like we have a connection. I know I'm going soon but I just wanted to… I don't know, leave you with something to remember me by." Jeez, that sounded dumber than she'd anticipated when the words emerged. "I'm not making much sense."

Maybe that had something to do with the way Rosie was staring at her now, a warm, soft stare full of gratitude and something she couldn't quite put her finger on.

"I love that you want to help," Rosie said, her gaze drifting to Olivia's lips and then back up. "I guess it's just not something I'm used to."

Olivia matched her soft smile. "All I'm saying is… take the sign down for now and give these changes a go. I'll help, and I know Gina will be on-board." She glanced around. "We can have this place ship-shape and ready to go in a few days, and then just see what happens."

Rosie was thinking about it, as Gina arrived at their table, carrying two plates laden with bacon, egg, sausage, tomatoes, baked beans, mushrooms and black pudding.

Olivia made room on the table, the smell of the bacon making her woozy with anticipation. She glanced up at Rosie as she picked up her cutlery. "You're having one, too?"

Rosie smirked. "No amount of pills can combat last night's alcohol intake. Sometimes, a fry-up is what's called for."

"You need anything else?" Gina asked, wiping her hands on a white tea towel draped over her shoulder.

"Just you," Olivia said, holding up an index finger. "If I come back when you close at four, can we sit down and go over your citizenship test?"

Gina's face quirked in surprise. "You and me?"

The Argentinean twang of her accent made Olivia think of smooth glasses of Malbec on hot summer nights. She nodded. "I'm going to make sure you pass the next one, so Rosie doesn't have to worry about losing you as her chef." She glanced over at Rosie, who was staring at her now with a puzzled look on her face.

"That would be so good," Gina said. "Thank you."

Olivia concentrated on eating her brunch, not looking at Rosie for a few moments.

"Where did you come from?" Rosie's tone was full of wonderment.

When Olivia looked up, Rosie shook her head, the warm smile still there. Her voice was low, her gaze unwavering. "You sweep into town like some mysterious stranger, you put Amy in her place and now you want to help my cafe. That's not even mentioning you're tall, dark and beautiful. I'm waiting for the punchline, but it hasn't come yet."

Her words reached in and grabbed Olivia's heart, making her draw in a sharp breath.

Rosie thought she was beautiful? Nobody had called her beautiful in a very, *very* long time.

"There's no catch — I just want to help you. After everything you've been through, you deserve it." She paused. "Plus, if anybody can help Gina brush up her language skills, it's me. I helped locals learn English when I was in Afghanistan, and if I can't help her pass her citizenship test, my mother would never forgive me."

Damn it, why did she keep mentioning her mother today? She must be on her mind.

"Then I'm all for it, thank you." Rosie was still looking at her like she'd landed from outer-space.

Olivia put down her cutlery, the food giving her energy, making her brave. If Rosie thought she was beautiful, maybe she should act on it.

"You'll think about the cafe plan, too? Just see if it works? Give it a few weeks?"

Rosie moved her mouth one way, then the other. "I don't know—"

"—You know what, don't decide now. We can do the facelift and rebrand this week, and then let me take you out this weekend and persuade you. And I'll show you what could be done. What do you say?"

Rosie arched a perfect eyebrow one more time. "You want to take me out?"

Olivia gulped. Yes, that's what she'd said. "I do."

"Like on a date?"

At Rosie's words, her heart began to boom. "A little like that, yes." She bit her lip, nervous now. "You know what, exactly like a date. Get dressed up." She leaned in, giving Rosie what she hoped was her best sexy stare. "I demand glad rags." She paused. "Do you have glad rags?"

Rosie gave her a look. "We're not that backward — we do have occasions for dresses even in Otter Bay."

"Then put your dress on. This Saturday, we're going out."

Rosie grinned. "Okay Miss London, you're on." She paused. "More to the point, do you have glad rags?"

Olivia's face dropped. "You know what, I don't."

Her mind raced. She'd have to contact her private secretary and get her to courier some down. And make sure she did it without anybody else knowing, or questions would be asked. "But I'm sure I can sort something out."

Rosie chewed her food before replying. "If you're really stuck, there's always Connie's boutique."

At that, Olivia let out a long, loud chuckle.

CHAPTER 14

"It's like an episode of *Homes Under the Hammer* and *Money for Nothing*...and I've just *Escaped to the Country*," Charlie said.

"Impressive knowledge of daytime television for someone with a full-time job." Rosie got up from her knees. She'd been covering the plinths with masking tape so they could start painting the wall first thing tomorrow.

Charlie still hadn't divulged more details about her life in London. In fact, Rosie didn't even know her last name, which made it rather difficult to google her and find out all the things Charlie wasn't willing to come forth with herself. But Rosie shouldn't think like that. Look at what Charlie was doing for her cafe.

A broad smile, a deep gaze into Rosie's eyes, and some marketing buzz words had been enough to make Rosie change her mind about selling the cafe, and she'd taken down the For Sale sign hardly an hour after she'd put it up.

Charlie just shrugged. She sat at a table, scrolling on her phone, which had buzzed a few times already with incoming messages. "Come look at this." She beckoned Rosie over.

After having spent the better part of an hour on her knees, Rosie was happy to sit on an actual chair for a minute.

"What do you think of these for the cafe?" Charlie showed her the phone screen.

Rosie stared at the image of a plate. It had an intricate blue pattern on it and looked decidedly different from the plain white plates Mark & Maude's had been serving full English breakfasts on for decades. Most of the plates they used were chipped in more than one place. But a plate was one of those things that you could keep on using forever — no matter how chipped or how many times it went in the dishwasher, it always continued to fulfil its purpose.

"Pretty, right?" Charlie asked, head tilted.

"Pretty price tag as well," Rosie said. Thirty-five quid a plate? Had the rebranding gone to Charlie's head? She seemed to have lost her sense of perspective completely.

"It's details like this that matter, Rosie," Charlie said. "If you want to attract the right crowd."

"Do you honestly mean to tell me that the pattern of the plate you eat your breakfast from makes a difference to your eating experience?"

"Of course. And look." Charlie flicked her finger over her phone screen a few times. She had one of the newer models with a humongous screen. Rosie still used the iPhone she'd bought second-hand from Dave three years ago. "This cutlery goes with it."

Rosie did Charlie the courtesy of glancing at the screen intently for a few seconds. Eighteen pounds for one fork? What world was Charlie living in? "I think we should perhaps focus on giving this place a fresh coat of paint before we decide on the details." She pursed her lips.

Charlie reached for the bottle of wine she'd brought and filled an empty water glass — the cafe didn't have any wine glasses. "Here." She handed Rosie the glass. "Maybe this will make you more amenable to my lofty crockery goals."

Rosie took hold of the glass. The memory of the other day's hangover had long faded. So much had happened since then. She'd decided to sell the cafe, then give it another go for a few more weeks. She could actually do with a glass of wine right about now. She took a sip, then pulled the bottle closer and examined the label. "Where did you get this? Not at the local co-op, that's for sure."

Charlie's features tensed for a split second. "At my friend's house," she said.

"Some friend." Rosie took another sip. "I'd like to get to know this friend of yours. Will you introduce me?"

"She's not local," Charlie said. "She just has a house here." She refocussed her attention on her phone, then turned its screen back to Rosie. "You never said what you thought of the cutlery."

Rosie needed another gulp of wine before she could say what she wanted to express. "I really appreciate all your help, but buying paint tomorrow is already going to cost more than I can afford. I can't add new plates and cutlery to that bill. And if I have to choose between the two, I choose the paint." She flashed Charlie a warm smile. "And the free labour you're so generously offering."

Charlie held up her hands. "Okay, we'll start with painting." She shoved the phone in Rosie's direction. "But you did like what I showed you?"

"I'm not denying you have exquisite taste." The wine was helping Rosie relax. She sneaked another glance at the eighteen-quid fork. She still thought the price was ridiculous. Then Charlie's phone lit up with a message. Before Charlie could pull it away, Rosie saw the name 'Jem' appear on the screen.

Charlie rolled her eyes. "You can never really leave London, can you?"

"A friend?" Rosie inquired.

Charlie bit her bottom lip before speaking. "My ex." She followed up with a wary grin. "Now don't go knocking back all that wine yet. We still have work to do today. Making over the entire cafe in one week is quite the challenge we've set ourselves." She jumped out of her chair. "What's next?"

Rosie looked up at Charlie. She wore a T-shirt with her tight jeans and that impressive shoulder line Rosie'd guessed at the previous night was gloriously on display. She pushed away the thought that Charlie might not be in Otter Bay anymore by the end of the week. Although she did seem to be able to set her own calendar. Or maybe all the texts she'd been getting — and had been looking quite guilty about — were from her family, demanding she come back to London, and back to work, pronto.

Rosie got up as well and, as she did, couldn't help thinking that, once again, Charlie had expertly changed the subject as soon as it had ventured in the direction of her private life. Not that Rosie was that keen to discuss Charlie's ex.

"Time to put those muscles of yours to the test," Rosie said. "I'd like to move that sideboard over there."

"Some girl power will be required," Charlie said, "but I've no doubt we can do it."

"Who needs men when you have two lesbians on hand to do the heavy lifting?" Rosie walked to the sideboard. It was about a million years old. She hoped it wouldn't fall apart when they moved it.

"Let me see what *you*'ve got in the gun department." Charlie had followed her and grabbed Rosie by the biceps. She encircled Rosie's arm and squeezed gently. "Hm," was all she said.

Rosie stuck her hands on her hips. "What's that supposed to mean?"

Charlie flexed her arm, her biceps bulging. The sight of

them made Rosie swallow hard. "It doesn't really compare does it?" Charlie stood there grinning.

"I can't go only on sight." She took a step closer. "I may have to cop a feel myself before I can reach an informed decision."

This time, Charlie took a step closer. They stood only inches apart. Charlie flexed her muscle a bit more.

Slowly, Rosie brought up her hand. Before she touched a finger to Charlie's upper arm, she stopped the motion of her hand. Her breath grew shallower. A hint of Charlie's perfume drifted up her nose. Rosie rubbed a fingertip over the swell of Charlie's upper arm. Her skin was smooth, the muscle underneath rock hard.

She glanced away from Charlie's arm and looked her in the eye. God, her eyes were the most peculiar kind of colour. Rosie had never seen that kind of green, flecked with tiny spots of gold.

Rosie tilted her head. She couldn't stop herself. She'd wanted to do this last night, when Charlie had ended the evening with a peck on her cheek. Rosie was going for her lips now. She closed her eyes, inhaling more of Charlie's scent. She let her fingers sink down deeper into her biceps and prepared for her lips to meet Charlie's for the very first time.

The door of the cafe opened. They both jumped and quickly took a few steps away from each other.

"I thought you could use some help," Paige said. She looked from Rosie to Charlie, then back at Rosie. "Unless you'd rather do this just the two of you."

"Don't be silly, any extra pair of hands is more than welcome." Charlie walked in Paige's direction. "Hi Paige," she said, "how are you?"

"I'm all right." Paige looked at Rosie again.

Rosie hoped her cheeks weren't too flushed, although she could feel them burning. How much had Paige seen? If only she'd arrived a minute later. Or two. Or ten.

Rosie tried to regroup. "Right, this sideboard." She tapped a hand against the piece of furniture. "Now that there are three of us, it definitely shouldn't be a problem."

They moved the sideboard away from the wall and Rosie put Paige to work behind it, applying tape and protecting the floor in preparation for tomorrow's paint job.

Charlie was back on her phone. Had she received another message from Jem?

Rosie wondered if she should take Charlie outside and say something. But what could she say? *Wanna have a go at that first kiss again?*

Charlie put her phone in her back pocket and looked around the cafe. "What are we going to do with these tables?" she asked. "Upcycle, I presume?"

"It's all the rage," Paige said from behind the sideboard.

Rosie tried to find Charlie's glance, but she kept looking away. Maybe that last message she'd received had given her an ultimatum to go back to London. Who knew, perhaps Rosie's tall, dark, beautiful stranger would be gone by tomorrow and she wouldn't even be there for the grand re-opening of the spruced-up Mark & Maude's.

Her stomach twisted at the thought. She walked towards Charlie and put a hand on her arm, guiding her into the kitchen. "Everything okay?" Rosie asked.

Charlie nodded. "Your sister has the worst timing." She gave Rosie a crooked grin that lit up her eyes — those eyes Rosie had nearly lost herself in earlier.

"Little sisters, eh," Rosie said.

"Tell me about it." Charlie seemed to be withdrawing again.

"Do you have one as well?" At least Charlie could give her the answer to that very simple question.

"I'm the youngest, actually." Charlie rubbed her arm. "I have an older sister."

"Oh, so you're the young brat of the family. That explains it."

"Explains what?" That crooked grin again.

Rosie ignored the question. "What's your sister's name?"

Charlie took a moment to reply. "Alex," she said then.

"Could it be that your parents wanted boys instead of girls?" Rosie smiled, happy she knew at least a tiny fraction more about Charlie, who definitely remained a mysterious stranger to her.

Charlie chuckled. "That could very well be." She straightened her spine and rose to her impressive full height, towering over Rosie a little. "Shall we get back to it?"

CHAPTER 15

Olivia's fingers slipped through her wetness and she groaned as she came, her orgasm slaloming through her body and making her shake. She brought herself to another quick climax, scrunched up her face as it skated through her, then stilled. She clenched and unclenched her calf muscles, letting a languid smile wander onto her face as the thought of Rosie on top of her, her naked full breasts pressed into her, made another wave of desire wash over her.

She had to stop thinking about Rosie.

She was going home soon and she was engaged to be married. That thought brought a frown to her usually smooth brow as she stretched her arms above her head, enjoying the last rattle of her orgasm as it skittled through her.

She needed to get up and make herself look presentable: the Queen had demanded an audience.

She glanced out the bedroom window. The rain lashed down outside, clattering against the pane. As long as she lived, she'd never understand British weather: brilliant sunshine one day, driving rain the next. She hoped it wasn't a sign of impending doom.

She closed her eyes, letting her fingers settle over them, the only sound her breathing, now returning to normal. She swung her legs off the bed and threw herself in the shower.

Today might be her last day in Otter Bay if her mother had her way.

Half an hour later, she was dressed in a green shirt that brought out her eyes, her hair styled and bouncy, make-up applied as if she was starring as the lead in a Hollywood production. Where her mother was concerned, appearance was key.

Now she just had to try to shift the image of a semi-naked Rosie from her brain, and she'd be all set.

She flicked on her tablet, called up Skype and pressed the button. She tried to ignore the butterflies in her stomach, her sharpened nerves.

Her parents answered almost immediately, and Olivia sat up straight, adjusting the screen so they could see her clearly. When she saw Jemima sitting in a third armchair in the palace's drawing room, her heart sank.

Shit, they meant business.

Jemima looked nervous, as she always did in front of the Queen.

Olivia gave her a sympathetic smile: she wasn't alone.

"Olivia," her mother said, crossing her legs in a no-nonsense manner. She was wearing a navy skirt and jacket, with a lemon-yellow shirt. Her mother didn't do casual. "How are you?"

Olivia cleared her throat. "I'm good, thank you. And you?"

"We'd be better if you were back home where you belong."

Okay, she wasn't standing on ceremony.

"Father said I could stay another week," she countered, already feeling out of control. Her mother had that effect on her.

"And that's up when? Tomorrow?" Her tone had gone up an

octave. "Tell me, what's so fascinating in Otter Bay? Have you forgotten you're engaged to be married?

Jemima gave a sarcastic wave. "Hi, Olivia. Nice to see you, finally."

"You, too," Olivia replied, her voice flat. Jemima had on a long red skirt, paired with a cream top that showed off just enough of her golden skin that seemed to go on for miles. She looked tired, but she'd gone heavy on the make-up to cover it up. If you didn't know her, you'd probably miss it. Olivia knew her.

"Olivia, I'm not going to beat around the bush." A slight smile from Jemima at those words, mirrored by Olivia. "You're coming home tomorrow, and that's that. We've given you time to sort yourself out, but honestly, you're taking advantage of your father's good nature. I think you'll agree we've been terribly patient. Plus, we've resisted plans to send you bodyguards, even though security is less than happy you being there alone."

She nodded. "You have, and I'm grateful." She needed a charm offensive if she wanted to stay a little longer — and she desperately did. There were still things to do, stuff to sort. Namely, getting Gina through her test, and getting the cafe set up for its new era.

A flash of her and Rosie's nearly-kiss rolled through her and she sucked in a breath.

If she was honest, Rosie was on her list of things to do, too, but that wouldn't be kind to Rosie or her. It would be sexy, satisfying and fulfilling, but not kind. Rosie deserved someone who could fulfil her dreams, who could appreciate her for who she was. And that someone wasn't Olivia — seeing her parents and Jemima had driven that home.

Still, Olivia could finish what she started before she left. It was the least she could do.

She sat forward, painting on her endearing smile. "You've been brilliant, all three of you. And I'm sorry I haven't been there, Jemima, I know you want to do some official engagement photos." *When you haven't got your tongue down Tabitha's throat.* "And I promise, I'll do all that when I'm back. The photos, an interview, the wedding plans — the works. But I need to finish off a couple of things here first — I've already said I'm going to help out in the local community this weekend, and they're counting on me."

A flash of thunder crossed her mother's face.

Olivia ploughed on. "What I'm saying is, I'm coming home, of course I am, but I just need to tie up a few loose ends. Another week, that's all I'm asking, and then I'm all yours." She beamed at them, bracing herself for her mother's tirade.

"Another week?" Her mother threw up her hands. "Don't you think I'd like to swan off for a month somewhere, hiding in a house in the country, no responsibilities, no ties. We all would! I know your father would." She glanced at her husband, but he just gave her a non-committal smile. "But life's not like that, Olivia, and the sooner you learn that, the better. Life as a royal *especially* is not like that. We do things for others, with no thought for ourselves."

Olivia tried to muffle her snort, but she wasn't as successful as she'd hoped.

Her mother's face hardened. "Don't scoff, Olivia. It's a very unappealing habit."

She winced. "Sorry, Mother. I know I'm asking a lot, but please, I just need this time. And as soon as I'm back, we'll do photos. Can you wait that long, Jemima?"

Jemima jolted slightly on hearing her name. "Sorry?" She hadn't even been listening.

"I was saying, one week and I'll be back to do everything, okay?"

She gave her a resigned shrug. "If that's what you're offering, I guess that's what I'll have to take."

"Hugo, this is not acceptable — will you please speak to your daughter."

Her father sat up, leaning forward so his head took up the whole screen. He'd never quite got the hang of using a video camera. "Olivia, your mother's right. You've been away for nearly three weeks, it's time to come home. For one thing, there are wedding details to sort out; for another, your fiancée has been left in limbo, wouldn't you say?"

With her mother, Olivia's first reaction was always to put up her fists, prepare to fight; her father had the opposite effect on her.

She stared at the screen, then nodded. "How about we compromise and say I'll come home Tuesday. Five days."

Her mother coughed. "Five days instead of seven? Not really a compromise. I want you back here for a photoshoot on Saturday or nothing."

"Monday?" Olivia's tone was light, so unlike the crushing sensation in her chest. She resisted the urge to count on her fingers: Saturday meant she only had two days left.

It was unthinkable.

Her father came to her rescue, as had so often been the case. "Monday will be fine. Nothing's booked, Cordelia," he told his wife, patting her hand. "Just make sure you're here for midday, okay?"

Olivia breathed out. "Okay."

Her mother squinted into the screen. "At least you listened with the haircut — the colour's not too bright and you look semi-respectable, not like you've just got out of prison like you did in the army."

She swallowed down her response. "I'll see you Monday."

Olivia stood up and walked to the kitchen sink, pouring out a glass of cooling water before drinking it down. Three weeks in Otter Bay and she'd almost managed to tune out her real life;

almost managed to forget her duties, her family, her upcoming wedding.

Almost.

But that call had brought it all sharply back into focus; once she was back in London, the slow pace of life and leisurely nights with Rosie would be a thing of the past. Soon, she'd have to go back to reality, and that thought made her rub her chest. Funny, but over the past three weeks, Otter Bay and Rosie had begun to feel like her real life.

Today was Thursday, and she had four days till she had to go back. She was going to make the most of them. The cafe was coming along, and with a bit more effort, it should be finished by their deadline. And she loved the paint colour Rosie had chosen: lemon yellow with shades of blue, just like her mother had been wearing today. The new chairs were being delivered on Saturday, and then that evening, Olivia was going to take Rosie out and show her a night she'd never forget.

A night that would make her stick in Rosie's memory forever.

Her phone beeping interrupted her thoughts, and she swiped right. Jemima.

'Make sure you do come home on Monday, because I'm just about done putting on a happy face for your mother. I'm in your corner here, don't forget it. See you Monday. x'

Olivia dropped her phone on the table and stared at the rain.

A cup of tea and some toast would make this better. She filled the kettle and switched on the radio, just as a song was coming to an end and the DJ began to chat.

"Big royal wedding news today: Kensington Palace has announced that the royal wedding cake for Princess Olivia and her bride, Jemima Bradbury, will be flavoured with elderflower and rose to emphasise the summery nature of the wedding.

More royal wedding news as we get it on Radio One — only nine weeks to go!"

Olivia flicked the switch, clutching the counter.

Nine weeks.

Fuck.

Real life was barrelling towards her at pace, so she'd better make these final four days count.

CHAPTER 16

Rosie peered into her closet. She had no idea where Charlie was taking her. She'd been told to put on her glad rags and Rosie had promised to wear a dress, of all things. She wondered what Charlie would look like in a dress. She'd only seen her in skinny jeans and Rosie couldn't really picture her in anything else. She didn't look like the dressing-up sort.

A knock on her open door startled her.

"Can't decide what to wear?" Aunt Hilary asked. She and Paige were watching *Casablanca* tonight. Rosie would have joined them, except she had a hot date. She still had trouble wrapping her head around the fact. A Saturday evening not spent in front of the telly or at the Dog & Duck. Her life was on the up.

"It's not as if I have that many fancy dresses to choose from." Rosie turned away from the closet.

Aunt Hilary cleared her throat. "The cafe looks great."

"Thanks. Charlie has been amazing."

"So it would seem." Her aunt leaned against the door frame. "What do you know about this Charlie, anyway?"

Rosie glanced at the clock next to her bed. Her aunt could

have picked a better time to discuss Charlie. But they'd barely had a moment alone since Rosie had reversed her decision to sell Mark & Maude's. Charlie had always been around, impressing Rosie with her enthusiasm for the cafe's make-over, although her painting skills left a lot to be desired.

"I know she's not Amy," Rosie said. "For now, that's enough for me."

"It's just that one minute you were sticking up the For Sale sign, and the next, you were taking it down again. This Charlie must have a lot of influence on you." Aunt Hilary pushed her glasses up her nose.

Rosie sat down on the edge of the bed. "It's hard to explain." She could hardly tell her aunt about the two almost-kisses she and Charlie had shared, and the many moments in between. "But it's not every day someone kind like Charlie comes along, lending a helping hand, and coming up with a bunch of great ideas for the cafe. She's inspired me in ways I've failed to do myself for a long time. She's jolted me back to life." Rosie shrugged. "And I really like her."

"That much is clear, but… I'd hate to see you hurt. After all you've been through."

Rosie nodded. "But looking at it from a different angle, I think I deserve a night out with someone like Charlie after all I've been through." She pulled up her shoulders. "And sure, I have no idea what will happen next. Charlie's not from here and I know next to nothing about her, yet, the past few weeks, she's made me feel more alive than I have in years."

Aunt Hilary stepped into the room. "You should wear the dress I gave you for your birthday last year."

Rosie didn't think so. It looked a bit too much like a Laura Ashley curtain for her taste. "I was more leaning towards this one." She headed towards the closet and took out the only other suitable dress she owned. A light blue number with a subtle blossom print stitched diagonally along the top.

"Ah, yes. Perhaps better for the occasion," Aunt Hilary said. She touched her hand briefly against Rosie's shoulder. "I'll leave you to get ready."

Rosie shot her aunt a warm smile. She meant well. She waited until Aunt Hilary had left the room, then held the dress along her body and looked at herself in the mirror. It should do nicely.

∼

Charlie had asked Rosie to stand outside her front door at 8.00pm sharp. Rosie had been glancing out the window for the past half hour, but only went out two minutes before eight. The moment she set foot outside the front door, a shiny black limousine pulled into the street. Rosie only realised it was Charlie picking her up when the car stopped in front of her house, the driver got out, and held the door open for her. Inside, Charlie sat beaming her a wide smile.

Rosie got in and sat opposite Charlie, who had shunned the skinny jeans for the occasion and was dressed in a pair of navy-blue trousers with a crisp white shirt.

"I'm stumped for words," Rosie said.

"Maybe this will help." Along with the smile she still sported, Charlie offered her a glass of champagne.

Rosie took it and held Charlie's gaze for a split second.

"Here's to our date," Charlie said and lifted her own glass towards Rosie's.

"I feel like a fairy-tale princess." Rosie was still trying to absorb the magic atmosphere Charlie had created.

"Everyone deserves to feel like a princess for an evening," Charlie said, and drank from the champagne.

"You look absolutely stunning." Rosie tilted her head. "In your glad rags, you actually do look a bit like Princess Olivia, but with short hair."

Charlie chuckled and took another sip.

"I haven't really been following the whole royal engagement hoopla," Rosie said. "Even though there was definitely a time in my life when a lesbian princess would have interested me to the point of obsession, but I'm a bit too old for that now." She drank some champagne. It was perfectly chilled and wonderfully dry. "But I did see the engagement photos of Olivia and what's-her-name. I don't remember. Something posh. And I didn't buy it for a second. It all looked so terribly put-on, which is a shame. Such a missed opportunity for some positive lesbian PR." Rosie glanced at Charlie. "But who knows, eh? And what do any of us know about what goes on in the royal family, anyway."

Charlie shrugged and shot Rosie another smile. "Have I told you how utterly gorgeous you look? You really glammed it up."

"I was asked to." Rosie put one leg over the other. Charlie was really turning it up tonight. "Now, where are you whisking me away to?"

"You'll see," Charlie said.

Fifteen minutes later, Rosie found herself in the fanciest restaurant she'd ever been to. One person took their coats, another guided them to their table, and yet another impeccably dressed waiter presented them with the menu — which had no prices next to the dishes.

Rosie glanced around. "I'm very impressed, but I can't help but wonder… where are all the other diners?"

"Elsewhere," Charlie said. "It's just you and me tonight."

"B—but," Rosie scanned Charlie's face, "how is that even possible? In a place like this?"

"Don't question it, Rosie. Tonight, you're a princess."

Rosie narrowed her eyes. "Who are you?" She burst into a smile. She could hardly believe another person would go to so much trouble for her. Rosie'd had to take care of herself for such a long time.

"Someone who likes you very, very much," Charlie said, making Rosie feel even giddier. "About the menu," she said. "No need to choose. We're having all of these dishes."

Rosie stared at the menu. She saw French oysters, a Thai seafood soup, Japanese sashimi, Argentinian beef and Moroccan couscous. "Very... diverse," she said, and glanced up again, looking into Charlie's sparkling green eyes.

"If you can't travel the world, the world will come to you."

Rosie's jaw slackened. This evening was turning out to be more than a dream — she could never have imagined something like this. But the best thing about the night was the woman sitting across from her.

Charlie nodded at a waiter, who promptly went into the kitchen, only to return a few minutes later with a very familiar woman by his side.

"Gina?" Rosie couldn't keep up with the surprises anymore.

"I asked Gina to cook for us tonight," Charlie said. "She's such an amazing chef."

"At your service, boss," Gina said and winked at them. "I need to get back to the kitchen. The *amuse-bouches* will be out shortly." Gina hurried off, leaving Rosie stupefied.

"*Amuse-bouches*," Rosie repeated. "Gina doesn't cook *amuse-bouches*."

"She does tonight." Charlie leaned over the table, offering Rosie a new angle on her cleavage.

"Some white wine, Madam?" the waiter asked. Rosie needed some alcohol to help her process the goings-on of the night. It was only half past eight and she'd been pleasantly surprised more times than in her entire life combined.

Four tasting courses and a few glasses of wine later, Rosie had to admit that even though she'd always loved Gina's food, she had, perhaps, been too preoccupied with keeping the cafe afloat to see Gina's full potential.

"You're right. Gina truly is amazing," she said.

"She's a keeper. And so is your cafe," Charlie said.

"I should be treating *you*. All you've done is help me. And the good times just keep on coming."

"All you have to do is be your glorious self, Rosie." Charlie's eyes softened. "That's more than enough for me."

Rosie wanted to snicker at Charlie's cheesy remark, but she couldn't. Because Charlie's words spread a new kind of warmth through her body. She was falling for her big time and, even though Charlie had a life in London, in that moment, it didn't matter. All that mattered were the two of them surrounded by soft lighting in a lovely restaurant, gorging on Gina's scrumptious dishes from around the world, enjoying each other's company.

∼

Back in the car on the way home to Otter Bay, Charlie sat next to Rosie instead of opposite her. They sat so close, their thighs touched, and Rosie could feel Charlie's body heat radiate onto her through the flimsy fabric of her dress.

It was just the two of them in the back of the limo. No one was going to walk in and interrupt them now. They'd had the most amazing evening and Rosie was more than a little tipsy. If ever there was a moment to kiss Charlie on the lips, it was approaching fast and hard.

Charlie reached into Rosie's lap and took her hand in hers. "On a scale of one to ten, how princess-like are you feeling?"

"At this very moment, I'm a bit too drunk to consider myself a princess." Rosie chuckled.

Charlie shook her head. "As if princesses never get drunk." She gave Rosie's fingers a gentle squeeze. Rosie's tummy tingled in response.

The car came to a stop. Had they arrived already? Just like

the rest of the evening, the ride had gone by in a flash. Rosie didn't want it to end.

Charlie turned to her.

"I don't know how to thank you for tonight," Rosie said. "I can hardly repay the favour."

"You don't have to thank me. I had the best night, Rosie. A night I would never have had if I hadn't met you." She slanted her head. "And if you really feel like you have to thank me, do it by making Mark & Maude's the success I know it can be."

Rosie shifted towards Charlie. "You're like a dream."

"I'm very real," Charlie said and leaned in.

Rosie slanted herself forward and, finally, felt Charlie's lips on hers. She leaned into the soft touch of their lips, breathing in deeply.

Charlie brought a hand to Rosie's jaw and drew her nearer. Rosie responded by folding her hands around the back of Charlie's neck.

Their lips opened and Rosie's tongue slipped inside Charlie's mouth. She forgot she was in a car outside her house, and that Charlie would be leaving soon — a sore subject they had expertly danced around throughout the evening. She forgot about everything and focussed only on Charlie's lips and her tongue twirling around hers. She surrendered herself to that delicious moment. And if it had to end after tonight, then at least they would always have had this.

CHAPTER 17

That kiss last night had been everything Olivia had expected and more. Rosie's lips had tasted of hope, of desire, of everything Olivia truly wanted in her life, but was afraid to reach out for. When she'd dropped Rosie home, she'd so wanted to ask her to come back with her instead. But how could she? It all went to making today that little bit harder.

What's more, she knew Rosie had questions — why wouldn't she? Every time the subject came around to Olivia and her life, she ushered it the other way; having had a lifetime of experience, she was a pro at doing so. But this time, she didn't want to. She wanted to be honest with Rosie, to tell her what she was feeling, the impossible situation she was in. An arranged marriage she was desperate to avoid, a future she couldn't think about without tears springing to her eyes.

So she'd gone over to the cafe this morning with plans to tell her. To confess it all. She was leaving tomorrow anyway, so it wouldn't be long before Rosie put two and two together and came up with four. But when she'd got to the cafe, Paige and Hilary had been there, and Rosie had been rushed off her feet, the new look and summer menu drawing in a roaring daytime trade. Olivia had eaten her bacon sandwich with a smile on her face as the Perkins family buzzed about the place, the cafe full of the aromas of ground coffee and freshly squeezed oranges. In one crazy week, they'd achieved what they'd set out to do: turn the cafe around. Now Olivia just hoped the evening menu worked as well, and their plans came to fruition.

When she'd realised Rosie was too busy to talk, Olivia had told her to come by her house tonight and given her the address: she couldn't do this anywhere else, they needed some privacy. Rosie had been stunned when she'd seen where she was staying, but Olivia had told her she'd explain it all tonight. Just to come around at seven. The cafe wasn't opening in the evenings till the following week, so Rosie had agreed. When she'd touched her arm as she'd left, they'd both stilled, sharing a look that said they still had unfinished business.

Olivia knew it, and Rosie did, too.

However, before anything could happen, Olivia had to tell Rosie the truth. She had to let her know who she was, why she was here and her reasons for keeping her identity under wraps.

She hoped Rosie understood.

If she didn't, Olivia didn't know how she was going to live with herself.

∽

Olivia opened the door to the manor house at just gone seven; Rosie stood on the doorstep, a slight frown on her face. Her dark blonde hair was full of static, showing it'd been freshly washed, and she was dressed in jeans and a black shirt. When she tried a smile she had some lipstick on her front tooth, but somehow, Olivia didn't think it appropriate to say.

The tension crackled between them as she stood aside for Rosie to walk past, her floral perfume filling Olivia's lungs. She closed her eyes as she breathed it in: she had to stay focussed tonight, or she knew things might go off course.

She ushered Rosie into the kitchen where she'd prepared a plate of cold cuts: Spanish ham, olives, mozzarella, fresh figs and Manchego cheese. She'd been surprised to find it all in the local supermarket, but she guessed that was the 'London influence' at work. A bottle of Tempranillo was breathing, and Olivia filled up the glasses, her heart fluttering in her chest. Rosie looked so confused, but also so beautiful; Olivia was nervous, because this mattered so much. This was bigger than Jemima, bigger than her parents, bigger than everything.

In a short space of time, Rosie had come to mean so much to her.

It was Rosie who broke the brittle silence.

"So, Charlie. You've avoided my questions the whole time you've been in Otter Bay, and now I find you're staying *here*." She cocked her head, trying to read Olivia's face. "How on earth are you staying in this place, by the way? Are you some kind of countess and you haven't told me?"

Olivia cleared her throat before answering, plotting out every word in her head before it seeped out of her mouth. "It's what I wanted to talk to you about," she began, her voice sounding calm. She was anything but. "It's kinda complicated, but let's just say I have connections."

Rosie smiled. "You must have. I mean, I knew you were posh — your accent is painted gold — but I didn't think you were staying here." She paused. "How did you even manage it? I mean, is it on Airbnb now?"

Getting the words out was harder than she thought. "I'm just lucky I guess, I went to the right school with the right people."

"That old chestnut — it's not what you know, it's who you know." Rosie eyed her. "But I guess, if you hang out with people who have it all, maybe it's a good thing. Like you with the cafe:

you didn't see the problems, you just saw the opportunity. It takes a special person to do that." She took a sip of her wine. "And guess what?" She sat up then, with a wide grin.

"What?"

"We had our best day ever today. Can you believe it? A lick of paint, some new menus, fresh flowers and boom! We took nearly three times the amount we did for the whole of last weekend in just one day. Whoever knew that Sunday brunch and bucks fizz was what people really wanted?"

She seemed genuinely baffled as Olivia laughed. "Mimosas, remember. Buck's Fizz makes it sound uncool — mimosas makes it sound positively exotic."

Rosie gave her a grin. "You see — that's what you get when you associate with people in high places — they know about shit like that. I never even knew I'd had a mimosa."

"You do now," Olivia replied. She leaned forward and put a hand on Rosie's arm. "And I'm thrilled about the takings — you deserve it all. Mark & Maude's deserves it all."

Rosie stared down at Olivia's hand, before covering it with her own. "I couldn't have done it without you."

Olivia's heart rose up and lodged in her throat as a trickle of want drizzled down her spine. She closed her eyes and when she reopened them, Rosie was staring at her like she'd hung the moon.

"I had a great time last night," Rosie said, her gaze never leaving Olivia. "I mean, nobody's ever done anything like that for me before. Gina's so fired up and..." She paused. "Thank you for reminding me there's more to life than the mundane. That things can be magical, that there's still room for wonder, for my breath to be taken away." She gulped, steadying her breathing before continuing. "Because last night, you took my breath away."

When Olivia locked her gaze with Rosie's, before letting it drift to Rosie's lips, the next move seemed inevitable. As if there was some director off camera yelling orders, telling them what to do. As the word 'Action!' rang out in Olivia's head, Rosie was on her feet, taking the starring role, reaching down and cupping Olivia's face, her eyes full of dark desire.

"You're so damn beautiful," she said, before closing the distance between them and pressing her lips to Olivia's.

Olivia let out a soft moan on contact. Her head swam in the moment, one that was rich with colour, bursting with life. As Rosie's lips slipped over hers and her fingers worked their way into Olivia's short hair, her plans to tell Rosie the truth were hushed. Instead, all Olivia could hear was the roar of her heart, and all she could feel was Rosie's body sliding onto her lap as she grabbed her hips and urged her there.

Her kisses tasted of honey and molasses; they were slow, sugary, long. But after a few minutes, Rosie pulled back.

Olivia's eyes sprang open, panicked. "You okay?"

Rosie gave a sweet smile and swung a leg, straddling her. "I just want to get closer to you." She reached down, staring into Olivia's eyes, her breath hot over her mouth. "And let's remove these glasses," she added, doing just that.

Olivia's breathing hitched as a surge of lust enveloped her.

Rosie brought her mouth to Olivia's neck, leaving a trail of hot kisses in her wake.

A warring duel of lust and guilt fought in Olivia's heart, and she couldn't tell which was winning.

But then something snapped: she had to be honest with Rosie, she had to tell her; she'd never forgive herself otherwise. "Rosie," she said, as Rosie ran her tongue up her neck again before eventually reaching her lips, this time slipping her tongue inside, too.

A punch of desire left Olivia breathless.

"Hmmm?" Rosie mumbled into her mouth.

"I need to tell you something," Olivia gasped, not quite

believing she was doing this. Her 20-year-old self would kill her.

Rosie drew back, eyeing her with naked desire. "Now?" she asked with a dazed smile.

She gave her another kiss, leaving Olivia punch-drunk.

"It's just... I'm leaving tomorrow." She drew in a lungful of breath. "I just thought you should know. I have to go back to London."

Rosie stilled in her arms, and Olivia braced herself for this to end. Her heart stalled.

"I knew it had to happen soon," Rosie whispered, pulling back. "In that case, we'd better make tonight count."

Rosie bent to kiss her once more, but Olivia stiffened, easing her back and clearing her throat. "But it's not just that... there's something else I need to tell you, too. Something big."

Rosie cocked her head. "Bigger than what's happening right here, right now?" Another sexy smile as she cupped Olivia's breast.

Olivia gulped. "It's pretty big."

Rosie stared at her with intent, her cheeks flushed. "Whatever it is, I'm sure it can wait." Desire coursed through Olivia as Rosie brought her lips back to hers in a bruising kiss. Olivia wilted at her touch.

And then, all the talk in her head ceased. She covered Rosie's mouth with hers, her tongue coming into play, her hands on Rosie's hips, pulling her closer. The only sound in the room was their ragged breathing and the soft meeting of lips.

And holy shit, Rosie could kiss; she was intoxicating. Olivia's mind jumped forward to what was beyond.

Rosie's pressure was soft at first, but the kiss soon escalated, with the two of them pulling apart after minutes had passed, staring at each other. The world shrank to this time and place.

Olivia couldn't wait any longer: she had to feel her.

Taking a deep breath, she popped the buttons of Rosie's

black shirt, slowly, carefully; when she laid a hand on Rosie's pale skin, her breathing stilled. With the pad of her thumb she brushed over the lace of Rosie's black bra, feeling her nipple harden under her touch, watching as Rosie's eyelids fluttered shut.

Her creamy skin stretched all the way up her long neck, and Olivia wanted to see it all.

She reached around and unhooked Rosie's bra with skilled fingers that brought an arch of a delicate eyebrow from Rosie; once her breasts were on show, Olivia pushed Rosie's shirt and bra off, before taking her breasts in her hands, sucking her nipples into her mouth, one, then the other.

Rosie ground down into her, and Olivia took note of how she wriggled when she clamped a nipple between her teeth and bit down lightly.

Rosie arched her back and her moan gained timbre.

Olivia grinned. She swept her hands up the contours of Rosie's naked back, as Rosie pulled off Olivia's top, then her bra, before staring down at her with a wicked grin. Just to make sure she had Olivia's attention, Rosie rolled her right nipple between her fingers.

Olivia felt it at her very core as she moved her hips, glancing up at Rosie, her breath hot and fast. "You want to do this here or somewhere a little more comfortable?"

Rosie leaned down and licked her way up Olivia's neck, ending with her tongue dancing on her lips. "I'll take whatever you're giving in any location you choose."

Heat flared in Olivia; Rosie was turning into her ideal woman before her very eyes. Suddenly she knew — she wasn't going to make it to the bedroom.

Olivia exhaled, before guiding Rosie off her and pushing the food and drink down the table. The last shards of evening sun cast shadows over both of them through the large kitchen windows.

Neither spoke as Olivia lifted Rosie up onto the table top, her breasts looking good enough to eat. So Olivia did, letting her tongue do the work, scraping her short nails down Rosie's back as she did. She inhaled Rosie's scent, before swirling her tongue around her neck, her earlobes, *her*.

Rosie moaned into Olivia's ear, pushing her hips towards Olivia, letting her know what she wanted.

The sound of Rosie's jeans being unzipped scratched the air, before Olivia worked them off. "You look incredible," she whispered in Rosie's ear, her fingers skating the edges of the black material covering Rosie's butt. Olivia pressed the palm of her hand between Rosie's legs.

Rosie threw an arm around her, her breath stalling.

Olivia pressed some more, revelling in Rosie's whimper. She allowed her finger to caress the edge of Rosie's knickers, then dip under them, groaning as she hit Rosie's wetness. Emboldened, she trailed a finger through it, and as Rosie closed her eyes, Olivia got her completely naked, spreading Rosie's legs and pulling her towards her.

"I've wanted to do this for so long," Olivia said, as she slid two fingers into her, marvelling at her warmth and how good it felt.

Rosie hissed into her ear, her hands on Olivia's back, their groans filling the kitchen.

Olivia drowned in the sweetness of it all as she pressed her lips back to Rosie, the drumbeat of this moment loud in her ears, the heat rising in her soul. Being inside Rosie was even better than she'd imagined, her fingers writing a love letter on Rosie's very core. She pulled her closer still, two becoming one, and they shared a momentary stare before Olivia fucked her harder.

Rosie let out a guttural moan and her eyes closed.

Olivia could feel herself gushing as she brought her thumb into play, circling Rosie's hard clit, her lover jerking in her arms as she did. She knew the fire had been lit, and now she just had to stoke it as best she could. She was going to give Rosie everything she had.

As Olivia circled and swooped, she fought back the unfairness of her plight; that this was happening on her final night, on the day she could put off reality no more. There was nothing she wanted more than to stay here, with Rosie, with this closeness, this emotion. She could feel it building, block by block, and it both scared her and left her exhilarated. Because what was she going to do with it when the sun came up? When she had to leave?

She pushed the thoughts aside as she nibbled her way along Rosie's collarbone, her thumb circling, her fingers exploring. Then she felt Rosie still, then arch her back.

"Don't stop!" Rosie gasped as she began to shake in Olivia's arms, her orgasm crashing through her.

Olivia never wanted to stop. She wanted this to go on and on forever, a never-ending stage of her and Rosie, in orgasmic bliss. She didn't let up, just as Rosie asked, and Rosie came one more time, crushing her fingers into Olivia's back, holding on for dear life. She squeezed and Olivia squeezed right back. The moment was bittersweet, but she couldn't tell Rosie why. She wanted to cling to it, stay being Charlie forever, but she knew it was impossible.

Despite that, Olivia couldn't help but smile when Rosie regained some power moments later, her face red and woozy.

Rosie kissed her hard, before reaching down and unzipping Olivia's trousers, her eyes dark pools of want that Olivia wasn't going to argue with.

"That was amazing," Rosie said, her words soaked with desire. "And I look forward to doing it again. But the whole time, I wanted to do something to you." She pushed Olivia's trousers down, regarding her underwear with a broad smile.

"Boy shorts. I knew you'd wear boy shorts." She trailed her tongue along Olivia's bottom lip and Olivia wobbled.

When she opened her eyes, Rosie was smiling at her. "You've been working hard," she said, pushing her down into the kitchen chair. Then she pulled off her boy shorts, before sinking to her knees and spreading Olivia's legs.

"And now I get to taste you, finally," Rosie said, her breath hot on Olivia's core.

Olivia shuddered, closing her eyes, waiting for the elixir from Rosie's tongue to overtake her.

As Rosie licked her way from Olivia's butt to her clit, Olivia's brain duly melted, her head falling backwards, her hands gripping the chair. Rosie's tongue on her was dizzying and disorientating, the pleasure oozing from every pore. Olivia hadn't experienced such mesmerising skills in quite some time, and she luxuriated in them, never wanting it to stop.

When Rosie added some fingers to the mix, Olivia moaned with pleasure, sinking her fingers into Rosie's hair, so close she could feel it.

Soon, she was toppling over the edge and freefalling to earth, a grin on her face, her heart a ball of happiness that was picking up speed with every second.

Rosie didn't let up. She made Olivia come for a second and third time, before Olivia stilled her with hands in her hair. Rosie sat back, looking up at Olivia, panting.

Olivia wanted to frame the moment, hang it on her wall, carry it in her heart. She was spent, sated, elated.

Until the next time.

"Shall we take this to the bedroom?" Rosie asked, getting up and holding out a hand to Olivia.

Olivia nodded, wordless.

If she was falling for Rosie before, she'd just hit the ground. Hard.

CHAPTER 18

Rosie blinked her eyes open. When she looked up, she didn't see the ceiling of her own familiar bedroom. In fact, she didn't see any ceiling at all. Instead, she found herself staring at the maroon canopy of a four-poster bed. She pushed herself up a little and looked at Charlie next to her. She was still asleep. Memories of last night flooded Rosie's mind. She indulged and allowed herself to reminisce for a few moments, before having to face the morning's cold hard reality.

Charlie was leaving today. She was going back to her life in London.

Anguish settled in Rosie's chest. She looked away from Charlie, who lay sleeping so peacefully, giving the impression that things could be so different. As long as Charlie didn't wake up, Rosie could hold on to the illusion that Charlie didn't have this other life — a life she had been more than happy to escape from for a few weeks.

At the same time, Rosie wanted Charlie to wake up, because they only had a little more time left together. Did she have to leave this morning or only tonight? Would she have time for one last meal at the cafe she had so deftly changed into a thriving business — something Rosie still couldn't wrap her head around.

She glanced around the room, which was about the size of the entire flat she and Paige shared. They hadn't bothered to close the heavy curtains hanging from the windows last night. They'd been too busy letting their hands roam all over each other's naked bodies. Rosie was no expert, but even she knew instinctively that the vase on the chest of drawers to her left was expensive, and the painting that hung next to it didn't look like it was picked up at a thrift store either.

Charlie really did have friends in high places.

Rosie felt a hand against her thigh.

"Morning," Charlie croaked.

"Morning, sleeping beauty." Rosie curled up next to Charlie, facing her. "Good night's sleep?"

"Best I've had in years." Charlie broke into a smile.

"Me too." Rosie kissed her on the tip of her nose. Do you really have to leave, Rosie wanted to ask, but she couldn't get the words past her lips. She wanted this moment to be about something other than goodbye. And Charlie wasn't moving to the other side of the world. Hundreds of people came down to Cornwall from London all the time. Surely Charlie could hop on a train and come see her?

"Please tell me you don't have to open the cafe." Charlie scooted closer to Rosie. "I'd like to keep you in this bed for a while longer."

"What time is it?" Rosie shot up. "I should call my aunt. She can open up this morning, but I shouldn't leave her alone for too long. Thanks to you, we're swamped."

"Argh," Charlie groaned. "I did this to myself then." She slung an arm over Rosie's belly.

"All these posh paintings on the walls, but not a clock in sight." Rosie pressed herself against Charlie's warm body. She didn't want to get out of this bed either. She also didn't feel like running downstairs and retrieving her phone. This house was so big, she might get lost on the way.

"Relax. It's not even fully light yet." Charlie pressed her fingertips into Rosie's back.

"You might be on an extended holiday, but I'm not." Rosie pushed herself a little more into Charlie's embrace. If they kept this up, she'd never get out of here.

A mobile phone started ringing downstairs. They both stiffened.

"That's probably Aunt Hilary wondering where I am." Rosie started to disentangle herself from Charlie's arms. "If you want to keep me here a little longer, I need to get that."

"Oh, all right." Charlie let go of her.

Rosie jumped out of bed, at the same time looking around for a piece of clothing she could cover herself with.

"Take the bedspread," Charlie said, and started pulling it off the bed.

Rosie wrapped herself in it and darted downstairs. The phone kept ringing and she had only to follow the intrusive sound it made to find the living room — if you could still call it that. It looked more like a ballroom to her.

The phone finally stopped ringing.

Rosie scanned the room. Her phone lay on top of her crumpled pair of jeans. She looked at the screen. No missed calls. It must have been Charlie's phone then. She might as well take it up to her, now that she was here. She spotted it on a sideboard that she was pretty sure she'd once seen on *The Antiques Road Show* being valued for a few hundred thousand pounds.

As she picked it up, it started ringing again. The name *Alex* popped up on the screen. Charlie's sister really needed to speak to Charlie this morning. Rosie checked the time. It wasn't even 7.00am.

She hurried up the stairs, taking two steps at a time. Maybe something had happened in Charlie's family. Rosie knew all about receiving the worst news when you least expected it, and she hoped, for Charlie's sake, that her sister was just the impatient kind.

"Your sister really wants to talk to you," Rosie said as she walked into the bedroom and thrust the phone in Charlie's hands.

Charlie shot up. "What?" Flabbergasted, she looked at her phone, which started ringing again a few seconds after it stopped.

"Are you not going to pick up?" Rosie shrugged off the bedspread and got back under the covers.

"Not now." Charlie switched her phone to silent mode.

"What if it's important?" Rosie asked, fiddling with her own phone. She needed to text Aunt Hilary.

"What's more important than this time with you?" Charlie put her phone away and turned to Rosie, a wide smile on her face.

Really bad news was usually not delivered by phone, Rosie concluded. If something had happened to one of Charlie's family members, the police would find her and break the news to her personally.

Rosie finished her text to Aunt Hilary, promising she would be there soon to help with the breakfast rush.

"Not much, I guess," Rosie said, and kissed Charlie on the lips.

∽

Charlie had promised to come by the cafe later for a last goodbye before leaving Otter Bay. Rosie tried to focus on that thought as she headed in the direction of Mark & Maude's. She needed the walk to clear her head. To process last night's events and etch every touch of Charlie's skin on hers into her memory. Last night had not just been sex with someone passing through the village. It had been much more than that. Despite Charlie only having come into her life a few short weeks earlier, she had changed it completely.

Rosie was headed towards a thriving cafe — a place she'd been so fed up with, she'd stuck an actual For Sale sign in the window. Then Charlie had waltzed in and changed her mind — and helped her turn Mark & Maude's into this quirky, cosy diner Rosie had not been able to see in it. Not until she'd looked at the place through Charlie's eyes.

The ride in the limo, the delicious dishes Charlie had asked Gina to prepare for them. That first kiss. Last night. It all seemed like a dream. But today, Charlie was leaving.

Rosie was about to cross the high street, when a small Jack Russell barrelled towards her. She knew that dog. She crouched down to pet Biscuit, while her heart sank. Biscuit was Amy's dog. She couldn't be far behind and Rosie would have no way of avoiding her. Such was the reality of life in Otter Bay.

A few seconds later, there she was. Rosie heard her footsteps approach but spent a little more time scratching Biscuit behind the ears.

"You're a bit far from home," Amy said.

"I needed a walk. Just like this little fella." She rose because it didn't feel very comfortable having Amy stare down at her like that.

"Look at how happy he is to see you." Amy cocked her head. "I know you're more of a cat person, but that dog is crazy about you."

Biscuit was trying to jump up, but his short legs didn't give him much height.

Rosie smiled. "I have room in my heart for both species."

Amy chuckled. "What's up with you this morning? You have a strange look on your face."

Rosie shrugged. "Nothing's up."

"Are you sure?" Amy took a step closer, as though she wanted to sniff Rosie to better suss out what was going on.

Rosie might as well save her the bother. "I spent the night at the manor up the hill. With Charlie."

Amy's face fell for an instant, but she regrouped quickly. "A night with the princess, eh."

"The princess." Rosie scoffed. "Staying at the manor doesn't automatically make you a princess."

"Not if you already are one." Amy arched up her eyebrows.

Rosie shook her head. "Look, I need to get going. Aunt Hilary's alone in the cafe."

"Come on, Biscuit." The dog perked up his ears at the sound of his name. "We're off." Amy continued in the opposite direction.

Rosie was glad she didn't have to walk the rest of the way with Amy by her side.

She marched on and remembered bringing Charlie's phone to her earlier that morning, the name Alex blinking on the screen in big white letters. What would have happened if she'd picked up? The phone had been ringing insistently enough. What would she have found out? What did Alexandra — Rosie presumed that was what Alex was short for — want from her sister at seven in the morning? Alexandra, like in Princess Alexandra, first in line to the throne.

Rosie shook off the thought. Alexandra was a very popular name — she'd had two classmates called that even in Otter Bay's tiny school. And as far as she knew, there was no Princess Charlotte, which she assumed Charlie was short for. Besides, Charlie might be mysterious, but she was much too kind to keep that kind of vital information from Rosie. It didn't fit with the Charlie who had transformed her life in the space of three short weeks.

She arrived at the gate of the cemetery. She briefly considered going in to visit her parents' grave, but she really had to get to Aunt Hilary. If this morning's crowd was anything like the ones they'd served the last couple of days, Aunt Hilary would be rushed off her feet — and her aunt was no spring chicken anymore.

Rosie walked on, upping her pace to make up for the time she'd lost chatting to Amy. She didn't need to see her parents' grave to think about them — to ask them for advice. Not for actual advice, of course. But talking to her mum and dad in her head often brought Rosie a kind of clarity that was hard to find when she didn't involve their memory in her thought process. They helped her see things clearer, enabled her to get to the point more quickly.

Rosie was sure of one thing. Her mum and dad would be pleased for her that she'd met someone. If anything, they had always believed in love. Being married for all those years hadn't made them lose their appreciation for each other. They'd worked side by side every single day, and Rosie had seen their love on display every single one of them.

What would they say about Charlie leaving today? At least you had the time you did with her, her dad would have said, and that's better than nothing. Not having her parents anymore, Rosie knew that one to be true.

What would they make of what Amy had just said?

"Nonsense, darling," Rosie heard her mother's voice in her head. "That girl's just jealous. That's plain as day."

Rosie nodded. That's right, she thought. *Utter nonsense.* She'd reach the cafe in about five minutes, and she knew what she was going to spend those five minutes thinking about: Charlie's deliciously muscled body all over hers.

CHAPTER 19

Olivia sipped her coffee and stared out the window to the back garden. The garden that had made Rosie's eyes widen last night, the same as they'd done with the entire house. With her intentions, she'd had no choice but to bring her back here, but she knew the house was a bit of a giveaway to her background. To Olivia, it was just another house; to Rosie, it was a manor where the rich lived. Olivia had seen the cogs whirring in Rosie's brain, and she'd fully intended to tell her, to come clean. She'd tried once, then twice, but Rosie hadn't wanted her to speak, and then the evening had spiralled out of control in the best possible way.

But she wasn't sorry she'd done it — how could she be? Last night had been incredible; this morning, too. Waking up with Rosie, she'd been overwhelmed with a sense of calm, as well as comfort and relief.

She'd been studying the relief bit for the past half hour. Relief? Was that the right emotion? But then she'd nodded to nobody in particular: relief was spot-on. Olivia was relieved she'd finally met someone who was real — and more importantly, who made her feel real, too.

However, now, with spectacular timing, she was leaving today. Going back to her Surrey estate, back to London to see her family, back to her real life. The very one where she could never be real. Wasn't that ironic?

Her phone beeping broke her train of thought and she looked down. She'd had four missed calls from Alexandra, but she'd ignored them. She got on well enough with her sister, but she wasn't in the mood this morning. Alexandra took her royal duties seriously, being next in line to the throne; Olivia, not so much. She wasn't built for the spotlight, she was built for a quieter life. But destiny had other ideas.

The text message wasn't from her sister this time, though: it was from Olivia's private secretary, letting her know that Gina had passed her retake, and her citizenship application had been fast-tracked — she could now stay in the country indefinitely. Olivia had even paid the fee for the visa, to ensure as little friction as possible when it came to Rosie's chef sticking around. She couldn't wait to tell both Gina and Rosie, and she grinned as she blew out a breath. She might be going, but she was leaving Rosie in a far better situation than when she'd arrived.

Her phone beeped again: this time, it was from her sister.

'Tried to call you all morning. Hope you're decent because I'm 15 minutes away and I'm dying for a coffee.'

Olivia closed her eyes as a familiar sinking feeling floated down her. Alexandra was coming here? Just what she needed.

Today was going to be hard enough, saying goodbye to Rosie. She didn't need an audience.

~

The wheels of Alexandra's shiny black BMW rolled heavily up the manor house's drive, and Olivia took a deep breath: she should know how to deal with her sister by now, but Alexandra still sometimes threw her off. She had a secret suspicion she was taking lessons from their mother, so similar were their methods.

Olivia opened the heavy front door just as her sister got out of the back seat, her shoulder-length black hair shining in the late-morning sun. Her eyes were covered with Dolce & Gabbana sunglasses, and she was wearing black heels and pristine dark blue jeans. She tugged the collar of her white shirt, straightened her black blazer and a smile crossed her face as she caught sight of Olivia. When Alexandra got to her, she pulled her sister into a brisk hug, and Olivia was surprised to find herself sinking into it.

She didn't want to go home, but it was nice to see a familiar face after she'd thrown her life into such an emotional blender over the past 24 hours.

When Alexandra let go and assessed her at arm's length, not moving her sunglasses, Olivia tried a confident smile. She could totally style this out, like her sister turning up on her doorstep was an everyday occurrence.

"To what do I owe this pleasure?" She folded her arms across her chest as Alexandra let her go.

Her sister let out a small huff. "I volunteered. Mummy and Daddy were concerned you wouldn't honour your agreement to come home today. She was going to send Malcolm."

Olivia's mouth formed an 'O', suddenly grateful to her sister: dealing with her mother's private secretary was the last thing she wanted today.

Alexandra nodded. "Exactly. So I told her I'd come instead, make sure you got home safely. And you'd better be grateful, because it meant leaving at an ungodly hour this morning to avoid the traffic. At least I wasn't driving, so I had a catnap in the car." Her sister paused. "Plus, it gives me a chance to get the full story of why you've spent so bloody long in this place." She took her sunglasses off and surveyed Olivia's face. "Because there's a story, of that much I'm sure. Jemima wanted to come, too, but I put her off." She raised both eyebrows. "So, I'd say you owe me big time."

"I'd say you're right."

Alexandra swept into the house, looking far more the part in the large, airy kitchen. She flung the back door open and stared at the patio and garden beyond, before turning to Olivia with a crooked smile. "Do you remember all the times we had here as kids?"

Olivia nodded. "It's one of the reasons I love it here — happy memories of summer holidays without Mother and Father on our backs. Just us two, Sophia and Nadia." The final two names belonged to their nannies who'd shepherded their childhood far more than their parents.

A wistful look crossed Alexandra's face. "I haven't thought about Sophia and Nadia in years," she said. "Did you put the kettle on, by the way?"

Olivia filled it at her command. "I've only got instant coffee, though." She waved the jar of Kenco at her sister, who gave her the exact face she'd expected.

"My god, you really are slumming it. No staff and instant coffee." She put her hands on her hips. "What's going on, Olivia?"

Olivia busied herself making the hot drinks, ignoring Alexandra's question.

She was successful, too, until she turned and Alexandra was standing next to her, closing in on her space.

"I just needed some space, like I told Mother." Stalling tactic; even she knew it was lame.

Alexandra scoffed. "You've been gone nearly a month! That's not space, that's another universe altogether." She walked to the table and sat, drumming her fingers on polished wood.

When Olivia glanced over, she tried not to think of a naked Rosie sprawled on that table last night, her fingers digging into Olivia's back as she came. She was only partly successful.

"What's really going on? You can tell me." Her sister had her concerned face on.

"Because you've always been so supportive of me and my relationships in the past."

"That's because I could see they wouldn't work!" Alexandra shook her head. "I know you were keen on Ellie, but she wasn't suitable for you long-term, you knew that."

Olivia rolled her eyes. "Keen on her? I was in love with her! But not one of my family could stand to hear that, could they?"

Alexandra gave her the same measured look the Queen was so fond of. "Love isn't always what matters, you know that."

"Talking of which, how is Miles?" Olivia spat the sentence.

Alexandra scowled. "He's fine, as far as I know." She avoided Olivia's gaze as she continued. "You know the drill. He has his life and I have mine. We show up for engagements and the camera. We get on well enough, and we have our arrangements as far as our needs are concerned." She licked her lips. "It could work just the same for you and Jemima, and she knows that, too. But she thinks you're getting cold feet, and so do some of the press pack." She paused, looking Olivia directly in the eye. "And frankly, so do I."

"So, Mother asked you to talk some sense into me?"

"Somebody has to, Olivia. It's one thing for you to take some time. It's quite another for the press to start wondering why they haven't had a photo opportunity of you and Jemima since the announcement. You need to play the game — and you can't do that if you're 250 miles apart."

"Fuck the press — this is my life."

That earned a steely stare. "You know as well as I do it stopped being your life the moment you were born."

Olivia blew out a long breath, before fixing her sister with her stare. She knew everything Alexandra was saying was true, but it wasn't what she wanted to hear. Especially not after last night. "You want to go for a walk? I need some fresh air."

Alexandra pursed her lips but got up, stretching her arms above her head. "Sure. And maybe we could go and get some proper coffee after that because this stuff is vile."

∽

Olivia made Alexandra wear a sun hat she found in the understairs cupboard, and gave her some trainers when she complained about walking in heels. "They'll make you far less conspicuous anyhow," she told her. "Me in trainers isn't that big a deal — but the future queen in a pair of Nikes? Nobody expects that."

They walked around the grounds of the house speaking about their parents and about Alexandra's two small children. After 20 minutes, Alexandra wanted to venture outside the grounds, to walk down to the cliffs she remembered as a child.

"If we do, you have to keep your head down. I've managed to stay under the radar with my hair and glasses, but you're far more recognisable."

"Promise," Alexandra replied.

They set off from the back of the estate, down a small lane with brambles and nettles either side. Oak trees lined the path, and to either side, rolling fields led down to the clifftops in the distance. Sheep filled up one field, corn the other. When they were teenagers, the sisters had often run through these fields and laid flat on their backs, discussing their future partners and future dreams. Neither of their lives had panned out quite as they'd once imagined.

"So, what's going on? You keep avoiding the question, but if I had to guess, I'd say there's another woman involved." Alexandra glanced to her left. "Am I right?"

Olivia swallowed down hard but didn't see any point denying it. "You're right." Her voice was only just audible.

"So, who is she?"

Warmth swept up Olivia and an involuntary grin settled on her face. Where Rosie was concerned, it just happened. "She runs a cafe in the village and she's just... perfect."

Alexandra slowed her pace and took her sister's arm. "Oh god, you've got that goofy look on your face." She put three fingers to her temple. "You can't be trusted to come down here for a few weeks and not fall in love?" She shook her head, like it was the worst thing in the world. "Olivia, you need to start living in the real world, not just in your bubble."

Olivia frowned at that. What was she talking about? This was just about as real as it got. "Ever thought being a royal is the unreal world?" She swept her arm from left to right. "Look around you — this is real life."

"For normal people, yes!" Alexandra was standing still now, frowning. "But you're not normal people — when are you going to understand that? You're a *royal*! Which means you can't just swan around like that doesn't matter — and it also means you have to marry within your circle. Jemima is the perfect choice." She closed her eyes briefly, before fixing her sister with her gaze. "But go on, tell me more about this woman."

Annoyance flared in Olivia's chest. "You make it sound like I fall in love like this all the time."

"You've done it once before."

"Yes, once! Excuse me for thinking I'm allowed to meet people and fall in love. You're as bad as Mother, you know that?"

Alexandra's face didn't move. "So, details?"

Olivia held her gaze. "Her name is Rosie, she's 28 and she's one of the kindest, smartest women I've ever met."

"Rosie." Alexandra winced as she spoke, chewing on the

name like it was the sourest taste ever. "Hardly the name of a future royal."

"If only you could meet her, you'd know she's different. She's so strong, hard-working and beautiful, and she makes me laugh. She makes me feel on top of the world. Like I want to shout about it from the rooftops."

"You can't do this again, Olivia! Mother will go into a tailspin, and you've already committed to Jemima. Don't make this any harder than it needs to be. You knew the score when you came down here. And what about this woman's feelings? Did you stop to consider that?" She moved her sunglasses up her head, frowning. "Does she even know who you are?"

Heat rose to Olivia's cheeks at that. "Not exactly," she mumbled.

"You're a bloody fool, you know that?" Alexandra shook her head with a smile. "You're getting married in eight weeks' time. Do the decent thing, follow through and have affairs like the rest of us. Love comes and goes, but what you need for a royal marriage is someone who understands your world, someone with class. I'm sure Rosie is lovely, but does she have the class needed to do this right? The answer is no."

"You haven't even met her!" How dare her sister write Rosie off without a thought.

"I don't need to, she runs a cafe in a village in Cornwall for god's sake!" Alexandra studied her sister closely again. "You've slept with her, haven't you?"

Olivia nodded slowly, heat burning her cheeks. "Last night."

Alexandra blew out another breath. "Then prepare to add Princess Heartbreaker to your list of titles. Because that's what you're about to be."

They came to the end of the small path and out onto the clifftop, the sea a glittering carpet of blue velvet in the distance. For a moment, all thought of what they'd just been talking about melted away as Olivia took in the magnificent scene; nature at its best.

"You know, I can see the attraction of this place," Alexandra said, sighing as she surveyed the scene. "It's absolutely beautiful."

Olivia nodded. "It is." *Just like Rosie.* She kept that thought to herself.

A yapping around her feet brought both of their attention back to the moment, and Olivia bent down to pet the Jack Russell. "Hello you," she said, rubbing behind its ears. Often, the highlight of a trip to the palace was seeing her mother's troop of corgis.

"Biscuit! Come back here!"

Olivia looked up to see Amy running towards her, dog lead in hand. "Biscuit!"

Alarm streaked through Olivia as she pressed the panic button, turning to Alexandra as Amy approached. "Run back down the path, she can't meet you," she hissed, as her sister took the hint, just as Amy pulled up beside her. "Hello Charlie, and is that—"

Amy peered under the rim of Alexandra's sun hat just as she whipped her head around and ran the other way.

"—just my cousin, desperate for the loo," Olivia said, giving Amy a fixed grin. The last time she'd seen her, she'd been face down on the pool table, so there was no love lost. "Lovely dog," she added.

Amy narrowed her eyes, nodding. "She is," she said. "Lively, too. A little like your cousin, who I would swear holds an amazing resemblance to Princess Alexandra. But of course, that couldn't be, because why would a princess be slumming it down here, right?"

Olivia ground her teeth together, her heart racing in her chest, a buzzing in her ears. It was going to come out eventually, wasn't it? But she'd prefer Rosie to hear it from her and not from Amy, so she wasn't going to give the game away.

"Why indeed?" Olivia replied, holding her nerve. If she admitted it, Amy would run straight to Rosie.

She might do that anyway, but not if Olivia could get there first.

Amy gave her a triumphant grin, before scooping up her dog. "You know, I'm suddenly feeling in need of refreshment, perhaps some lunch. Maybe at Mark & Maude's. If Rosie's there, she might like to know who she's *really* been dealing with. Who's *really* been feeding her lines to get her into bed before rushing back to London to get married." She shook her head, giving Olivia a look of utter contempt. "I knew there was something off about you, but this is deception of epic proportions."

"Amy," Olivia began. She balled her fist by her side to stop her hand from shaking.

"Save it," Amy said, turning to walk away. "Rosie deserves so much better than you. You might be a princess, but you've got absolutely zero class."

Olivia stood with her mouth ajar as Amy hurried away from her, clutching her precious dog.

Fuck, fuck, fuck!

Her mind whirred with the implications of what had just happened, before her body clicked into gear. She had to get to Rosie before Amy did. Rosie simply couldn't hear this from her — it would kill her, and it would crush Olivia, too.

She took a deep breath, then turned and sprinted down the path to the house.

Could she outrun Amy? She was about to find out.

CHAPTER 20

Rosie had no time to enjoy the new look of the cafe. Since she'd arrived that morning, a bit tired but with a spring in her step nonetheless, she'd been rushed off her feet.

"Two Tuscan chicken sandwiches for table three," she said to Gina. "Probably the last order for lunch."

"Coming right up, boss." Gina winked at her. Not only was she a fabulous chef, but she was able to keep her cool during busy times. Rosie hoped she'd be able to remain in Otter Bay. Working alongside Gina almost every day had made her part of Rosie's very small family.

Rosie took a minute to catch her breath. All but one of the tables she and Charlie had up-cycled were full. Why had she not seen this? That with a little TLC this place could reach its full potential. It had a great location on Otter Bay's high street and, Rosie thought — a smile spreading on her lips — very friendly service. Maybe she'd no longer been willing to see Mark & Maude's potential.

"What are you grinning about?" Paige asked, bumping her shoulder into Rosie's. Now that Mark & Maude's had been done up, her sister often ate lunch there before going back to school.

"This place," Rosie replied.

"Are you sure that's all it is?" Paige scanned her face. "Because your bed wasn't slept in last night." Paige shot her a toothy grin.

A flush crept up Rosie's cheeks.

"Excuse me." A customer at a table by the window waved at Rosie.

"Sorry, sis. Duty calls." Rosie hurried to the customer, hoping her flush would die down soon. She pushed the insistent memories of last night to the side.

When she reached the table, something scurrying past the window caught her eye. A Jack Russell.

"Biscuit," Amy's voice rang.

Rosie turned her attention to the customer, fervently hoping Amy wouldn't come in.

No such luck.

The customer had just asked for the bill when the door of the cafe swung open. Amy fixed her gaze on Rosie. "I need to speak to you. Urgently," she said, sounding out of breath, like she'd been running.

"Not now, Amy. I'm a little busy." Rosie suppressed the triumphant smile she wanted to give Amy. She looked a bit distressed.

Rosie headed for the till and printed the customer's bill.

"I'm serious, Rosie. It's important." Biscuit yapped at their feet.

"Table three's ready," Gina said from the kitchen.

Rosie stepped into the kitchen to pick up the plates. Amy followed her inside, blocking the doorway. The nerve of the woman.

"Can I get by, please?" Rosie squared her shoulders.

Amy shook her head. "You're not going to believe who I

just saw near the manor house." She paused. "Princess Alexandra." She brought her hands to her sides. "And guess who she was chatting to?" Amy pursed her lips. "Your new girlfriend Charlie. Or should I call her by her real name: Princess Olivia."

"W-what are you talking about?" A cold fist gripped around Rosie's heart. Her hands started trembling and she put the two plates down. Rosie inhaled deeply. "If this is another one of your schemes to get me back, you're pushing things way too far."

"This isn't about me, Rosie. Or about us." Amy found her gaze and held it. "It's about you being lied to. As I live and breathe, Charlie *is* Princess Olivia. Can't you see that? Why else would Princess Alexandra be there? And why else would she be staying at the manor house?"

"You're full of shit, as usual," Rosie said, her voice breaking. "Trying to stir things up between Charlie and me because you're jealous."

Behind Rosie, Gina cleared her throat. "I'll take these to table three," she said. She left the kitchen and closed the door behind her.

"Come on, Rosie," Amy said. "I just don't want you to get hurt. You know how I feel about you."

"Just… get out." Rosie's voice had shot up. "You're the one who's hurting me with your stupid lies." Rosie couldn't bear to look at Amy's smug face any longer. "Leave."

"Fine," Amy said. "But please know I'm here if you need to talk." She had the audacity to touch her palm to Rosie's arm.

Rosie shrugged Amy off of her. How had she ever been able to enjoy this woman's touch?

Amy shot her one last look, then turned on her heel and left the kitchen.

Rosie steadied herself against the counter. Amy's words swirled through her mind. She took a breath to collect her thoughts. The name lighting up on Charlie's phone screen this morning. *Alex.* Could that really have been Princess Alexandra?

It couldn't possibly be because that would mean that Charlie had lied to her all this time. They'd slept together. Charlie would never make such a fool out of Rosie. It was impossible. Yet, the seed of doubt had been planted.

"Are you okay?" Paige appeared in the doorway. "Amy's gone, by the way."

Rosie looked at her sister. "She came to tell me she's convinced Charlie is Princess Olivia."

Paige's eyes grew to the size of saucers. "You're joking."

"I don't know." A whoosh of air flooded out of Rosie. "I'm not sure what to think. Amy's willing to stoop very low to get me back, but she's not stupid. She wouldn't just say something like that. She claims to have spotted Princess Alexandra, talking to Charlie."

"But Princess Olivia is engaged to…" Paige scratched her hair. "Jemima Bradbury."

"What did you say? Who's she engaged to?" Rosie leaned her full weight against the counter.

"Jemima Bradbury. Some posh chick with a pedigree."

Rosie racked her brain. Where had she seen the name Jemima. Probably in the newspaper if she was, indeed, Princess Olivia's fiancée. But no, that wasn't it. The name 'Jem' had lit up on Charlie's phone when she'd been showing her the overpriced crockery for the cafe — was it short for Jemima?

"Shit." Rosie looked at her sister. "I think Amy's telling the truth." The cold fist that had wrapped itself around her heart was squeezing tightly now. Rosie had been lied to. For three weeks Charlie had been pretending to be someone else.

"Do you have your phone on you?" Rosie asked.

Paige nodded and fished it out of her pocket.

"Can you google an image of Princess Olivia?"

Paige nodded and started tapping.

If this was really true, how could Rosie not have seen this?

"Here." Paige handed her the phone.

Rosie peered at the screen. There was no doubt. Take away Charlie's thick-rimmed glasses and imagine her with longer, blown-out hair, and there she was. Staring back at Rosie from her official engagement portrait. Rosie would recognise those eyes anywhere after peering into them so deeply last night. That curly hair she'd gripped between her fingers when she came was nowhere to be seen. That smile — although in the picture it was merely a hint of how Charlie had smiled at her when they'd said goodbye this morning.

"It's her." Rosie gave the phone back to her sister. She threw her head back and took a deep breath. No wonder Charlie had to go back to London today. She was getting married soon.

If she followed the logic of her brain, Rosie had to believe it. That was Charlie in the picture she'd just seen. It had been Princess Alexandra calling her younger sister Princess Olivia on the phone she'd carried up the stairs of the manor house this morning. But her heart refused to believe Charlie was capable of such deception.

Rosie had only to cast a glance at the cafe to remember Charlie's kindness. At Gina, who was feverishly ringing up bills for customers as Rosie stood nailed to the ground, staring at her sister. She only had to think of last night to be utterly convinced of Charlie's good heart. Yet, good heart or not, Charlie had lied straight to her face.

Paige walked up to her and put a hand on her shoulder. "Are you sure?"

"Look at the picture and tell me that's not Charlie." Rosie desperately glanced at her sister, hoping that, if she looked at Princess Olivia's picture, she could miraculously unearth some evidence of her not being Charlie. Of her not being engaged to be married. Because that was what stung most of all. Charlie — Princess Olivia — was not a single woman looking for some peace and quiet in the Cornish countryside and making a silly local fall in love with her in the process. She was in a relationship. She was bloody well engaged. So much for Jemima being her ex. She'd not only deceived Charlie, but her fiancée as well.

"It's her," Paige said. "No doubt." She patted Rosie on the shoulder. "We've all been bamboozled."

Gina entered the kitchen. "Rosie, there's someone here to see you."

She moved away from the doorway, revealing Charlie standing behind her.

At the sight of her, a tear welled up in the corner of Rosie's eye. She blinked it away. She wasn't going to cry in front of this woman who had so cold-heartedly lied to her about who she was. Who had changed the subject whenever her family came up and was mysterious about her job. It all made perfect sense now. And Rosie had been enough of an idiot to fall for it.

"Do you want me to stay?" Paige asked.

"It's fine." Rosie barely managed to get the words past her lips. Her throat was too constricted with grief — and anger.

Paige left them alone and Rosie stood face to face with the woman she'd laid her heart bare to. She had told Charlie about her parents, about what she wanted to do with her life. She'd made love to her. Now none of that meant anything anymore.

CHAPTER 21

"Rosie, I can explain it all," Olivia began, not really believing it herself. A prickly heat crept onto her cheeks, and she clenched her right fist by her side.

"Can you?" Rosie's voice was low, controlled. So unlike how it had been this morning when she was lying on top of her, naked. Rosie clutched the counter behind her, as if anchoring herself. "Go on then, explain, *Olivia*." She shook as she said the name.

Olivia hung her head. "I guess Amy got here before me," she said, then cringed when she saw Rosie's face harden.

"Is that why you came running in here? Was it a race to see who could tell poor, gullible Rosie that the woman she's fallen for, the woman she slept with last night is actually not who she told her she was?" She was shouting now. "That she's actually *engaged to be married*."

Olivia's heart stumbled at Rosie's words. She knew it sounded bad. Mainly because it was bad.

"Rosie, it's not how it sounds."

"Isn't it?" Rosie's tone was no longer controlled; emotion

was seeping from every word. "Tell me how it is then, princess."

Olivia winced. She hated being called princess.

"Look, I know I lied to you, and I'm sorry. But you have to see it from my point of view. I don't want this marriage, and I needed some time to think, to process—"

"—to have one last roll in the hay with some unsuspecting mug before you committed to marriage." Her icy stare sliced through Olivia's defences.

"It's not like that," she replied. "I came down here to get away from the madness that is my life at the moment."

"Boo hoo, poor little rich girl."

Okay, she deserved that. "I know I don't deserve any sympathy, but when I got here, if I'd turned up and said, hi, I'm Princess Olivia, nobody would have talked to me and the press would have been all over me before I could blink."

"So, you lied through your teeth and told me you were someone else."

"It was the only way you would have talked to me!" Olivia took a deep breath, trying to stay calm, but it wasn't easy. She'd been in war zones she'd felt in more control of. Bombs hadn't fazed her, but Rosie's disappointment just might.

She was in danger of unravelling on the spot. "I wanted a bit of normality, so I used my army nickname, Charlie. And it worked. You talked to me, and I liked you. I still really like you. Everything else I told you was the truth — all of it, Rosie, you have to believe me."

Rosie narrowed her eyes at that, looking at Olivia like she was dirt on the bottom of her shoe. Like she just wanted to get rid of her, scrub her out of her life and never see her again.

"I have to believe you? You've got some fucking nerve. You've spent the last month lying to me, leading me on, buttering me up, before finally getting me into bed last night." She was shaking as she spoke, her eyes wild. "Just tell me —

was it a bet with your posh friends? Perhaps even with your fiancée, I've no idea how your world works—"

"—what do you mean how my world works? It works the same as yours."

Rosie scoffed. "I think we both know that's not true." She stared at her. "Are you honestly telling me this world," she swept her hand around the kitchen, "is the same as the one you come from? Do you often stand around in kitchens with the commoners?"

Olivia lowered her head, but she knew she'd already lost. Why should Rosie listen to her? She didn't deserve it.

"Was it a bet? Just answer me that."

Olivia ground her teeth together. "I don't know what you mean." Why did she keep asking about a bet?

"A chance to sow your royal oats? A chance to get someone into bed before the big day? Your last bit of rough before you settle down into aristocracy?"

Olivia gave her a sad, slow shake of the head. "You have to know that's not true." Didn't she? Surely Rosie didn't doubt everything? "The last few weeks have made me see there's another life I could lead. I came here to escape — but I never imagined I'd meet someone like you. And if I'd told you the truth, you'd never have treated me as an equal." She cleared her throat, her heart hammering in her chest. "I'm falling in love with you, Rosie. Every single part of that is real."

Just at that moment, Gina poked her head around the kitchen door, hesitation painted on her face. "Sorry to interrupt," she said. "But I need to get in here to do some orders."

"That's fine, Olivia was just leaving," Rosie replied, not responding at all to what Olivia had just said.

"And if you don't move soon, I might just throw you out," said another voice. Olivia turned her head to see Hilary standing with her arms crossed at the kitchen doorway, Paige beside her. This family that she'd grown to love, all of them were now looking at her with utter contempt.

She'd fucked this up royally, hadn't she?

She held both her hands up, palms out, as if Rosie was pointing a gun at her. "I'm going, I know when I've outstayed my welcome," she said. "But think about what I said. This past month, I've never been happier. And I know I should have told you who I was, but I couldn't. But everything I've told you, everything we shared, it's all real." She held Rosie's gaze, tears pricking the back of her eyes. "You've shown me real life in the past month, and I've never been happier. I don't want to marry Jemima, I want to stay here."

Rosie's eye roll was enormous. "And that's going to happen, is it? You're going to go home, tell your parents, and then come back and live in Otter Bay?"

Olivia cast her gaze to the floor, not daring to look Rosie in the eye. Alexandra had been right all along. She was living in her own bubble; she saw now it would never work.

"I didn't think so." Rosie blew out a long breath, gathering herself. "So, whatever you convinced yourself you were doing, the truth is you're engaged and you're a princess — and you can't run away from that." She sighed. "Just go home, Olivia. Take your lying arse and leave. Go back to your life and forget we ever met. It's what I intend to do."

"Really?" Olivia shook her head, her breathing erratic as she spoke. "Can't we see if we can make this work? Can't you give me some time to try to work things out?"

But Rosie was having none of it. "I think we both know that's not going to happen. The princess and the cafe owner." She threw back her head. "I haven't even got a degree, for fuck's sake."

"You've got a degree in living."

"And you've got one in lying, so I guess that makes us almost equal."

Olivia felt the blow of her words, before standing up tall and turning to leave. As she took one step towards the door, Rosie cleared her throat.

"You know, I've had some dark days in my short life — getting that news about my parents was a particularly harrowing one. But this? This is right up there. So well done. You said you wanted to leave me something to remember you by. You've broken my heart and deceived me like nobody else; you've achieved your goal."

∼

Leaving the cafe had been an absolute nightmare, with every single customer clutching their phone to get a shot of Olivia's stricken face as she'd fled, no longer able to bear any of Rosie's looks or words. If Rosie had taken a knife to her soul, her words couldn't have cut her more.

The trouble was, she deserved them all. Yes, her heart had been in the right place, but Olivia knew she was in the wrong. If she was in Rosie's shoes, she'd probably have acted the same way. None of which made it any easier.

As she'd left Mark & Maude's, Connie had been standing on her boutique's doorstep, trying to lure Olivia in. Olivia hadn't stopped. She ran past the surf shop she'd never gone in to; past Amy's parents' cafe-bar; past the butcher's, then the supermarket. All the places that made up Otter Bay, her temporary home, and one she was no doubt barred from forever. Because in deceiving Rosie and breaking her heart, Olivia knew she'd deceived the whole village.

Her name was dirt here now.

She ran all the way back to the house, as much as to rid herself of all the energy she had circling her body, but also to try to escape this whole nightmare as quickly as she could. Because now the whole village knew, it was only a matter of time before the whole world knew. Olivia's stomach lurched at the thought.

When she turned into the lane that ran up to the manor's driveway, there were already cars parked there.

Shit.

As she approached, she could see they were reporters. News had clearly spread faster than she could run.

Two men in jeans and button-down shirts thrust a microphone in her face; she put her hand up, covering her face so they couldn't get a good shot. She buzzed herself into the estate, clanging the tall black iron gate behind her. She sprinted up the gravel driveway, but stumbled halfway, letting out a cry of pain as she came crashing down on her left knee. When she looked down, there was blood seeping through her jeans. Through the gaps in the gate, she heard the whir of cameras. Oh god, this was going to be all over social media in minutes, wasn't it? She couldn't believe it was only this morning she'd woken up with Rosie in her arms. It might as well have been another lifetime.

Tears spilled down her cheeks now, the enormity sinking in. Even though her knee protested all the way, she hauled herself up, not looking back once as she heard the men shouting her name. When she got to the house, Alexandra was waiting for her, a look in her eyes Olivia couldn't work out.

If her sister shouted at her now, she might collapse. Olivia knew she'd buggered everything up, she didn't need to be reminded. Her sister was all about duty, and Olivia had neglected it. She braced herself for Alexandra's inevitable onslaught.

However, instead, her sister pulled her into the hallway, slammed the door shut and silently, took Olivia in her arms.

The action was so compassionate, so unexpected, it caught Olivia off-guard. As Alexandra's arms wrapped around her and her lips kissed her cheek, she finally gave in and her sobs split the air in the long hallway, echoing off the surfaces all around. As she stood in her sister's embrace, her heart breaking into a thousand tiny pieces, the past month whizzed through her mind; the beach, karaoke, dinner, the cafe, last night.

All of it involved Rosie. All of it was now gone.

It had all been a lie, hadn't it? A fantasy she'd wanted to believe. But she knew now her sister was right.

And from the look on Rosie's face, she'd meant what she said: she wanted to just forget they'd ever met, forget any of it had ever happened.

Could Olivia do that, too?

She took a deep breath as she stepped back, steadying her hands on her sister's upper arms.

Alexandra's eyes were glazed with sympathy, and Olivia dredged up a vague memory of a similar situation in her sister's life. Alexandra's Rosie had been a man called Dean — was that where this sudden rush of empathy and love had come from? Was Alexandra remembering her lost love, too, before she settled with Miles?

"You don't do things the easy way, do you?" Alexandra said, her eyes warm.

Olivia gave her an exhausted shake of the head, before sniffing and rubbing her eyes. "Apparently not."

"I've already called the palace press office and they're going to come up with a damage limitation strategy. But that only stretches to the rest of the world, not within the palace walls."

Olivia gave her a stoic nod. "I know." She'd deal with her mother and Jemima when she had to: there was no room in her head at the moment.

Alexandra rubbed her arm and chewed her lip. "You want to get packed so we can get out of here?"

Olivia nodded. After all, there was nothing left to stay for anymore, was there? "Give me half an hour and then let's go face the music."

CHAPTER 22

Rosie ran a finger over the sharp edge of the brand-new menu. Her gaze fell on an item she still wasn't used to: halloumi salad with spring onion and flatbread. The last time Charlie had a meal at the cafe, she'd eaten this. She'd smacked her lips and had looked decidedly un-princess-like. She'd suggested the dish for Mark & Maude's new menu and now it was listed on this piece of laminated paper, taunting Rosie. Even her own cafe reminded her of Charlie, the lying, heart-breaking princess.

"These look really lovely," Aunt Hilary said. She took one of the menus in her hand and studied it, as though it was the first time she laid eyes on it. "You've done such a great job, Rosie." She put a hand on Rosie's shoulder.

Rosie sighed in response. *That's what sleeping with a princess gets you.* She should really stop feeling sorry for herself. Charlie — or no, Olivia — was gone. What had started as a dream may have ended in a nightmare, but at least it was over. All Rosie had to do was allow herself to get over it, and then she could move on with her life. Enjoy the rebranded and refurbished cafe.

Easier said than done.

"How about I make you a nice cappuccino?" Aunt Hilary's hand lingered on her shoulder.

"That would be nice." Rosie tried a smile, but it didn't quite stick.

Aunt Hilary gave her one last pat on the shoulder and headed to the coffee machine.

The door of the cafe opened and a man in overalls walked in. His van was parked right outside the cafe.

"Delivery for Rosie Perkins," he said.

Rosie wasn't expecting any deliveries today.

"I'm Rosie."

"Can you clear a spot for me, please, love? I've got some fragile goods for you."

Fragile goods? Rosie scratched her head, then emptied the table closest to the door.

A few minutes later the delivery guy brought in two big boxes and put them on the table side by side.

"If you could just sign here," the man said.

Rosie signed for the boxes of *fragile goods*, even though she didn't know what their contents were.

"What's this then?" Aunt Hilary brought over her coffee.

"Your guess is as good as mine."

"I'll get a boxcutter so we can find out."

Rosie sipped from her coffee while she eyed the boxes. She spotted a label on the side. Cooking Up A Storm, it said, with an address and phone number below it. It didn't ring any bells.

"Here we are." Aunt Hilary cut open the first box. She opened the sides and peered inside. "Crikey. These are beautiful." She rummaged in the box, her hands making a rustling noise, then held up a plate with an intricate blue pattern.

Rosie's heart sank. She put down her cup of coffee because her hands had started shaking. "Don't get too fond of those. We're going to have to send them back."

"Were they brought here by mistake?" Aunt Hilary pressed her lips into a thin line and examined the plate she was holding further. "They look a tad expensive, I must say."

"Charlie—I mean, *Princess Olivia* must have sent them. We can't keep them."

"Ah," was all Aunt Hilary said.

Rosie stared at her aunt with the plate in her hands. That had been such a wonderful evening, when Charlie had shown her the website with the plates that cost thirty-five pounds apiece. When had she ordered those? Rosie believed she'd made it clear they were too expensive and she didn't want them, but maybe princesses were not used to listening to anybody else's opinions and did only what they felt like doing.

"Shall we put these away then?" Aunt Hilary asked.

Rosie nodded. She hoped Aunt Hilary would take care of it because she didn't even want to touch these plates. They were just another reminder of Charlie's deception.

Gina walked in, flapping about a large brown envelope. "Guess what this is?"

Rosie couldn't handle any more surprises that morning, but it was an easy enough guess.

"You passed the citizenship test," Rosie said. This time, she couldn't hold back a smile, because she was genuinely happy for Gina — and for being able to keep her on.

Gina jumped up and down, which was a funny sight. She didn't make it very far off the ground. She threw her arms wide. "And my brand-new work permit." She curved her arms around Rosie and hugged her tightly. "It's a miracle."

"Hm." Inside her, gratitude for what Charlie had done for Rosie battled with contempt. Apparently everything was easy when you were a member of the royal family.

"I'm happy for you," Rosie said when Gina let her go.

"I know she's not your favourite person right now, but I do owe this to Charlie."

"Princess Olivia, you mean," Aunt Hilary said.

"To me, she's Charlie. That's the woman I met," Gina said. "A good-hearted, genuine, and generous woman."

"Yeah right," Rosie scoffed. "If only she wasn't a liar and a cheater as well."

Gina tilted her head. "I know she hurt you, but this is very real to me. In fact, it's life-changing. And Charlie made that happen. That's not the work of a liar or a cheater. That's the work of a good person."

Rosie shrugged. "She probably had to make one phone call to push it through."

Gina grabbed a new menu off the table. "What about this, then?" She pointed at the freshly painted walls. "Look at all the things she left behind and tell me again she doesn't also have goodness in her heart."

Rosie pressed her eyes shut for a moment. Sure, Charlie had left some very real tokens of her kindness behind, but she'd also trampled all over Rosie's heart.

"She's engaged to be married, Gina. There are no excuses for omitting that particular piece of information."

Aunt Hilary came to stand next to Rosie again. She took the cup of coffee Rosie had put down earlier and gave it back to her. "Your cappuccino's getting cold, dear." She took the opportunity to put a gentle hand on Rosie's shoulder. Her aunt only ever got touchy-feely when she saw one of her nieces in utter distress. She hadn't touched Rosie's shoulder this much since her parents had died.

"Could you call the shop those plates were sent from, please?" Rosie asked her aunt. She couldn't possibly make that call herself. "Ask them to pick them back up. We'll pay whatever it costs to have them sent back."

"Consider it done," Hilary said.

"Rosie, I know you're hurting and a party is out of the question, but I'd like to celebrate this."

Rosie shook her head. "Of course we can celebrate you passing the test, Gina, as long as we can make a deal. No more mention of Charlie and how wonderful she is. At least not for a good long while."

"Deal." Gina nodded before heading into the kitchen.

Hilary was bent over the box of plates, probably trying to read the phone number on the label.

Rosie took a deep breath. If one more thing reminded her of Charlie today, she might actually burst into tears in the middle of the cafe.

∼

When Paige arrived at the cafe after school, the first thing she said was, "Princess Olivia is the talk of the town." She shook her head. "I just saw a clip of her on YouTube. She doesn't look very happy about it all."

"Please, Paige, not you as well," Rosie said. "It's bad enough that there are press all over Otter Bay." She sighed. "Can we please make an effort to get through one day without mentioning Charlie?" Rosie had trouble calling her by anything else other than her nickname. Every time she thought of Charlie as Princess Olivia, it felt like that moment when Charlie had left the cafe for good all over again. That horrible moment of having her heart broken and being so incredibly stupefied by the new information she'd been forced to process all at the same time.

Why couldn't she just have told Rosie who she really was?

Rosie's phone buzzed in her pocket. She'd turned it to silent so it wouldn't keep chiming with message notifications. She looked at the screen. Another text from Charlie: 'I'm so sorry. I miss you. xo'.

It made Rosie wonder about the message Jemima had sent Charlie that evening they'd been looking at the expensive plates and cutlery. Had Charlie's fiancée told her that she missed her, too? While she was busy flirting with another woman, calling her fiancée her 'ex' with whom things where 'complicated'. Charlie had looked a little preoccupied perhaps, but once she'd fixed her gaze on Rosie again, all that preoccupation had fled her. She was a two-faced princess, that was for sure.

"I guess I shouldn't show you these then." Paige stared at her phone screen.

Another war waged within Rosie. Should she hazard a glimpse of Charlie's face? No, she'd been reminded of her enough for one day. For one lifetime.

Paige sat shaking her head. "I hardly recognise her," she said.

Rosie couldn't fault her sister for getting so swept up in the whole thing. All her classmates were probably talking about the royal engagement and the rumours surrounding it.

"Show me," Rosie said. She sat next to Paige and they both looked at the phone screen.

Displayed on it was a full-length picture of Charlie and Jemima, a very green, manicured garden as its backdrop. Paige was right. The woman in the picture, who was supposed to be Princess Olivia, was hardly recognisable as the Charlie Rosie had met. No more skinny jeans and trainers. Charlie was all dolled up, all the curly deliciousness blow-dried out of her hair — which was now brown instead of copper — making it look longer and a lot more boring. The glasses were gone too, only the green in her eyes remained. But Charlie's eyes didn't sparkle the way they had when Rosie had looked into them. They looked as dull as the forced smile on her face.

Jemima was all long legs and delicate features. Rosie didn't think she'd ever seen a woman who was more the opposite of herself. Yet this was the woman Charlie was going to marry. What a mind fuck.

Objectively, Jemima looked very pretty, but something was missing in her glance as well. Joy, perhaps. Understandable when your fiancée had been cheating on you. For a brief moment, Rosie felt sorry for Jemima. Then a pang of jealousy shot through her, because she was the one holding Charlie's hand. The hand that had… No, Rosie pushed the thought away. She looked away from Paige's phone screen. It hurt too much to see Charlie like that.

"They might not get married, you know," Paige said.

Like most of the country, Rosie had watched every royal wedding on television. She could hardly picture herself watching this one. She'd need to find something fun to do that day — preferably on another continent where no one cared about a British princess getting married.

"They should," Rosie said. "If that Jemima still wants to marry Charlie after what she did to her, they deserve each other."

"It can't be easy for her, though," Paige said.

Rosie looked her sister in the eye. "Please, don't you start as well."

Paige shrugged. "It's true."

"It might very well be true, but if I'm going to move past this, I need to stop hearing about how wonderful Charlie is and how hard this must be for her. How about how bloody hard it is for me?" Rosie was instantly sorry for yelling at her sister. "Sorry." She drew Paige into a quick hug. "I didn't mean to snap at you. None of this is your fault."

Paige waved her off. "It's fine." She put away her phone and glanced around the cafe. "How amazing does this place look?"

Rosie knew she meant well, but even the cafe that had belonged to her mum and dad, where so many of her best memories had been made, now reminded her of Charlie. Or no — of Princess Olivia. And Rosie didn't know the princess, she only knew Charlie. Princess Olivia's army nickname. Only this morning, while browsing one of the newspapers they always had lying around the cafe, Rosie had caught a glimpse of an article about Princess Olivia's army days. At least she hadn't lied about that. She'd served in the army and her fellow officers had called her Charlie.

Charlie was the one Rosie had lost. Princess Olivia was the one she despised.

CHAPTER 23

They'd driven back to London in Alexandra's car, the tinted windows hiding their pensive faces. The ride had been quiet; Alexandra seemingly lost in her thoughts, and Olivia willing herself not to look back. After such a torrent of emotions that morning, the rhythmic motion of the car had been soothing, and she'd tried not to think about how she'd messed up being in love before. Was she destined to make the same mistake again? The odds were stacked against her.

When they'd got back to Olivia's home, it had been swarming with press. So much so, she'd been given instructions from the palace press office to stay away and move to her sister's central-London home. Alexandra and Miles lived in a far more spacious and secure residence than Olivia, and it had been deemed more appropriate for the time being. Her sister had been amenable, so Olivia was now lying on the bed in one of the house's guest suites, staring at the high ceiling with its intricate cornices and cream ceiling rose.

It all meant nothing.

When she closed her eyes, all she could see was Rosie's crushed expression on repeat.

When she swallowed down, all she could taste was regret.

She'd tried to make it better with apologetic texts and the crockery order, but Rosie hadn't replied.

Last night, she'd lain awake till the early hours, wrapped in a blanket of shattered dreams.

A knock on her door interrupted her thoughts and she waited a beat before answering. "Who is it?"

"Me," Alexandra replied.

Olivia swung her legs off the bed and stood. "Come in."

Today, she'd spent an uncomfortable afternoon with Jemima, posing for stilted photos and plastering on fake smiles — they were now no doubt all over the media, which she was steadfastly avoiding. Her fiancée had been icy, and Olivia was hyper-aware she wasn't pleasing any of the women in her life: Rosie, Jemima or her mother. Olivia hadn't had a chance to speak to Jemima alone, but she knew it had to happen soon.

Her sister sashayed in wearing some relaxed trousers and an elegant black top, giving her a nod. "You've dyed your hair back to normal."

Olivia shrugged. "I'm not Charlie anymore, am I? Time to return to Princess Olivia who's a brunette."

"I guess it is." Alexandra walked over to the tall wooden fireplace on the right of the room before turning to face her with a grimace.

Olivia's spine stiffened. "What's that face for?"

"Do you want the bad news or the bad news?" She didn't wait for an answer. "So, let's start with the worst news first." Alex turned towards Olivia. "Mother wants you at the palace for supper."

Olivia checked her watch. Supper was always 7.30pm, which meant she had three hours. Not much time. "Okay. What about the rest?"

"The car's arriving in an hour, and Penelope is coming to brief you on the way." Penelope ran the palace press office.

A cloak of heaviness settled on her. "Right."

"And when you've got through those two adventures, Jemima will be waiting in the drawing room for after-dinner drinks so you can talk."

"Mother's invited her to the palace?" Olivia was pretty sure her mother didn't even like Jemima — she just liked what she represented.

Alexandra nodded. "To patch up any 'misunderstandings' the press might be circulating, apparently."

"Jesus."

"He won't be there."

"You might as well throw him in," Olivia replied.

Alexandra threw her a sad smile. "At least you're keeping your sense of humour." She winced. "There is one other thing you may or may not want to know, but better forewarned when you meet Jemima later."

"What?" Olivia's breathing slowed to a crawl as she prepared for what might fall from her sister's lips next. "Is Rosie okay?" A chill ran through her veins.

"It's not connected to her — well, not directly." Alexandra cleared her throat. "Remember I was joking about how you might get a new title after this? Princess Heartbreaker? Well, it's come true — it's currently a trending hashtag." She sucked on the inside of her cheek briefly. "Although there are other versions that are not quite so complimentary."

"That's complimentary?" Olivia's voice was shrill.

"Compared to the other versions, yes."

She blew out a breath. "At least I know what I'm dealing with."

Her sister was still staring, her cool green gaze matching her own. "There is one final thing."

"What?"

"They're going after Rosie, too. Trying to get her story."

Now she was listening — all the rest was noise, but she

didn't want Rosie to suffer: she'd done nothing wrong. She simply couldn't cause Rosie another drop of harm.

"So far she's not saying a word, insisting you were just good friends," Alexandra continued. "But they know she's a lesbian already because her ex is telling everyone. You might need to have a word, just for damage control. If you don't do it, Penelope will."

Olivia sat back on the bed. Amy's reaction didn't surprise her one bit, and neither did Rosie's. She was the wronged party, and yet she was still protecting Olivia.

Perhaps there was still hope?

Or perhaps Rosie was just an honourable person who liked to keep her private life just that: private.

Alexandra walked over to the antique drinks cabinet in the corner, pulling out two crystal glasses, along with a bottle of Glendronach. She poured two large measures without consulting Olivia, before sitting beside her on the bed. They both took a long slug before anything else was said.

"Was this what it was like with Dean?"

Alexandra dropped her head, taking another pull on the whisky. "Exactly the same. Except I had to see him every day."

Dean had been the Palace's chief of staff.

"Until Mother fired him," Olivia finished.

Her sister looked into the distance. "Yes." She put a hand on Olivia's thigh, before squeezing. "I know what I said earlier, but seeing you these past two days… I don't know." She turned her head, gulping as she continued. "It didn't work out for me, I have to live someone else's dream. But one of us should be happy. Whatever you decide, I'm behind you."

Olivia squeezed her hand right back.

∾

Supper with her parents had been a stilted affair, but Alexandra had been true to her word and never left her side. The Queen had been officious, outlining duty, tradition and royal oaths. But as far as Olivia was concerned, she hadn't signed any oaths — she'd just had the bad luck to be born.

Her mother hadn't been in the mood for her lip.

"You don't know your luck," she'd snapped after staying calm for a good five minutes. "You don't even have to be Queen — your sister gets that honour. Your job is to look pretty and have a trophy wife on your arm. But most of all, you must behave like a royal and produce an heir to replace you. The royal family demands respect, and you need to start giving it." She'd sat forward to deliver her final line. "You are getting married to Jemima, because doing otherwise weakens the crown, and that weakens me."

That was the crux of it: if there was one thing her mother hated more than anything, it was showing weakness.

And the killer blow? Her father had nodded his head in silent agreement.

Olivia had never gone against his wishes.

It said a lot that she was relieved to be in the drawing room waiting for Jemima. She poured herself another whisky, then sat on one of three velvet antique wing-backed armchairs, tapping her burnished brown brogue against the polished wooden floor. Alexandra had told her to keep her photoshoot dress on for supper, but Olivia was feeling rebellious. She'd changed into her best black suit, her sharpest white shirt and her shiniest cufflinks. If she was going down, she was doing it looking like the best lesbian in town.

She was pretty certain she was one of the most famous right now.

A knock on the door signalled Jemima's arrival, and seconds later she strutted into the room. She'd changed since this afternoon's shoot but was still looking delectable in a flowing midnight blue off-the-shoulder number, the necklace that sat on her chest twinkling with more sparkles than Blackpool. When she sat in the armchair opposite Olivia, she crossed her leg, showing a vast expanse of smooth, tanned skin through a side split.

Ten years ago, Olivia's head would have been turned.

Now, she looked away, feeling like she was cheating on Rosie.

She kept having to remind herself there was no her and Rosie anymore.

She'd sent another flurry of messages thanking Rosie for her silence with the press. Still no reply.

"Are you going to offer me a drink?"

Olivia stood up, getting Jemima what she needed. Then they stared at each other for a few moments before Olivia spoke first.

"How's Tabitha?"

Jemima let out a hollow laugh. "You want to play that game? Because from what I hear, you had your own plaything in Cornwall."

Olivia's jaw muscles twitched. "She was many things, but she was not a plaything." Dammit, that was too defensive.

Jemima's eyes narrowed as she sat forward, swirling her drink. "Let me make this very clear. It's not just you in this engagement and this marriage — I'm in it, too. And yes, I know I'm second fiddle, but I'm still part of it. And you know the deal with such a marriage. We put up a united front, we smile for the camera and we sleep with who we want to. But the one thing we don't do is fall in love because that wrecks things." She held Olivia's gaze. "I would never have agreed to this if I knew you were in love with someone else."

Olivia cast her eyes to the ground, steeling herself.

"You have a duty, you are a royal." Her mother's words went round and round her head.

Her father's pleading gaze burned into her soul: "She's right, Olivia," he'd reinforced.

"Bottom line, Olivia," Jemima said. "If we do this, you can't see this woman again, because I can tell she's got under your skin."

Olivia's heart stalled: could she commit to never seeing Rosie again? She threw her head back, biting her lip to stop the tears.

Her mother, her father, Jemima; they all wanted the same thing.

She desperately wanted to see Rosie again, but their paths were unlikely to cross now, weren't they?

Could she give up her life to being a royal like the rest of her family had? Did she have a choice now Rosie was lost?

"Do we have a deal?" Jemima asked, her stare heated. "No more falling in love, and we can make this work."

Olivia looked at her, this woman she hadn't even kissed in over a year.

Jemima was offering her a compromise, and maybe that's all she could hope for anymore.

"Olivia?"

She looked up, ignoring the crack of her heart breaking, and slowly nodded her head. "We have a deal, Jemima."

CHAPTER 24

Rosie stretched to the tips of her toes, hoping it would relieve the ache in the balls of her feet. The cafe had been a mad rush again and, while it was good that she was so busy, as it kept her mind from wandering to the same person every single time, she was exhausted. It didn't help that she had trouble sleeping and that, every time she set foot outside, she now had to be wary of a paparazzi snapping a shot of her or, even worse, a camera crew barrelling in her direction, asking her the same question over and over again: Did you and Princess Olivia have an affair while she was engaged to Jemima Bradbury?

It had been like that every single day this week and every time Rosie wondered if what they'd had between them was 'an affair'. What was an affair, anyway? In her heart of hearts, she knew what it was, yet she couldn't let that feeling come to the surface ever again.

Rosie stopped her feet gymnastics and glanced at Amy. She wasn't sure why her ex had chosen Mark & Maude's to have brunch today. Her family owned plenty of brunch spots in Otter Bay. Either she was here for Gina's food, or for Rosie.

Rosie didn't have any resolve left to resent Amy showing up. In fact, she was quite happy to see a familiar face — as opposed to having a camera lens shoved into hers.

Amy looked up from the newspaper she was reading and smiled at Rosie. She leaned back and said, "Join me for a minute?"

Rosie nodded and took the seat opposite Amy. This was the quiet time just before the lunch rush would begin. And Aunt Hilary was here. Rosie could afford to sit down for a few minutes.

"You look tired," Amy said, giving Rosie's face a once-over, "and like you've lost weight."

"Having a princess break your heart will do that to you." Rosie followed her statement with a chuckle. She didn't need Amy's pity.

"I can't say much about the princess bit, but I can definitely tell you what heartbreak feels like," Amy said.

What was Rosie supposed to say to that? She hoped Amy wouldn't take this opportunity to put the moves on her again. Rosie was too tired to put up that particular fight.

"Thanks for telling me about Charlie." Rosie shook her head. "I still can't believe I didn't see it." Rosie supposed she only saw what she wanted to see: a kind, gorgeous woman who was interested in her.

"Just so we're clear." Amy leaned over the table. "I didn't get any joy out of giving you that information. I hate to see you like this. I really do."

"Is that why you're here?" Rosie asked.

"No." Amy tapped the newspaper she'd been reading. "It's for your free copy of *The Daily Mail*, of course."

"Of course." Rosie had vowed to end the cafe's subscription to *The Daily Mail* many a time, but even she had to admit it was the most read newspaper at Mark & Maude's by far. She'd basically been outvoted by her customers. "Please don't tell me what they have to say about me today."

"It says here you used to go out with Otter Bay's most eligible lesbian bachelorette Amy Davies." Amy snickered at her own joke. At least Rosie hoped it was a joke.

"As long as it doesn't have too many unflattering pictures of me in there," Rosie said on a sigh. The other day, she'd glimpsed a headline above a picture of her in, admittedly, rather frumpy clothes: *Rosie in Rags vs Jewelled Jemima!*

Rosie worked in a cafe so she dressed in jeans and comfortable shoes. What did Jemima do with her days? Probably go fancy shoe shopping and get photographed in all the right places.

"A picture of you could never be truly unflattering." Amy was laying it on a bit thick.

The cafe's phone started ringing and Rosie was glad to have an excuse to get up, but Aunt Hilary had answered it already.

"Sorry," Aunt Hilary said. "Dinner service is fully booked for the next two weeks."

Rosie's brain still had a hard time computing the words her aunt had just spoken. Firstly, they had a *dinner service* now. And secondly, it was so popular, they'd had to turn away customers.

Amy stared at her, her eyebrows drawn all the way up.

"Yes?" Rosie asked.

"Fully booked, eh? Congratulations."

Rosie wasn't about to confide this in Amy, but every time she took a call for a booking, her heart sank a little more. At first, she thought it was because Mark & Maude's revival was so inextricably linked to Charlie, until it started dawning on her that there might be a different reason.

"Thanks," Rosie said. "Who'd have thought?"

Rosie wondered what would have happened if she hadn't taken the For Sale sign down. Would the cafe have sold yet? And now that it had been all done up and was doing so well, could she ask a higher price for it? She pushed the thought away and focussed on Amy.

"A bit of gloss and the place looks like new," Amy said.

Rosie looked at Amy, at the spot she was sitting in, but instead of seeing Amy's face, she saw Charlie's. This was the table she always chose, away from the window. That made sense to Rosie now. Even though she'd worn that expensive Paul Smith jacket, Charlie had looked decidedly un-princess-like when she'd ordered her first pot of tea at Mark & Maude's. Then the whirlwind of the subsequent weeks played like a movie in Rosie's head again, like it had done so many times before.

The details of it killed her. The most random memories turned out to be the most heart-breaking ones. Charlie leaning over the pool table at the Dog & Duck. Charlie chatting to Gina, telling her she would fix things for her. Charlie walking up to her at the cemetery on the anniversary of her parents' death. Charlie kissing her chastely on the cheek outside her front door.

All of that had happened, yet here Rosie sat. The walls might be a different colour, but she was still the same Rosie Perkins taking orders at Mark & Maude's — now *with* dinner service. Or was she?

Sticking up the For Sale sign, for about thirty minutes on the day she'd made the decision to sell, hadn't only made her incredibly nervous. It had also shown her a glimpse into a different life. A different future.

The point was that on that day, after many months of consideration, Rosie had made a decision. There were many reasons why she'd backtracked on it, but the main reason behind it at the time — Charlie — was gone forever.

Rosie slanted her torso over the table and whispered to Amy, "I still might sell it."

Amy narrowed her eyes. "Don't tease me about this, Rosie. You know I'm dead serious when it comes to business."

"Oh, I definitely know that." She kept her voice down because she didn't want Hilary to overhear. "If I do sell it, it would come with certain conditions."

Amy nodded. "It can come with a million conditions, I'll honour all of them."

∽

When Rosie got home, she found Paige hunched over her laptop. She seemed utterly absorbed in whatever she was reading. Rosie hoped it wasn't another article about Princess Olivia. It seemed as though there was no other news in the country anymore. She was secretly hoping for a juicy political crisis to take the nation's attention away from the upcoming royal wedding.

Rosie cleared her throat. Only Cher had noticed she'd come home.

"Oh, hi," Paige said absent-mindedly.

"What are you so caught up in?" Rosie sat down next to her sister.

Paige straightened her spine. "I think I've made my decision and I've decided on Bristol. It looks great and I won't be too far away, so I can come back home regularly."

Rosie tried to decipher Paige's smile. It failed to convince her that Paige was one hundred per cent certain about her final choice.

On her short walk home, Rosie had made a choice as well. It was time both she and her sister started supporting each other's real dreams, not the ones they conceded to because of concerns for one another.

"Bristol Uni is really your first choice?" Rosie inquired.

"Not my first choice, per se, but close enough."

"Close enough to what?"

"It's a great university and I could come home during terms. See how you and the cafe are doing. Maybe help out a little."

Rosie shook her head. "What's your actual first choice?"

"Durham," Paige said, as quick as a flash.

"You should go with your first choice."

"B-but it's too far away and that would—" Paige started protesting.

Rosie shook her head with a bit more fervour this time. "You don't have to choose Bristol for me. We need to start making our own choices."

"Well, yes, but this particular choice isn't just about me. And going to Bristol wouldn't exactly be a hardship."

"But it wouldn't be your first choice." Rosie turned fully towards her sister. "Would it be easier for you to choose Durham if I told you I might not be here to come back to?"

Paige tilted her head. "What do you mean?"

Rosie took a deep breath before speaking. "What if I sold the cafe?"

"But you've just spruced it up," Paige said.

"Which will only make the price go up." Rosie's heart was beating in her throat. "I think the reason I didn't take the initiative to give the cafe an overhaul, apart from lacking the funds, is that it was never *my* dream. I never really had the chance to figure out my dreams. After Mum and Dad died, all I knew was that I had to come back here. But if you'd asked me before they died what I wanted to do with my life, it would never have been run a cafe in Otter Bay. Not even one that's been done up by a princess."

Paige giggled at that. "Are you sure about this? I mean, what will you do?"

"That's what I need to figure out. But I definitely want to go travelling."

"Wow." Paige sank against the backrest of her chair. "Everything would change."

"Everything will change regardless." Rosie eyed her sister. "You're all grown up now. You're starting your own life in September. I don't want you to be held back by thoughts of me."

"You could never hold me back." Was that Paige's voice breaking? "After all you've done for me." She grabbed hold of Rosie's hand. "If anyone deserves to follow their own dreams, it's you."

"And you'd be all right with selling Mum and Dad's cafe?" Rosie had trouble fighting back a tear.

"Their memory lives on in our hearts, not in a pile of bricks," Paige said.

"When did you get so wise?"

"Must have been my older sister's influence." Paige shot her a smile.

Rosie scooted a little closer and threw her arms around her sister. Perhaps she hadn't done such a bad job of raising her after their parents were gone.

As if she wanted in on it, Cher jumped into Paige's lap.

"Who's going to look after this furry monster if we both leave?" Paige asked.

"I hope Aunt Hilary feels up to that terrible burden." Rosie scratched Cher under the chin.

Paige took the cat in her arms and walked to the sofa. She sat down and addressed Cher as if the animal could actually understand what she was saying. "What do you think, Cher? Do you want to go live with Aunt Hilary?" She shook Cher's paw. "She has agreed," Paige said with a smirk on her face.

"Now we only have Aunt Hilary to work on." Rosie crashed into the other sofa and stretched out her legs. She was so knackered, she felt she could fall asleep in a heartbeat.

Paige switched on the TV and immediately they were

assaulted with more images of Charlie and Jemima. Paige switched the channel, but it seemed like every single one was covering a press conference the princess and her fiancée had given.

"It's okay," Rosie said, the adrenaline of seeing Charlie's face again jolting the fatigue from her system. "Let's see what happened." Part of her didn't want to know, but the overriding part was curious. Maybe they'd called the whole thing off?

They watched in silence for a few minutes. Princess Olivia — because that was not Charlie on the screen — confirmed that the wedding would take place in five weeks' time and that all the rumours the press had been spreading were false. She and Jemima were in love and firmly committed to this engagement.

"It's like it's not really her, is it?" Paige said. "Like she's a totally different person."

For a split second, Rosie allowed herself to think that, in a way, Charlie had been right. Rosie would never have fallen for Princess Olivia. She could only ever have fallen for Charlie, the ex-army officer who had swept her off her feet. But Charlie was gone and had been replaced by that stiff and joyless woman on the television. Sure, Princess Olivia smiled, but the smile never reached her eyes. Didn't anyone see that?

Rosie felt sorry for Charlie and, for the first time, came close to understanding why Charlie had lied. But she could understand it all she wanted; Charlie was still marrying another woman.

CHAPTER 25

The press conference and the numerous photoshoots they'd organised seemed to have done the trick, and the press had moved on to newer stories that seemed easier to break. Olivia never thought she'd be grateful to the Labour party and their eternal infighting, but if it knocked her off the front pages, she hoped they'd fight on forever.

Nothing more had surfaced of her time in Otter Bay, and for that, she knew she had Rosie to thank. Numerous other residents could have blown the whistle on her — anyone from the Dog & Duck, the cafe, Connie from the boutique, even Amy — but their total loyalty to Rosie meant the story had never gained traction. Plus, now she and Jemima were on the front pages every day in a huge show of togetherness, the press had to accept the marriage was going ahead.

If only it was that easy for Olivia.

The cooling of the story also meant Olivia had been allowed home, where she could finally breathe again. The past couple of weeks had been filled with non-stop social engagements, dresses and make-up, all of which made Olivia want to scream. Now she was back in her own house, she was calmer.

Jemima was coming over later and they were going to choose a menu for the wedding, something they both wanted to eat. Malcolm had chosen one that involved venison, grouse and caviar, none of which would make it into Olivia's top 100 foods, never mind her wedding meal. Jemima had agreed, so they were taking back that tiny piece of control. They might not be in love, but at least she and Jemima agreed on many things — and lately, they'd been getting along just fine.

There were definitely worse people she could be married to, as Miles had reinforced in her time living with her sister. Had it not been for the company of her niece and nephew at dinner a couple of evenings, his attitude would have made her say something. It pained her to see her sister living this way, but it was also an insight into just what she'd given up, and how much Alexandra was prepared to put up with for the crown. Not that she had much choice, but still.

Now she was back in her own home, one other thing Olivia could do was ride — she'd missed it greatly.

Olivia approached the stable block, greeting Eddie, her stable hand, before going to her favourite mare, Britney. Tall, dark and elegant, Britney had been named after Olivia's favourite pop star of her youth — and also to enrage her mother, which it duly had. Olivia had told Britney all her secrets and ridden her throughout some challenging times, and her spirits automatically lifted on seeing her. Whatever else was going on in her life, when she was riding Britney, Olivia was invincible.

"Riding out today, madam?" Eddie asked, tightening Britney's saddle before giving her a firm pat. "Lovely day for it."

"Can't wait," Olivia said, staring up into the cloudy sky. That was another thing that had changed since coming back from Cornwall: the weather. There, the days had been carpeted with sunshine; back in London, there were always clouds overhead. The weather seemed to be echoing her mood. "Have you been keeping her fit in my absence?"

Eddie nodded. "As instructed, madam. Nothing but the best for Britney."

Olivia smiled. "Thanks, it means a lot." She mounted her horse, squeezed her sides lightly and steered her out of the paddock. Just like always, a grin slid onto Olivia's face as she cantered across the fields, freedom hugging her like a long-lost friend.

She leaned forward, doing the same to Britney. "I've missed you, girl," she said, patting her neck as the horse got into her stride. "And you have no idea what a mess I've made of my life since I last saw you. I've fallen in love with one woman but I'm marrying another. Can you believe that?"

In the 21st century, she'd mistakenly thought any issues over her marriage would be based around her marrying a woman, not the *right kind* of woman. But Olivia had underestimated the power of class and tradition.

She kept falling for the wrong women, according to her mother.

"But if I've fallen for them, surely they're the right ones, don't you think?" she whispered.

The wind whistled past her face as she gripped Britney's reins, enjoying the pull of muscles she hadn't used in a while. What was Rosie up to, now? She'd been in contact with Gina after her test and permit had been passed, and she knew the cafe was doing well. Gina had told her some of the clientele were tourists who'd come to eat at the same cafe Olivia had used, but if that was pulling in customers, Olivia was thrilled.

She glanced at her watch as the horse slowed slightly: 3.45pm. Rosie would just have finished the lunch rush and be prepping for the evening service. Hilary would be hovering in the background as she always was, the much-loved family matriarch; and Paige would be having a coffee after college, talking about where she was going to university. Had she chosen yet? She'd confided to Olivia she'd love to go to Durham but feared it might be too far away. Olivia had been to Durham and was all for it. She'd told her to tell Rosie; Paige had been hesitant.

"Rosie." Saying her name out loud made her seem more solid, more real. She was so far away in distance and in spirit, it often felt like what had happened had been a mirage. But it wasn't, Olivia knew that. Her feelings weren't a phase, or something that would go away. She loved her, and if Rosie's face was anything to go by when she'd left, Olivia was willing to bet Rosie felt the same way. "Rosie!" she shouted into the air, her heart thumping out its own rhythm. "I love you, Rosie Perkins!"

Fuck.

~

Olivia returned from her ride an hour later, and jumped straight in the shower, her head clearer. Exercise and fresh air always did that for her. She thought back to Otter Bay, to the idyllic afternoon walks along the clifftops and down to the deserted sandy coves beneath. She'd give anything to be back there now, with Rosie.

She checked her phone as she did all day every day: no texts. She was getting the message loud and clear. Rosie had meant what she'd said, they were over. And who could blame her? She'd probably seen the news, too. Olivia and Jemima were getting married.

Damn it all.

She was in black jeans and a black T-shirt, her hair still damp when Jemima walked in, her heels scraping along the slate tiles of the kitchen. Olivia spun round at the sound and gave her a smile. Jemima was wearing dark jeans, too, but they were paired with a summer blazer, jet-black heels and much bling.

"Hello, future wife," Jemima said, giving her a wink.

They were hardly love's young dream, but at least they could share a joke. "Hey yourself," Olivia replied. "You want a drink?"

Jemima nodded. "A coffee would be nice," she said, glancing around. "Where's Anna?"

"I gave her the week off," Olivia told her, flicking on the kettle.

"How are you surviving?" Jemima's voice was filled with horror. "Who gives their housekeeper a week off?"

Olivia shrugged. "I got used to doing things myself in Otter Bay and I just wanted my own space for a while longer." She looked up at Jemima, staring at her bright blue eyes. "Because soon, I'm going to be sharing my space with you, aren't I? Call it making the most of my last days of freedom." She tried to make a joke of it, but every muscle in her body tightened.

Jemima gave her a smile. "Get this out of your system now because there will be none of this nonsense when we're together. Housekeepers and cooks are essential to my lifestyle, as you well know."

Olivia swallowed down her unease, a glimpse of Rosie popping up in her head, running her own business, tackling life head-on. Jemima would fall apart even making a cup of coffee.

"And tell me you've got proper coffee? From Italy? I don't want any of that Fairtrade stuff — I know it's for charity, but it tastes disgusting."

Olivia sucked down her immediate reply and waved the cafetière at Jemima. "Will this do, your highness?"

That brought a smile from her fiancée, who leaned against the kitchen counter, raking a hand through her long, blonde hair. She was still beautiful, but Olivia's pulse only ticked up for one woman these days.

"Do you think they're going to decide on my title, soon?" Jemima said, licking her lips, her gaze pinned to Olivia. "I know they were talking about maybe making me the Duchess of Bath, but surely that's a bit small, don't you think?" She frowned. "You're the Duchess of Sussex, a whole county. Alexandra's got a county, too. Bath seems a bit… insignificant?"

Olivia's actions stilled as she took in Jemima's words, a sour taste dropping into her mouth. Really? There was so much else to worry about in this marriage, yet Jemima was only concerned about her title and whether or not Bath was big enough for her ego?

Olivia stared at her, her mouth dropping open slightly. "After all these years, you still have the power to take my breath away." She was being sarcastic, but Jemima narrowed her eyes as the corners of her mouth tweaked into a smile, reaching her index finger out to trail up Olivia's bare arm.

Olivia got goose bumps, but it was all on the surface. Inside, she was frantically pumping the brakes.

"I thought, maybe, you know," Jemima continued, raising an eyebrow. Her finger moved higher, running along Olivia's exposed collarbone. "If you could have a word with your mother about it, see if we could at least upgrade to a bigger city, I could make it worth your while." She took a step closer, her tongue trailing along her bottom lip, her gaze trained on Olivia. "Plus, we're going to be married and living together, so we should at least have a welcome-home fuck, for old time's sake." She was so close now, Olivia could feel the warmth of her breath. "You have to admit, that was never bad between us."

Another second and their lips would meet, but Olivia wasn't going to let that happen.

She yanked her arm from Jemima's grip and stared at her like she'd gone mad. "You want to sleep with me so my mother will make you Duchess of somewhere bigger?"

Jemima frowned, looking confused. "That, and you've got

that whole 'just got out of the shower and looking sexy' thing going on." She stepped back. "We are getting married, Olivia. You don't think we're going to have sex?"

Olivia's eyes widened. Was that what Jemima thought? They'd actually sleep together again?

It wasn't that outrageous, she supposed, but her head had just been filled with Rosie, and she hadn't given anything else much thought. Sure, in these royal marriages the deal was you slept with other people, but even Alexandra had spawned two children with Miles. She tried to picture her and Jemima naked, but she kept drawing a blank. All she saw was Rosie, deliciously naked and all hers. Nobody else's.

And just like that, Olivia knew she couldn't do this. What had she been thinking? She couldn't stand up in front of Jemima, never mind in front of the whole country and god, and swear to be faithful to someone she didn't even love. It was ludicrous.

Judging by Jemima's expression, every thought Olivia was having was being broadcast across her face.

She moved closer again, studying her. "You weren't going to sleep with me, were you? Like, ever?" She sucked in a breath. "Jesus, Olivia, I know we're not going to be faithful, but I thought at least I might get the odd roll in the hay. It's one of the reasons I agreed to this — sex is important and we're good at it." She turned, leaning her back on the counter, tipping her head to the ceiling. "But we're not going to do this, are we? Because you are in love with that woman, aren't you?"

Olivia bit the inside of her cheek and gripped the counter to stop her shaking. It only partly worked. "I can't stop thinking about her," she said, after a few moments.

"Have you contacted her?" Jemima was still looking up.

"She won't talk to me, why would she? She thinks I'm getting married. I wouldn't talk to me, either."

Jemima looked at her, shaking her head, her eyes soft. She

put out a hand and led Olivia over to the large kitchen table, pulling out two of the eight wooden chairs. Then she leaned forward, head in her hands.

"Jem?" Olivia's stomach fell to the floor.

Jemima held up a hand, before shaking her head, bringing herself back upright. "I knew this might happen, but it's still a bit of a shock."

Olivia winced. "For what it's worth, I'm sorry."

Jemima's mouth twitched as she took in a lungful of air.

"But it's not like you don't love someone else either, is it?" Olivia said. "You and Tabitha?"

Jemima shook her head again and let out a strangled laugh. "It doesn't matter if I love her or not, does it? She's marrying Henry, keeping up appearances." She paused. "I will always love you, though, you know that, right? You were my first love."

Olivia gazed at her with a sad smile. "I know." She paused. "And it was one of the reasons I said yes to this — we get on, I know that."

"But it's like you said in the beginning — it's not enough for you, is it?"

Olivia sighed. "Not now, no. Not when I've met someone else and fallen for her."

"Tell me about her."

Olivia sat up. "Really? You want to know?" It wasn't what she'd expected Jemima to say.

Her fiancée just smiled. "If I'm being usurped, I'd like to know who's doing the usurping."

Olivia reached over and took Jemima's hand, giving it a gentle kiss. "You're amazing, you know that?"

"I've been thinking about it over the past few weeks — even when you were down in Cornwall. I knew something was up, but you wouldn't talk to me." Jemima pursed her lips. "The thing is, it's like we said, we both need to be in this one hundred per cent for it to work. If I'm married to you, I want you to be my partner in a lot of ways. I want the occasional bit of razzle dazzle, the occasional fuck, a laugh, a joke. From what my sisters tell me, that's more than most couples experience in their marriages. I look around and I agree. Are arranged marriages that different to other marriages? Not from where I'm standing."

She was dead right. When Olivia looked at her own life, all the marriages she knew — arranged or otherwise — were pretty dire.

"Why do you think people want to get married then?" Olivia asked.

Jemima shrugged. "It's what you do, a life marker. Or maybe you are actually in love. I don't hear that one much these days." She dropped her head. "And I don't really want to hear about this woman, by the way. I was trying to be nice, but I might have taken it a step too far."

Olivia's heart went out to her. "Just know, it would take quite a woman to knock you off anybody's list."

Jemima winced. "That doesn't make it any easier." She sighed. "But you really do love her?"

"I really do." Olivia's heart lit up just talking about her. "Walking away was the hardest thing I've ever done. She just makes me feel alive. She got to know the real me and not a title, and that means so much."

"Does she love you, too?"

Did she? When everything had blown up, Rosie had never had a chance to tell her. "I think so. I hope so," Olivia replied. She wasn't sure, but she was willing to risk it all to give it a shot.

Jemima stared at her. "If you think there's a chance, maybe you need to go and ask her, find out for sure. And if she does, you should marry her, not me. I don't want to be married to a grump all the time, like you have been for the past few weeks."

"I haven't been that bad," Olivia replied, even though she knew she had.

Jemima gave her a look. "You get away with much more being a princess, let's just agree on that." She gave Olivia a resigned smile. "So, I guess we're not deciding on the wedding menu tonight, then?"

"I guess not." Olivia got up and pulled Jemima up with her. Then she wrapped her arms around her, kissing her cheek, breathing in her expensive smell. "Thank you," she whispered in her ear. "Thanks for understanding, I'll never forget it."

"You'd better not," Jemima replied. "I do have one condition, though." She pulled back, looking Olivia directly in the eye. "I want to be out of the country after this has broken and I've done my duty of looking happy about it."

Olivia nodded. "I'll take the fall, don't worry."

"Damn right you will," Jemima said. "But I want use of your family's house in Bermuda for at least a month. I do not want to be here when this all blows up. Make that happen and I'll do whatever you want."

Olivia stared at her, then nodded. "Life's not the fairy tale we were promised in childhood, is it?" She paused. "But there's someone out there for you, too, I'm sure of it. It's just not me."

CHAPTER 26

Rosie glanced around the wine bar. Even though it had been open for quite a few months, she'd never set foot inside before. It was a matter of principle — and having just broken up with Amy around the time of The Lounge's grand opening.

Amy's parents had just called it *The* Lounge, which was so typical of them. Granted, it was the only wine bar in Otter Bay, but the name got on Rosie's nerves nonetheless.

"Thanks for meeting me here," Amy said. "I got you a glass of Sancerre."

"Thanks." Rosie decided to let it slide that Amy had ordered for her. She knew she meant well. When they were still together, Rosie had professed her love for Sancerre numerous times, and Amy wasn't one to forget something like that. It was actually kind of sweet.

"Our last chat has been on my mind," Amy said. "And I've talked to my parents."

Rosie was still taking in the rather sterile ambiance of the bar, and Amy wanted to talk business already. She had definitely inherited some of her parents' ruthlessness. You didn't monopolise most of Otter Bay's food and beverage industry without making some enemies — although industry was perhaps too big a word for it.

"I'm fine, thanks, and how are you?" Rosie said, grinning.

"Sorry." Amy looked up from her glass of wine. "I'm just excited about this." She held up her glass.

"A toast already?" Rosie lifted her glass towards Amy's.

"I suppose we can toast the fact that we can now be civil with each other. That's something. At least to me it is."

Having been brutally hurt herself, Rosie felt a bit more compassionate towards her ex. "I'm sorry if I hurt you," she said. "But you and I, we were never really right for each other."

"According to you." Amy drank her wine.

"Well, yes. There are usually two people in a relationship and if one of them thinks—"

Amy stopped Rosie by putting a hand on hers. "It's fine. We don't have to go there again. My feelings for you aren't mutual. I'm starting to get over that fact." To Rosie's relief, she withdrew her hand swiftly. "We're not here to rehash the past. I want to talk about the future."

Rosie took a sip of wine. Its cool crispness slid down her throat and relaxed her a little. "Okay, let's talk about the future."

"As I said, I talked to my parents. They haven't failed to notice how well Mark & Maude's is doing. I'm here to make you an offer on their behalf."

Rosie tried to keep her cool. She wouldn't have agreed to meeting Amy at The Lounge if she hadn't suspected this was going to happen, but Rosie was determined not to let her excitement get in the way of her negotiation skills. She nodded. "That's great."

"I know you have conditions," Amy said. "And we're willing to honour them because why change a winning team? We definitely want Gina to stay on as chef. And Hilary is part of the fabric of the cafe so we'd love for her to stay as well, if she wants to, of course." Rosie wasn't so sure about that. "We want the place as it is." She cocked her head. "We may change some details, like the crockery. But all in all, you've done a good job doing it up. It's got oodles of Cornish charm."

Rosie wanted to hop off her barstool and jump up and down with glee. But she didn't know what they were offering yet.

"Thank you," she said instead. "That sounds like music to my ears."

Amy fished inside her purse and got out a notepad and pen. She scribbled something on the piece of paper, tore it off and folded it in half. She then slid it across the table to Rosie.

Rosie peered at the piece of folded-up paper. "I feel like I'm in a gangster movie."

"Otter Bay style," Amy said.

Rosie reached for the piece of paper. Her pulse picked up speed as she unfolded it. Her eyes went wide, her mouth as dry as the paper she was holding. This was much more than she had expected. This amount of money would pay for Paige's entire university education, while leaving more than a good chunk for Rosie to go travelling with.

"I—I don't really know what to say." She glanced at Amy. Was there a catch somewhere?

"Otter Bay is on the up," Amy said. "It's reflected in the offer." She pulled her lips into a smirk. "You didn't think I was going to low-ball you, did you?"

"I guess you'd be getting rid of your last competition in town." Rosie glanced at the number again. "What about the name? You won't change it to *The* Cafe, will you?"

Amy chuckled. "My dad went to school with yours. He was very fond of Mark. I think he'll want to keep the name."

"That's a lot of sentiment for a Davies," Rosie joked.

"We're not cold-hearted arseholes, you know. We love Otter

Bay. And isn't it better that a local family owns it instead of some multinational chain rolling into town, taking all its personality away?"

"It's only a matter of time before Starbucks claims its stake in Otter Bay."

"Over my dead body." Amy spat out the words.

"When your parents ever retire, they'll leave their business in good hands with you."

Amy rolled her eyes. "Better in mine than in Grant's, that hormonal little twerp."

"Give your little brother a break. What were you like when you were twenty years old?"

"I was at uni and working full shifts in the pub when I came home."

"Yes, the youngest ones always get spoiled more." *Except for my little sister who had other things to deal with.*

"So." Amy nodded at the piece of paper. "What do you think?"

"I need to discuss this with my family, Gina included."

"Of course." Amy painted a smug smile on her face. She knew very well this was a once-in-a-lifetime offer.

So did Rosie.

∾

It was a Friday night so Paige was still up, watching *Riverdale* on Netflix, Cher in her lap, as usual.

Rosie casually walked past her and dropped the piece of paper she'd been clutching in her hand all the way home into Paige's lap.

Cher lazily lifted a paw but didn't seem further bothered by it.

"What's this?" Paige picked up the piece of paper.

"You might want to pause your show." Rosie sat down on

the coffee table. Her cheeks were starting to hurt from grinning.

Paige pressed pause and flattened the piece of paper. She glanced at it, her brow furrowing.

"This could be your university fund." Rosie couldn't keep her mouth shut any longer.

"Did Amy make you an offer?" Paige readjusted her position and Cher glared at her in response.

Rosie nodded.

"Oh my god." Paige kept staring at the piece of paper.

"And they've agreed to keep Gina and Aunt Hilary on, if they want to stay." Rosie looked into her sister's elated face and, for the first time since that dreadful moment with Charlie in the cafe's kitchen, she felt a rush of pure happiness surge through her. She may not be able to be with Charlie, but at least she could make some of her other dreams come true.

"You can go travelling." Paige was getting so excited, Cher hopped off her lap in search of a more peaceful spot to spend her evening.

"I know."

"Where will you go?"

"Hold your horses, sis. We need to speak to Aunt Hilary and Gina first."

"There's no way Aunt Hilary could be against this kind of offer." She waved the piece of paper in the air between them. "And not that much will change for Gina."

"She'll have the Davies as her boss." Rosie pursed her lips together.

"They're not that bad," Paige said.

"Says the girl who fumed against Amy just as much as I did."

Paige shifted her weight around again. She sucked her bottom lip into her mouth and looked at Rosie rather coyly. "Amy and her family are doing right by you now, aren't they?"

"Yes." Even Rosie couldn't deny that.

"Because… the thing is…" Paige called Cher over. The cat ignored her.

"What?"

"I didn't want to tell you because you were so down in the dumps about Charlie." A small smile appeared on Paige's face. "But the past few weeks, Grant Davies and I have been sort of seeing each other."

"Amy's brother?" In her head, the words Amy had used earlier that evening to describe Grant blinked in big red letters: that hormonal little twerp.

"He's nothing like Amy," Paige blurted out. "He's so sweet."

"Amy can be very sweet when she wants to be. It's only when she doesn't get her own way that the claws come out."

"I really like him." Paige's cheeks turned pink. "I've been dying to tell you, but I just couldn't do it. Not with the whole Charlie thing."

"Come on." Rosie leaned over and patted her sister on the knee. "You're my baby sister. You can always tell me anything."

"Correction, I'm your grown-up sister, who can and always will take your feelings into account."

A fuzzy warmth spread through Rosie. "I'm happy you've met someone you really like. At least, as far as looks go, the Davies gene pool isn't too bad."

Paige chuckled and smoothed the wrinkles out of the piece of paper she was holding in her hand. "I wonder if Grant had any say in this."

"Why don't we find out? Invite him to dinner. I'd like to spend some time with him."

"You mean you want to appraise him?" Paige balled up the piece of paper she'd just carefully levelled out and threw it in Rosie's direction.

"That as well."

"Shall we double date then? You and Amy plus me and Grant?"

Rosie threw the piece of paper back at her sister. She hoped it would suffice as a no. Now that she and Amy could have an adult conversation again, she didn't want to get her ex's hopes up.

"We should plan your travels," Paige said. "Where will you go?"

Rosie thought for a moment, but she didn't have to contemplate this question very long. She knew exactly where she wanted to go. "Venice."

"I wish I could go with you," Paige said.

"Then do." Rosie looked her sister in the eye. "Come with me."

Paige's mouth fell open for a split second, then closed. She started nodding enthusiastically. "We can go to all the spots Mum and Dad took pictures of. Relive their last, happy moments."

They both fell silent for a while.

Paige was the first to talk again. "Maybe you should go to Monaco as well."

"Monaco? I agree that the Davies made us a good offer, but I don't think we should consider tax evasion just yet."

"With your magnetism to royals," Paige said, "maybe you can attract another princess."

Rosie giggled along with her sister, hoping she was successfully hiding the anguish ripping her apart inside.

There would only ever be one princess for her.

CHAPTER 27

Sweat dripped off her forehead and onto the sweet-smelling grass under her feet as Olivia leaned over, hands on thighs, her breathing still returning to normal. She glanced up at the full trees above, the sky a mass of white clouds, the only sound around her birdsong. She was glad she'd made the decision to run this morning, to get rid of some of her excess stress. Seeing as today was the day she planned to tell her parents she wasn't marrying Jemima, stress management was at a premium. This morning's run around the woods in the grounds of her Surrey estate had been just what she needed. Her mind was a jumble of emotions to begin with, but by the end, the only thing she was processing was the wind on her face, and the snap of twigs under foot.

She stopped by the kitchen for a glass of water, replaying the scene with Jemima last night. She'd taken the news remarkably well — almost as if she'd been expecting it — and Olivia could only hope her parents would be the same. Somehow, she couldn't see it. But if there was one thing meeting Rosie had brought into sharp focus it was that this was her life, and she only got one shot at it; her next move was the critical one, and she wanted to get it right. She just had to hope, once she cleared the hurdle of today, that Rosie was on the same page, too.

She picked up her phone and saw she had a text: as usual, her stomach fluttered. It wasn't from Rosie, it was from her sister.

'Are you seeing the parents today?'

Olivia messaged back telling her she was.

Alexandra's reply was almost instantaneous. 'Let me know the time and I'll be there.'

Olivia's heart swelled: her sister was coming to support her, and in this situation, there was nobody more qualified to stand in her corner. Her sister having her back meant the world to her and made her hopeful for the future. Today was a battle between the current queen and the future one. When the time rolled around for her niece and nephew to get married, she hoped this conversation would never have to be repeated.

∿

Olivia was in the drawing room, whisky in hand, staring into the fireplace. As the wooden grandfather clock in the corner ticked around to 7.30pm, supper time, her mind went increasingly blank. Should she have prepared cue cards for this? She rubbed a hand on her cheek, before remembering the sheen of make-up she was wearing, and swore. She got out a mirror from her handbag and checked herself: she still looked perfect, ready for battle. She'd decided on a simple black dress that would please her mother; tonight, what she had to say was the most important thing, and she didn't want anything distracting from that.

The door was flung open, and Olivia looked up as her sister walked in, giving her a grin. She gave Olivia a bruising hug, before drawing back and holding her at arm's length.

"Ready?" she asked.

"As I'll ever be," Olivia replied.

Her sister squeezed her arm. "It's not just us, by the way. I've called more back-up."

Olivia crinkled her brow. "What does that mean? If Sebastian's coming, I'm not sure that's going to help matters."

"Just trust me — you'll see."

They were called into the dining room moments later and took their places; Olivia and Alexandra to the right of their mother, their father to the left. Their chat was stilted while the staff brought wine, water, bread and starters; once they'd left the room and Olivia had eaten half of her cream of tomato soup — the Queen's favourite — she put down her spoon.

"There's something I need to talk to you both about," she said, her voice coming out far more confident than she felt. As Alexandra had told her, just keep calm, speak slowly and hold eye contact.

"I hope it's good news about the wedding. Malcolm told me you wanted to change the menu." Her mother's stare was laser-like. Somehow, even when she wasn't wearing her crown, it still felt like she was. "Did you both manage that at least?"

Olivia met her gaze, every muscle in her body locking up. "We did meet to discuss that." She took a deep breath before continuing. "But then we made another decision, a major one." She cleared her throat and looked first at her father, then at the Queen. *Remember officer training — shoulders back, stomach in.* "I want you to know that we didn't arrive at this decision lightly, but Jemima and I have decided that we don't want to get married." A shudder ran down her as her heart-rate slalomed. Olivia gripped the table as she continued. "I'm here tonight to let you know that — we're calling off the wedding."

Her mother's face curdled, her solid-silver spoon stopping in mid-air. "You are what?"

"We're not getting married." White noise played in Olivia's

head, but she ignored it. "I know this isn't what you want to hear, but it's better to call this off now rather than a few months down the line."

Her mother put her spoon on her side plate, wiping her mouth with her starched white napkin. She glanced at her husband, and then back to Olivia. "We have already had this discussion, Olivia. This is not your decision to make. The wedding is happening as planned." Her mouth was a straight line across her face, her eyes narrowed.

Olivia left it a few beats, then looked back up at her mother. "No, Mother, it's not. I know it's not what you want to hear, and believe me, I'm not doing this to upset you, but this wedding isn't happening."

Her gaze didn't falter, even though inside, she'd already run screaming out of the palace gates.

The Queen cleared her throat. "Did you know about this?" She was addressing her sister now.

Alexandra nodded. "I did."

The Queen cocked her head. "And what do you think about it? Do you think your sister should be allowed to ride roughshod over the whole institution of royalty like she's the chosen one?"

Alexandra cleared her throat. "I'm behind her in this, yes."

Olivia could have kissed her. She glanced to her right and saw her sister's hand shake as she continued.

"I followed your orders, but times have moved on. Olivia loves someone else and if she marries anyone, it should be her."

The Queen slammed her hand on the table. "How many times do I have to have this conversation? Marriage is not about love, it's about duty."

"And I'm happy to do my royal duties, I've never said otherwise," Olivia said, keeping her cool. "I just want to do it with the right woman by my side."

"Jemima was the right woman."

"No, Mother, she wasn't!" Okay, maybe she wasn't so calm anymore. "Jemima is a lovely woman, but she's not in love with me — she's in love with Tabitha Middleton."

The Queen furrowed her brow. "Tabitha Middleton who's engaged to Henry Maston?"

Olivia closed her eyes. "Yes, that one."

"My god, is everyone in the world depraved these days? In my day, you only had affairs with men."

Something inside Olivia burst. "Depraved? Is that what you think? That being a lesbian is *depraved*!" She pushed back her chair and stood up, shaking as she did. "You know what is depraved, though? Marrying someone you don't love and making your life and their life a misery in the process." Olivia was on a roll now, not to be stopped. "Look at you and Father," Olivia continued, waving her hand between the pair. "How's your married life been? Were you madly in love when you got together?"

The Queen pursed her lips. "Nobody is madly in love when they get married — that only happens in films, not real life."

"But what if it did happen in real life? What if it happened to me?" Olivia pressed her index finger to her chest. "It did happen to me, when I was in Cornwall. I met a woman who loved me for who I was and I fell in love."

The Queen pushed her chair back and stood up. "This again? This woman? This woman who runs a cafe? That is whom you want to marry?"

Olivia gave a firm nod. "Yes, it is."

The Queen threw up her hands. "Well, go ahead," she said. "See how that works out. You don't even know her, she doesn't even know you. You won't last a month. The press will have her for breakfast and she won't be able to cope with the scrutiny. You'll be destroyed by the demands of the title, and then you'll come running back here and realise that you should have married someone who understands, who knows the role. Someone like Jemima. Someone with background and class."

"You're wrong and I'm going to prove it to you. Rosie might not be a duchess or have gone to Oxford, but she's the smartest woman I've ever met. I don't love Jemima, I love *Rosie*. And I haven't yet asked her to marry me, so I'm not saying she will. But I'm going to do everything in my power to convince her to give us a try."

An arm curled around her shoulder, and Olivia turned to see Alexandra by her side. "She's right, Mother. You keep going on about tradition, but it's time to start a new one in this family. Olivia should marry who she wants. Look around this room. You and Father, me and Miles — are any of us happy?"

"Life isn't about happiness. It's about getting the job done."

"Olivia can still get the job done," Alexandra replied. "But wouldn't it be better to get the job done with someone she loves by her side? I know it would have made my life a whole lot easier."

"Your life is easier with Miles than it ever would have been with *that man*."

Alexandra's stare was made of ice. "That's a matter of opinion."

Just then, the door opened and the royal butler announced: "Her Royal Highness, the Queen Mother."

In walked Grandma, looking resplendent in red, her grey hair elegant in a bun. Even in her 70s, she was still a bundle of energy. "Sorry I'm late," she said. She gave her granddaughters a kiss. "Traffic was frightful."

For once, the Queen looked off balance. "What are you doing here?"

Olivia wasn't sure, but she turned to grin at her sister: the back-up had arrived. If there was anyone in the family who would understand her predicament, it was Grandma. Unlike the Queen, Olivia's grandmother had an unwavering faith in love, one that was wholly out of step with her background.

She walked over and sat her daughter back down in her chair. "And hello to you, too, my darling girl."

Olivia's father got up and pulled out a chair for Grandma, with the staff scuttling about, setting another place for her.

"Apologies for gate-crashing the party, but I was alerted to the fact my presence might be needed. So, what have I missed?" Grandma asked.

Olivia cleared her throat. "I was just telling Mother that I'm not marrying Jemima because I love someone else."

Grandma nodded, picking up a bread roll. "Good, she was never right for you. Far too much make-up on her all the time." She paused. "Who's this other woman?"

"She's called Rosie and she lives in Otter Bay," Olivia replied.

"And she's a commoner who knows nothing of royal tradition," the Queen added, her face stony.

"Good," Grandma countered, staring at the Queen. "That's just what this family needs — someone new, fresh blood." She turned to Olivia. "What does this Rosie do?"

"She runs a cafe," Olivia replied.

Grandma nodded. "So she's business-savvy and smart." She paused. "I bet she's strong, too, if you were drawn to her — am I right?"

Olivia's face lit up. "She's the definition of strong, Grandma."

Grandma took a sip of wine and turned to Olivia's father. "What do you think about this, Hugo? Are you behind your daughter going after love and being happy?"

Her father dipped his head to his chest, then sat upright. "I told her to obey her mother, but I've been rethinking." He glanced at his wife, then at Olivia. "I'm sorry Cordelia, but I have to agree with your mother. I trust Olivia and I think you should, too. If there's one thing we got right it's our children — look at them, they're both fantastic. And if Olivia thinks this woman can survive marrying into this circus of a family, then why not? I think we should allow her to live her life and trust her instincts."

Olivia turned to her mother and sucked in a breath, waiting for her response. Her whole future was on the line; she already knew the path she was going to follow, but it would be so much easier with her mother's blessing.

The Queen's mouth twitched. "Fine," she said, through gritted teeth. "You're all ganging up on me, what can I do? Go after this woman, marry who you like, but don't come crying to me when it all goes wrong."

Heat rose through Olivia's body as she tried to process what her mother had just said — somewhere, hidden among it, she detected a tacit acceptance. For once in her life, the Queen had acquiesced. Olivia could do nothing but beam.

"And that is about as much of a blessing as your mother gives," Grandma said, chuckling. "Do get a grip, Cordelia, the world will carry on spinning if Olivia marries someone who speaks with an accent." She turned back to Olivia. "And if she's the reason my granddaughter is wearing that smile, I can't wait to meet her."

CHAPTER 28

Rosie sipped from her Cornish cider and it made her think of Charlie and the face she had pulled when she'd tasted it. But Rosie was at the Dog & Duck with her family and they were here to celebrate, so she ignored the pang of regret in her chest and looked her sister in the eye instead. Paige shot her a tight smile, then glanced at her watch.

"I'm sure he'll be here soon," Rosie said.

"He'd better be," Paige said, in a tone that sounded more as though she and Grant had been married for twenty years, instead of being newly in love — and him about to be introduced to the family.

Rosie had to chuckle. Oh, to be filled with nerves at the prospect of the person you were in love with arriving. Such a delicious feeling. She was happy for her sister.

And Rosie might have been hurt, but she was making a fresh start. Starting a new life. There was no better way to get over a princess.

Gina studied the pub's menu, then looked up, and said, "I may need to have a chat with the Davies' about their pub menu."

"Well, well," Aunt Hilary said. "Listen to our Gina." She held up her glass of wine. "Let's drink to new beginnings."

Just then Grant arrived, rubbing his palms on his jeans. Sweat pearled on his forehead. When his gaze slid to Paige, however, the frenetic glint in his eyes softened, and his lips curved into a lop-sided smile.

Paige seemed to melt on the spot. Rosie looked forward to teasing her about that on the way home.

Grant waved sheepishly at the four women huddled around the table. "Nice to meet you all. I mean, not that we, um, haven't met before," he stammered. "How about some more drinks?"

"Sit down, Grant," Aunt Hilary said. "I'll get you a drink so you can join our toast."

Grant did as he was told. Perhaps Paige had warned him to obey Aunt Hilary when she was in a boisterous mood — and she sure was tonight.

He kissed Paige chastely on the cheek and Rosie felt another pang of something in her chest. Nostalgia at the memory of time gone by. Covering Paige with a blanket after she'd fallen asleep in the sofa — again. Trying to help her little sister with her homework but Paige knowing everything so much better than Rosie. Visits to the cemetery, Paige tucked against her side, both of them sniffling but trying to hide their tears from each other.

Aunt Hilary returned with a beer for Grant. Rosie glanced at him for a second. He had the same big brown eyes as Amy.

"Let's try again," Aunt Hilary said. She raised her glass again and everyone followed suit. "To new beginnings."

Aunt Hilary wasn't one to take early retirement and she had agreed to stay on at the cafe along with Gina. Rosie was glad because with her aunt staying, it felt like a piece of her mother — and a piece of herself — would still be present at Mark & Maude's.

"Don't you girls forget where your home is," Aunt Hilary said.

"I'll only be away a few months," Rosie said.

"And I'll be at uni." Paige turned towards Grant. "Please keep an eye on this one for me while I'm away."

"I'll have fresh pasties waiting for you whenever you get back," Gina said.

"Hello, hello," Amy's voice came over the speakers.

"Good grief," Grant groaned. "It's starting." He rolled his eyes. "My sister loves doing this way too much."

As long as she doesn't launch into song, Rosie thought.

"We've all agreed to sing a celebratory song tonight," Paige said. "What are you singing?" She smirked at Grant.

"Me?" Grant's eyes grew wide with horror. "I'm not singing. I want the customers to have a good time, not have their ears bleed. Besides, Amy would never let me." He relaxed, sure of his case.

Rosie tuned out the rest of their conversation and looked at Amy on stage. She'd done right by her in the end. As long as she didn't burst into *I Will Always Love You* again, Rosie could enjoy this evening out with her family.

"Normally, I would kick off the evening's events," Amy said. "But tonight, I'd like for someone else to do the honours." She stood there with a smug grin on her face, her gaze glued to their table. For an instant, Rosie feared Amy might call her to the stage. "My baby brother's here tonight and he's *in love.*"

Grant's cheeks grew pink all the way to his ears. "That bitch," he muttered under his breath.

"Doesn't look like you have much choice," Paige said.

"Of course I have a choice. My sister has been tormenting me since the day I was born. I've learned how to stand up to her." To prove his point, he rose. "I wouldn't want to take away your most fun moment of the week, Amy." Grant had raised his voice so the entire pub could hear him.

Aunt Hilary rolled her eyes. "Sibling rivalry."

Amy ignored what her brother was saying. "Please everyone, help me lure Grant up onto the stage." She had the advantage of a microphone in her hands. "Grant! Grant! Grant!" She started chanting the poor boy's name so that it reverberated through the pub.

Paige joined in and started shouting her boyfriend's name.

Poor Grant. Rosie knew all about Amy's persistence. Maybe, in the future, she and Grant could bond over that.

"Come on, Grant." Amy nodded at Dave behind the bar. "I've got your favourite song cued up."

"To think I was actually beginning to see her good side again," Rosie said to Aunt Hilary.

"Thank goodness you and your sister were never like this with each other."

"I'm sure we had our moments," Rosie said.

"Not that I can remember." Aunt Hilary shot her a smile.

Most of the pub was now yelling Grant's name. Rosie could barely make out the music over the frantic shouting.

"Come on." Paige egged him on. "Sing me a song then." Maybe she and Amy would get along better in the future, because she seemed to enjoy her torturing her boyfriend.

"You asked for it," Grant said. "But no complaining afterwards."

"I'll enjoy every note of it." Paige blew him a kiss.

Grant made his way to the stage. Some people were still screaming his name. Maybe he enjoyed the attention — he was a Davies, after all.

Amy mock-curtsied and handed her brother the microphone.

Paige leapt to her feet and started clapping.

"He hasn't even started yet," Aunt Hilary said.

"Ah, young love." Gina gazed at the stage with a silly grin on her lips.

Dave restarted the track and Rosie recognised the song this time. Amy really was a bit of a bitch. Grant wasn't even born when this was a hit. She waited with bated breath for Grant to start singing. Once he did, a collective sigh echoed through the pub. Grant didn't let it get to him and delivered a truly horrendous version of Robbie Williams' *Angels*.

The second time the chorus came around, everyone joined in to drown out the tone-deaf noise Grant was producing with his vocal chords, and it reminded Rosie of how much she loved this place.

No doubt Grant would be teased mercilessly once he got off the stage, but it would all be in good cheer. And Rosie had to applaud him for the heart he was putting into his performance. It sounded as though angels were being murdered instead of being sung about, but he was strutting around the stage and beckoning the crowd to sing along.

Paige had found a good guy.

"I'm not sure I'll ever be able to enjoy that song again," Gina said.

"Let's make sure he never does that at the cafe. No microphones allowed in there," Aunt Hilary said.

"I may have to reconsider this relationship," Paige said with a wide smile on her face.

The crowd whooped as Grant headed off the stage. There had been nothing romantic about his performance, yet Paige welcomed him back to the table as though he had just sung her the most heartfelt serenade.

"You actually made me sad that Amy didn't open the singing tonight," Rosie said. She took a long sip from her drink and chuckled.

"Don't pretend as though I didn't do you a big favour by taking the spotlight from her," Grant said, jesting, as though he was part of the family already. He emptied his beer. "Another round?" he asked. "Singing makes me thirsty."

Rosie got up. "I'll get it. You get the next one." She had a feeling they were going to be here for a while. She took the opportunity to visit the loo. When she was washing her hands, she could swear she heard the opening bars of *Royals* by Lorde come on. Once her favourite song — now forever tainted.

She hurried back into the pub to see who was singing it. Rosie usually picked this song for herself on karaoke night — and most people in Otter Bay knew this. It was probably a weekender from London, stealing her song. She could already make out that it was a woman's voice. Whoever it was, she was welcome to it. Rosie didn't plan on belting this one out any time soon. Too many memories were attached to it now for her to enjoy singing it.

She turned the corner and looked at the stage.

This couldn't be. Rosie blinked, but when she peered at the stage again, it was still the same woman standing there, singing.

Their gazes met and locked. Now there was no doubt left. It was her. Charlie had come back to sing for Rosie. She didn't look anything like the woman Rosie had seen in the newspapers the past few weeks, in her designer dresses and with layers of makeup on her face.

This wasn't Princess Olivia on the stage at the Dog & Duck. It was the Charlie, the ex-army officer Rosie had met two months ago. The person who had wooed her. The gorgeous woman Rosie had spent one glorious night with.

Rosie stood nailed to the floor. How had this happened? And where was Jemima?

The people on the table to her right started jabbing each other in the arm. Even though Charlie didn't look much like the woman who had been dominating the more frivolous bits of the news of late, she was being recognised. She could no longer hide. Yet, she had decided to go up on stage and sing, for Rosie.

A girl walked to the edge of the stage and started filming Charlie on her phone. She was soon joined by two more people. Rosie wanted to stop them, wanted to tell them that, although this was a public place, this was a private moment.

And in that instant, she understood that for Charlie, when it came to love, there was no such thing as a private moment.

Flashes were going off all over the place now. If anyone posted this on social media, the paparazzi would be here soon. These were the sort of things Charlie had to concern herself with. Rosie had been hounded by the press enough over the past few weeks to know how utterly exposed that could make you feel.

She walked closer to the stage but remained behind the people with their phones out. Charlie kept looking at her as though Rosie were the only person in the pub.

There could only be one reason Charlie had come here and exposed herself like this.

She was doing this for Rosie.

The song ended and everyone in the pub went wild. Charlie gave a quick bow but kept eye contact with Rosie. Once she had risen back to her full length, she grinned, and rushed off the stage.

Rosie followed her and met her at the side of the stage. She took Charlie by the hand and dragged her outside, hoping no one would follow.

CHAPTER 29

Rosie gripped Olivia's hand as they stepped out into the demi-gloom of the pub car park, and the feel of Rosie's skin against hers was everything. Compared to the deafening roar of karaoke and Friday night fervour inside the pub, outside was an ocean of calm. Rosie didn't look at her, just pulled Olivia through the car park and down towards the clifftop, away from any stragglers and their smartphones. As they neared the bench where they'd sat before, where Rosie had shared about her family and her story, a wave of relief washed through Olivia. Rosie was still entertaining her, and she guessed that after everything that had happened, it was her turn to share.

Rosie turned to check for any followers, but they seemed to be alone. Then she stared at Olivia, before her face creased and words came tumbling out. "What the hell are you doing here?" Rosie didn't seem to know what to do with her arms or facial expressions — she was clearly flummoxed.

"I came to the cafe to find you, but then I saw the sign on the door saying you were closed for a celebration — and if there's a celebration, I knew you'd be at the pub." She paused. "What are you celebrating?"

Rosie shook her head. "You don't get to show up and ask the questions, that's not how it works. Why are you here, and why are you looking like that?" She waved her hand up and down Olivia's tall frame. "You look like Charlie, you don't look like Princess Olivia anymore."

Olivia reached out and put a hand on Rosie's arm, before looking down at herself. Black jeans, leather boots, a white-and-grey striped top — she didn't think she looked that bad. "I wanted to blend in," she said, frowning.

"You're a princess, you don't do blending in," Rosie replied.

Olivia fixed her with her gaze. "I do when it matters — and tonight mattered."

If Rosie's attention had been wandering, she snapped into focus now. "But..." She shook her head. "What are you doing here looking like Charlie? You're getting married to Jemima whatshername. You can't just come back to Otter Bay in a pair of skinny jeans and sing karaoke, like a normal person. Isn't that against royal code?"

Olivia smiled. "Have you been talking to my mother?"

At Rosie's continued frown, she stepped forward, and sat her down on the bench. Their bench. Olivia turned her body towards Rosie and took her hands in hers.

"I know this is out of the blue, but you haven't been far from my mind ever since I left all those weeks ago."

"But you're getting married — everyone knows that. I saw the venue in the paper."

Olivia shook her head. "I'm not."

"I read a piece where they interviewed the designer of your dress." Rosie scrunched up her face.

"Rosie," Olivia said, a sharpness to her voice.

"And your cake's elderflower and rose — I remember

thinking I would never have elderflower in my wedding cake, I always think it tastes a bit like wee—"

"—Rosie!" Olivia's voice slapped the air. "Listen to me." She brushed a thumb over Rosie's knuckles.

Rosie looked down, then back up.

"Ready? Watch my lips. I'm not getting married."

Rosie frowned. "You're not?"

Olivia shook her head, arranging her face in the most convincing way she knew how. "I'm not, I've called it off. Jemima and I… we were never really together. We're exes who run in the same circles, and that was enough for my mother to get us married because apparently I've reached a certain age. But we haven't even kissed each other since the engagement was announced, and the thought of doing that again only got worse after I met you. Because how can I kiss Jemima — let alone marry her — when my heart belongs to someone else?"

As realisation slid down Rosie's face, Olivia sucked in a breath and waited for a response.

"Well say something! I don't make a habit of coming to seaside villages and singing karaoke — never mind *Royals*. It's not a particular favourite for any of my family."

That brought a sound from Rosie, finally. A small spark of laughter, which hugged Olivia's ears.

"You're not getting married?" Rosie's voice was low, but clear.

Olivia shook her head. "I'm not. I couldn't, not when all I could think of was you." She brought Rosie's fingers to her lips and kissed them lightly. Her insides shivered — she'd missed Rosie and what she did to her. Olivia glanced up to see Rosie staring at her, her eyes dark and questioning. Olivia hoped she felt the same, otherwise she might throw herself off this cliff.

"But what about everything else? It's not just any wedding — you're a royal for fuck's sake. The whole nation has been counting down, as I've become very aware of since you left. Can you just... up and leave?"

Olivia winced, kissing Rosie's hand once more. She caught a shudder as she did so and smiled. At least that part still worked. "Let's just say, my mother's not happy with me, but she'll get over it. We've done an official statement and it's getting released tomorrow morning."

Rosie sat up. "Won't you get in trouble for the karaoke stunt you just pulled?"

Olivia shrugged. "The Palace press office will be pissed off, but I was only out singing a song — there's no law against it. Plus, tomorrow's big announcement will blow that out of the water anyway — but I couldn't wait till tomorrow to tell you." She paused. "I missed you so much, and I'm so sorry about it all, you've no idea." Olivia looked up into the hazy sky, the ocean slapping the rocks below. When she took a deep breath, it was coated with hope. "I wanted to tell you, to come clean, but I didn't know how. And then you liked me for me, for being Charlie, and part of me wanted to keep it that way."

"And honestly, if I had known, I'd have run a mile." Rosie shook her head. "I keep thinking I was stupid not to have known. How could I not see who you were?"

A smile creased Olivia's face. "You see what you want to see — I wanted you to believe I was Charlie, and you did. Nobody would think a princess would eat in their cafe every day, would they?"

Rosie laughed, shaking her head. "I didn't even think princesses ate fry-ups — I thought you survived on dust."

"That's my sister, not me." Olivia paused, stroking Rosie's soft fingers. "I had a magical time here with you, and everything I told you was true. I fell in love with Otter Bay first, and then I fell in love with you."

Rosie sucked in a breath at that, biting her lip. "You really fell in love with me?"

Olivia nodded. "With you, with your family, your cafe — but mainly with you. And when I left, I couldn't stop thinking about you. But I thought I'd fucked everything up so much there was no going back. I sent you the crockery, the flowers, the texts, but you didn't respond." She gave her a sad smile. "I thought we were done, that I had to do my duty, because that's what my mother kept telling me. My royal duty to the crown and to the country. So, I agreed to carry on with the marriage. But the closer it got, the more wrong it felt, until eventually, I knew I couldn't go through with it." She paused. "I can't marry one woman when I love another, it's just not how I'm built."

Olivia shuddered. Had she left it too late? Did Rosie feel the same? Had she buggered it all up again? "Leaving you and this place was the hardest thing I've ever done, and I'm so sorry for all the upset I caused you. I know it must have been a shock."

"Understatement of the year." Rosie quirked her mouth into a semi-smile. "It was good for business, though. Turns out you're quite the celebrity, and everyone who came in wanted to know where Princess Olivia had sat."

"I hope you didn't show them photos of me with baked bean sauce dripping down my mouth, I have an image to keep up."

"I think you just punctured that by singing *Royals* in the Dog & Duck."

"You're probably right," Olivia said, sweeping some hair from Rosie's cheek. Rosie still hadn't responded to her declaration of love, and her heart was still waiting, everything crossed. "I've missed this, I've missed you," she said. "Most of all, I've missed us. That night we shared is still seared in my memory."

"Mine, too," Rosie replied. "But then everything happened and I didn't know what to think." She paused, staring into Olivia's eyes. "But despite it all, I don't regret it, and I don't regret meeting you — Charlie, Olivia, whatever your name is. Because yes, you might be a princess, but to me, you were just you." She gazed at her. "And whatever happens, you changed my life for the better."

Olivia's heart boomed — at least she'd done something right.

But Rosie wasn't done. "I've got something else to tell you, too."

Olivia's stomach dropped. "What?"

"You know you were asking what we were celebrating."

Olivia nodded.

"We were drinking to new beginnings." Rosie licked her lips. "Paige leaves for Durham in September, and I've sold the cafe to Amy."

Olivia's mouth dropped open. "After everything? I thought it was doing better?"

"It was — it is! And that's all thanks to you." Now it was Rosie's turn to bring Olivia's fingers to her lips.

Her touch made Olivia's heart stall, but she forced herself to concentrate on what Rosie was saying.

"But when you left, when Gina was sorted and the cafe started to do so well — I realised that, despite it all, it still wasn't what I wanted to do. This was my parents' dream, not mine. And with Paige leaving and Amy's offer on the table, I decided to do what I wanted for once — and I'd never have had the courage to do that if I hadn't met you. You made me see there's a big world out there and I want to be a part of it."

Olivia shook her head. "Wow — you never stop amazing me, you know that? The easy thing to do would be to stay here and run the cafe — chasing your dreams is always the harder route."

"Isn't that what you've chosen?" Rosie asked, her gaze heating Olivia's skin.

Olivia smiled. "Coming back here was the easiest decision to make. Coming back to you." Olivia kissed Rosie's hand again. "When I was with you, I felt myself. When I lost you, nothing was right. I knew I was in love with you because every time I saw you, I never wanted to leave you." She couldn't hold back anymore. "But I have to ask — do you love me? Or at least think you could, in time?"

Rosie's gaze was so deliciously warm, Olivia melted.

"Of course I love you — how could I not? You've changed my life." Rosie cocked her head. "Plus, you look hot in a pair of skinny jeans."

"I do?" Olivia wanted to punch the air, but she stayed put.

Rosie quirked an eyebrow. "Very much so," she said. "But how can this work? Last time I checked you were still a princess, and I'm still me. We live in very different worlds, that hasn't changed." Sadness crossed her face. "I'm not really royal material, and maybe Jemima was."

"Jemima's my past — you're my future. Or at least, I'd like you to be." Olivia had never meant anything so much — it was a future she could already see forming in her mind.

"Don't," Rosie said, shaking her head. "This can't work, Charlie… I mean, Olivia." She threw up her hands. "I don't even know what to call you anymore. How's that for ridiculous?"

"I don't care what you call me, so long as you call me something."

"Aren't all the stars telling us this isn't destined?" Rosie said, glancing up to the sky, before coming back to Olivia. "It hasn't exactly been the perfect start to a romance, has it?"

"No but we could make it the perfect ending."

"But I'm leaving — I'm going travelling."

"You're leaving?"

Rosie nodded. "Uh-huh."

"Shit." Olivia's forehead creased, then she sat up. "Then I'm coming with you."

"What? You can't do that — don't you have royal things to do?"

"They can wait." And they could: sorting this out with Rosie was her top priority, nothing else mattered.

Rosie shook her head. "But—"

"—No buts. Just one question. A simple one. With a yes or no answer." Olivia paused. "Do you love me?"

Rosie's whole body softened. "You know I do."

"And I love you. We should be together — you know it and I know it. Nothing else matters when I'm with you." Olivia swept her thumb across Rosie's cheek as she brought her lips within inches of Rosie's once again. Back where they belonged. "I'm not letting you go, Rosie. Not for a second time."

And then there were no more words as Olivia closed the gap between them and pressed her lips to Rosie's, putting everything she had into that kiss.

What she'd said was true — nothing else did matter — apart from the two of them, together. Just like this. Lips locked, Olivia's hands sliding to Rosie's breasts, Olivia groaning into Rosie's mouth as her tongue slid into hers. She wanted to start over, a fresh chapter. What better time was there than right now?

After some long moments, Olivia pulled back, her breathing shredded, her heart just wanting more. More of Rosie, more of them, more of this moment. "You want to get out of here and go somewhere more private?"

Rosie nodded. "God, yes," she said, her voice scratchy.

"Then let's go," Olivia said, pulling her to her feet.

CHAPTER 30

Rosie fumbled with the keys in the lock. It wasn't every day she had a princess breathing heavily into her neck when she entered her and Paige's tiny flat. But after Olivia's declaration of love, there was no way they'd waste time walking all the way to the manor house. Their place was hardly fit for royalty, but it would have to do. The way Olivia was pressing her weight against Rosie's back, she didn't think the princess minded where they ended up — as long as it was private and had a bed in it.

Of course, once inside, Cher was waiting for them, breaking the sexy mood.

"Goodness, what a cutie." Olivia crouched down and scratched Cher behind the ears.

"Don't waste all your affection on the cat." Rosie locked the door behind them.

"I'll try," Olivia said, but she'd already scooped Cher into her arms.

Cher's purr was so loud, Rosie could hear it from where she stood. "I'm going to text Paige. Tell her not to expect me back in the pub tonight." *And not to come home too early.*

"Hello, Miss Fluff," Olivia said to Cher, not responding to what Rosie had just said.

As soon as Rosie had finished texting her sister, she went to stand in front of Olivia, hands on her hips. "Excuse me, but how am I supposed to take your heartfelt declaration of love seriously when you're so loose with your affections? You seem to fall in love at the drop of a hat — or the purr of a cat."

"Sorry." Olivia smiled sheepishly. "I think I'm the only cat person in my family. The Charltons are more exclusive dog lovers."

"Yes, well, I know Cher is adorable, but, you know." Rosie batted her lashes.

"Your cat's called Cher?" Olivia burst into a giggle.

"Paige chose the name." Olivia shook her head. "It can't really be explained."

"Bye, Cher." Olivia finally put the cat down. She took a step closer to Rosie. "Is this more to your liking?"

"Much."

They were still standing in the small hallway. Olivia didn't seem to have much eye for her surroundings. She fixed her green gaze on Rosie.

An arrow of lust burrowed its way through Rosie. It was time they finished what they'd started on that bench. She grabbed Olivia by the hand again, as she'd done when she'd walked off the stage earlier, and, this time, led her to her bedroom.

Rosie hadn't exactly been expecting company, so her bed was unmade, and there was a pile of clothes on a chair in the corner.

"Don't mind the mess," she whispered. "I'm only a commoner."

"You're *my* commoner now." Olivia pushed the door shut behind them and pressed Rosie against it.

"Oh," Rosie said. "Is that how it's going to be?"

Olivia paused and scanned her face for an instant, then she curved her lips into a slow smile. "This… is how it's going to be." She slanted forward and gently kissed Rosie on the mouth.

Rosie drank in the scent of Olivia, her very presence. The miracle of her turning up after Rosie believed all had been lost. And now here they stood. Olivia's toned body pressing into hers. The princess's lips on hers.

When they broke from their kiss, Rosie couldn't help but smile.

"What's so funny?" Olivia asked, mirroring Rosie's smile.

"Last time we did this, I didn't know who you were yet. I didn't know you were a princess."

"I tried to tell you." Olivia spread Rosie legs with her knee. "But you were too delicious and distracting that night."

"Oh sure, blame it on me." Rosie sank her teeth into her bottom lip.

"Allow me to make it up to you." Olivia narrowed her eyes and leaned in again. Her tongue darted between Rosie's lips. Rosie pushed her hands into Olivia's curls. She looked so much more scrumptious out of her princess garb, with her hair wild and her face free of makeup.

Rosie would very much like for Olivia to make things up to her all night. She had no idea what the future would bring, but she had a clear inkling of what tonight would be like.

Olivia's knee pressed a little harder into her and Rosie pushed herself against it. She lowered her hands from Olivia's head to her top, wanting to get it off her — desperate to clasp eyes on her spectacular shoulders again.

Olivia gave her a helping hand and leaned backwards long enough for Rosie to hoist her blouse over her head. Even though she'd seen Olivia like this before, the effect of seeing her naked body again seemed to have amplified. Maybe because everything was different now. Rosie was different, too. Meeting Olivia — Charlie — had changed her.

Olivia tugged at Rosie's T-shirt and Rosie lifted up her arms, wriggling so that Olivia could remove it.

"You're so beautiful," Olivia whispered. "I missed you." Olivia came at her with such hunger in her eyes, Rosie had no choice but to believe every word she said. There were no more lies between them, no more omissions of truth. The heaviness of heart that had weighed her down since their confrontation in the cafe's kitchen, had lifted the moment Rosie had realised it was Olivia singing on the stage at the Dog & Duck. Singing for her. Now, she felt as light as air. Like a new version of herself. The version that was about to take a princess to bed.

Rosie had met Olivia when she was pretending not to be a princess. No matter what happened, that would always be part of their history. But so would this.

Olivia ran the back of her fingers over Rosie's belly, making her shiver. In response, Rosie traced her fingertips over Olivia's naked biceps. She could look at those wonders of arms for days. How could they be so perfectly shaped?

Rosie lifted her glance back to Olivia's eyes. Her green gaze was as wild and riotous as her hair. Rosie wasn't sure she'd ever encountered such desire staring back at her, mirroring her own so perfectly.

"God, I missed you too," Rosie said on a sigh, before melding her lips to Olivia's again.

Things moved fast then. They fidgeted with the buttons and zippers of their jeans, hurried out of their shoes, and tumbled onto the bed, clad only in underwear.

"I dreamed of this so many nights," Olivia said, staring down at Rosie. "Of you."

Rosie couldn't speak. A wave of happiness crashed over her — the kind of joy she'd believed was no longer in the cards for her. But this woman had made it possible, had unlocked something in her.

Olivia kissed her again, and the touch of her naked skin

against Rosie's made her pulse pick up speed. The hardness of her muscles underneath that satin-like skin was playing tricks with Rosie's mind.

Even though she hadn't allowed herself to feel it, not if she could help it, Rosie had missed Olivia too. She'd missed her intense stare when she listened to Rosie, and the kindness on her face when she looked at her — a kindness that had been sorely lacking in any portrait of Olivia in the newspapers.

But it wasn't Princess Olivia in bed with her, not the princess the world thought they knew. Because hidden underneath the glossy veneer of royalty, was Charlie. Rosie had fallen for Charlie and Charlie would always be a part of Olivia — of them.

Rosie couldn't wait any longer. She reached for the fastening of Olivia's bra and undid it. Olivia manoeuvred out of it and threw the garment into the semi-darkness of the room.

Olivia traced a fingertip over the cups of Rosie's bra. Rosie's nipples rose to meet her caress. They hardened, pushing against the fabric, needing release. Slowly, Olivia peeled down one cup, and freed a breast from its fabric prison. Olivia slanted forwards and licked Rosie's nipple before taking it into her mouth.

Pleasure burst open between Rosie's legs, unleashing the full extent of her desire. She wanted Olivia all over her, wanted to feel all of her. So much want, so much need. Rosie'd never experienced the likes of it.

Olivia repeated the process with Rosie's other nipple and doubled the anticipation coursing through her veins. When she retreated, Olivia looked Rosie in the eye as she removed her bra, tossing it behind her with the same nonchalance she had disposed of her own.

Rosie took the opportunity to push Olivia onto her back and kiss a trail from her lips, along her neck, to her breasts. She cupped them in her hands and feasted on Olivia's nipples as the pressure between her legs grew.

Rosie paused her exploration of Olivia's body to cast a glance at her face. Olivia's eyes sparked with lust, giving Rosie the confidence to continue on her path. She kissed Olivia's belly, dipping her tongue into her belly button, before plunging down.

She trailed her tongue just above the waistband of Olivia's boy shorts, then lifted it a fraction to plant one teasing kiss on her curly hair there.

Olivia's fingertips pushed into the flesh of Rosie's shoulders and she relished the touch. It spurred her on to continue downwards. Over the fabric of her underwear, she planted wet kisses on Olivia's lower lips. Olivia's hips rocked up and Rosie got the message loud and clear.

She rose and slid Olivia's shorts off her, baring her. Olivia reached for Rosie's behind and started to pull down her undies. Someone was impatient.

"I want you," Olivia said, her voice ragged.

Rosie got rid of her underwear and shuffled closer to Olivia. Olivia grabbed her by the hips and moved underneath Rosie, pulling her down. Rosie's clit pulsed as Olivia's hot breath tickled her sex.

When Rosie looked down, Olivia was spread out before her. A tingle of lust started at the base of her spine and travelled all the way up. Rosie lowered her head. She wanted Olivia to feel the same delicious sensation of hot breath between her legs.

But the sweet hotness of Olivia's breath was already being replaced by a different kind of heat. Wet and insistent, Olivia's tongue swept over Rosie's pussy and Rosie had to use all her strength to not crash through her arms.

At the same time, the gush of desire engulfing her encouraged her to mirror Olivia's actions. She hunkered all the way down and pressed her lips against Olivia's sex. She inhaled her and as Olivia's tongue swept over her, Rosie gave into her own desire to do the same. She slid her tongue between Olivia's lips and sucked Olivia's clit into her mouth.

The simultaneous sensation of feeling Olivia's tongue while her own was tasting all of Olivia's goodness proved too much for Rosie's flimsy stamina. She'd wanted Olivia all over her — and now she had her. All her wants and needs were being met — and then some.

Rosie tried to give as good as she was getting, even as she felt the beginnings of her climax take root deep inside of her. That delicious warmth travelled to the surface, until it burst out of her. Olivia's one hand was clasped around her thigh while the other... Oh, a finger at her entrance. Olivia slid it deep inside of Rosie while her tongue flicked over her clit.

"Oh god," Rosie moaned. There was no stopping this any longer — and why would she want to stop it anyway? She'd waited for her princess long enough.

An orgasm ripped through her like a shooting star. She did crash through her arms then, her cheek falling onto Olivia's belly. Olivia's finger kept moving inside her, her tongue swiping back and forth. However this princess didn't seem to get satisfaction from delivering only one climax — maybe princesses had higher standards than most.

Rosie clenched her hands around Olivia's strong thighs, bracing herself as yet another wave of pleasure washed over her. She lay panting on Olivia's belly, giving herself totally up to her.

When she came to, Rosie could barely shuffle off of Olivia's body. It was Olivia who manoeuvred from underneath her and crawled up to her, then cradled her in her arms.

"Jesus Christ," Rosie said. "You didn't give me any chance."

"You'll get plenty of chances." Olivia held Rosie tight to her chest.

Rosie could hear her heart thumping wildly.

"I might not have been in the army, but I have a code of honour too." Rosie kissed the curve of Olivia's upper arm before freeing herself from her embrace and pushing her down.

"I have zero objections," Olivia said, a wide grin on her face.

"Good." Rosie kissed Olivia on the lips, then made her way down again, adamant that her second attempt at pleasing the princess would not be so easily thwarted.

CHAPTER 31

⚜

Olivia woke the next morning and took a moment to acclimatise. White walls adorned with a framed world map, clothes all over the floor, the satisfying twang of under-used muscles in her groin... Oh yes, it was all coming back to her now — she'd had minimal sleep after a night in Rosie's double bed. She rolled over and nuzzled the back of Rosie's neck, receiving a muffled groan into the pillow in return. Olivia slung an arm around her lover's waist and pulled her close, luxuriating in their closeness, breathing in her smell. When she licked the back of her neck, she tasted of salt and sex; Olivia emitted a satisfied sigh as a smile took over her face.

"Someone's feeling pretty invincible this morning?" Rosie's voice was still muffled.

Olivia wriggled closer. "Invincible and a little broken," she replied. "But I like feeling broken, especially by you."

Rosie rolled over and cracked open an eye. "A broken princess — that could be the title of a very sad romantic movie."

Olivia grinned. "Maybe that can be your next career —

screenwriter, breaking all the royal secrets one film at a time. You'd have a string of directors queueing up to work with you."

"Are you sure your family would approve of that? Wouldn't I get sent to the Tower or something?"

A fleeting image of her mother's reaction skated through her mind, and Olivia shook her head. "Let's just say, my mother is an acquired taste. I'm still not there yet." She kissed Rosie's shoulder. "But I'll pull some strings to make sure you don't end up in the Tower."

"Thanks," Rosie said, twisting now, and placing a kiss on Olivia's lips. "Morning, by the way."

A grin, followed by a surge inside. Yes, they might have been up all night, but staring down at Rosie's naked breasts, Olivia just wanted more. "Morning." She kissed her lips, then her perfectly full breasts. And then her phone buzzed, making Olivia cringe and flop onto her back. "I'd better get this, I promised Penelope I would."

"Penelope?"

"Palace press officer."

Rosie bit her bottom lip. "Right."

Olivia grabbed her phone, before sitting up in bed, pulling up the blue-and-white striped duvet. "Don't look so worried, you haven't done anything wrong."

Rosie frowned. "It feels like I have — I am involved in this."

"Yes, but this is on me. I want you to know I'm going to keep you out of this for as long as I can. We might have to lie low for a bit, but I'll sort it out. And remember — the press can speculate all they like, but until we confirm it, it's not the truth. First rule of dealing with them: nothing looks as guilty as a denial, so the best thing to do is smile and say nothing."

Rosie nodded, looking unconvinced. "I have a lot to learn."

Olivia sucked on the inside of her cheek; she wanted to reassure Rosie, but she could only go so far. This was all new territory for her, too, and she knew the ride would be bumpy before it began to get better. She put her phone back on the bedside table and lay down, with Rosie scooching in beside her, laying her head on Olivia's shoulder. Olivia would have been content to lie there all day, just like this. This was the window into the other life she wanted, and it was already so tantalising, she could taste the sweetness on her tongue.

"Do you have to go today?"

Olivia exhaled. "I do — got to go and face the music once the news is out. I should really be on the road by eleven." She stroked a hand through Rosie's hair, soft and dark gold. "I wish I didn't have to go, but this will all calm down soon. It's just the first hit that will be hard."

"I know," Rosie said, kissing her collarbone.

Even that slight touch sent a rocket of want through Olivia, and she kissed Rosie's hair. "But before I do — what are you cooking me for breakfast?"

The sound of Paige swearing loudly somewhere in the flat made them both smile.

"Is she okay?" Olivia asked.

"She's probably just late and being her usual morning self — Hilary's opening up the cafe, and Paige said she'd give her a hand." Rosie wriggled upwards. "I better just go and check."

Rosie jumped out of bed, before turning back and scurrying over to Olivia on all fours.

"I thought you were going?" But Olivia wasn't complaining one bit.

"You're too delicious to leave," Rosie said, eyeing her suggestively. "But I hope you'll take pity on your subject and come back to fuck her again soon?"

Olivia growled and pulled her down, making Rosie shriek as she toppled onto her in a heap. "For you, I'll make a special exception."

Rosie kissed her again before clambering off the bed,

putting on some denim shorts and a blue T-shirt and running a brush through her hair.

Olivia sighed. "You look sexy as hell, you know that."

Rosie blushed. "Get up, princess, and I'll make you some toast."

Olivia gave her a salute as she left the bedroom, before throwing on yesterday's clothes and following Rosie. Somehow, even being in a different room from her felt all wrong. Even as that thought ran through her mind, she wanted to slap herself. She really needed to get a grip, especially if she was doing a press conference with Jemima later.

That thought slowed her progress in the hallway as she heard Paige and Rosie's chatter from the kitchen.

She had to push that aside: this morning was for her and Rosie and nobody else.

"Morning," Olivia said as she walked into the kitchen, giving Paige a grin as she sat down opposite her, banging her shoulder on the bright yellow wall as she did. The kitchen was just about big enough for a small wooden table shoved up against a wall with three chairs, but Olivia was impressed at how homely it felt, with posters on the walls and kitchen gadgets the colour of sunshine everywhere she looked.

"Morning," Paige said, her cheeks colouring red.

Rosie spun round and gave Olivia a smile that could have stopped traffic. "Tea or coffee?"

"Tea would be great," Olivia replied, as toast popped from a yellow toaster on the counter.

Rosie fished it out, swearing at the heat before flinging it onto a plate and placing it in front of Olivia. A tub of Utterly Butterly and a jar of marmalade already sat on the table, a trail of crumbs in the spread showing Paige had got there first.

When Rosie brought their teas seconds later and sat down — leaning in to give Olivia a peck on the lips — she looked at her breakfast companions before raising a single eyebrow.

"What's going on — why is nobody talking?"

Paige chewed on her toast, looking down, avoiding eye contact.

Rosie reached over and nudged her. "What's the matter with you?"

Panic ran across her sister's features as she shook her head. "Nothing," she said, before pointing. "It's just… we've got a princess at our table and she's eating toast and marmalade." Her tone was incredulous. "I mean, that isn't normal, surely? Don't you usually have something posher? Caviar on toast at least?"

Olivia's face cracked a smile. "Not really — my mother has toast and marmalade every morning. Kind of a royal tradition."

Paige dropped her toast. "Your mum being… the Queen." More head shaking.

"Last time I looked, yes."

Rosie slapped Paige on the arm. "Stop being so rude. Just because she's royal doesn't mean she doesn't like normal food."

"My mother's favourite meal, in fact, is fish and chips," Olivia said, nodding to back up her claim. "But she can never have it at banquets — she always has to have venison or monkfish. But give her cod and chips any day." Olivia wasn't lying — although her mother's watchful eye on her waistline also prevented her from indulging too often. Whereas Olivia would rather eat and work it off. She hoped with Rosie in her life, those workouts were only going to get more frequent and more strenuous.

Paige's mouth dropped open at that before she frowned. "Are you winding me up?"

"No!" Olivia crossed her finger over her chest. "I swear on my sister's life."

"And she likes her sister, so no more quizzing her. Let Olivia eat her toast in peace." Rosie gave Paige a look and Olivia knew that would be the end of it. She'd been on the receiving end of that look enough from Alexandra. Did they teach it at big sister school?

Paige shoved the last of the toast in her mouth and scraped her chair back, gulping down her tea. "Better go, otherwise Aunt Hilary will be moaning at me, too." She gave Rosie a sly grin, before sloping out of the room.

"Paige!"

She popped her head back around the corner, her dark hair hanging in her eyes.

"Say goodbye to Olivia — she's back off to London today."

Paige gave her a wave. "See you soon?"

Olivia nodded. "I'll be back — and I can give you the lowdown on Durham if you like."

Paige grinned. "That would be awesome!" Then she disappeared, the front door slamming minutes later.

"You've done a brilliant job with her, you know — you should be so proud." Olivia leaned over and gave Rosie a sticky kiss on the lips. When she pulled back, they stayed staring into each other's eyes for a few beats, and Olivia's heart swelled. It wasn't going to be easy to leave again, but at least this time, it wasn't for long.

"Where are we going travelling, anyway?" Her gaze never left Rosie, and she never wanted it to. It seemed insane that she'd even entertained marrying someone else in four weeks' time, but she had. Still, after today, that would be old news. In a few weeks, she'd introduce the world to Rosie, the woman she really loved.

"The question is more where aren't we going. Europe, South East Asia, Australia and New Zealand for starters. Gina told me we have to go to visit her family in Argentina, but I don't know if I have the budget or the time to stretch to South America, but we'll see." Rosie sipped her tea, staring at Olivia. "Are you really coming with me?"

Olivia nodded. "I really am." She couldn't imagine a life

without Rosie anymore. More to the point, having lived without her for the past few weeks, she was determined it wasn't going to happen again.

"Does that mean I might have to change where I stay? I'm guessing you're not really a hostel kinda girl." Rosie crossed her right leg over her left as she spoke.

"How about you choose where you want to go and let me take care of the travel and accommodation. We might have to alter a few things, but if we're savvy, we can still fly under the radar. So long as you're happy with me wearing my glasses again, no make-up and you get to call me Charlie."

A wide grin stretched over Rosie's face as she got up, slinging an arm around Olivia's neck and sitting in her lap. "I get to travel with you and I get the old Charlie back? The one who charmed me with her gorgeous smile and seduced me on a kitchen table? This trip is sounding more and more inviting by the second."

Olivia wrapped an arm around her waist and squeezed her tight, holding Rosie's sapphire stare before replying. "Stick with me, and I guarantee a wild ride."

CHAPTER 32

Olivia shook her head again as the engine sputtered. They'd said their goodbyes. Olivia was going back to London to deal with the press and the subsequent fallout of cancelling a royal wedding. But the car gods were plotting against her.

Olivia opened the car window. "Looks like the car is voting to stay in Otter Bay."

"Instant coffee and cars that don't start." Rosie was glad to have Olivia with her a few moments longer. "Royal standards are beginning to slip."

Olivia gave it a few more tries, but the engine refused to come alive. "You don't happen to have car repair skills as well, do you?" Olivia said on a sigh. "Mother's going to kill me if I'm late for this press conference."

"It goes against all stereotypes, but I'm no good with cars," Rosie said. She pointed at her Toyota. "I would offer mine, but I'm not sure it'll get you where you need to be in one piece."

Olivia got out of the car. She checked the time on her phone. "I'll have to take the train instead."

"I'll take you to the station," Rosie said, and took the opportunity to draw Olivia into another good-bye hug.

~

The car shuddered as they turned into the station's parking lot.

"Your royal behind's not suffering too much?" Rosie asked.

Olivia shook her head. "And to think I truly believed I was past the age of being teased about my pedigree."

Rosie put a hand on Olivia's knee. "I wasn't teasing. It's genuine concern." Just then, the car bumped savagely. "Oops. Didn't see that pothole. Do you have any contacts in the Otter Bay council? That has been here forever."

Olivia rubbed her back in an exaggerated fashion. "Do you know the penalties for hurting a princess?"

Rosie parked the car and looked at her. "Nope. But I do hope the punishment is doled out by the princess herself."

"Wait until I get back. I'll show you then. Or…" Olivia looked at her watch. "My train doesn't arrive for another fifteen minutes. I could show you now."

Rosie glanced around the car park. "Just making sure the coast is clear."

Olivia grinned, then fell back against her seat with a sigh.

Rosie put her hand back where it had slid off earlier. "Not looking forward to going back?"

"It's not every day I have to face the press and tell them the royal wedding they've been going nuts over for weeks is being cancelled." She put her hand over Rosie's. "Even though it's being cancelled for the best possible reason."

Rosie scanned Olivia's face. In the beat-up car, with her hair rioting in all directions, she looked decidedly un-royal. She looked like Charlie. "Come back soon."

Olivia nodded. "Shall we get out? I'm a little antsy and I'll be stuck on a train for the next few hours."

"With a bunch of commoners," Rosie joked. She gave Olivia's knee one last squeeze and opened the door. "I don't envy you."

"You were much nicer to me before you knew who my mother was." Olivia grabbed Rosie's hand and they walked to the empty platform.

"Falling in love with a princess has taken its toll." Rosie gave Olivia a quick peck on the cheek, lest she think she wasn't joking. Rosie scanned their surroundings. There was no one on the platform yet, but other passengers would soon be arriving. "Come with me," she said.

Rosie led them past the waiting room, around the corner of the station's building. "We should have some privacy here."

Olivia nodded and stood in front of Rosie. "About what you said earlier." She drew her lips into a small smile. "Being with me will come with challenges, there's just no other way." She inclined her head. "Please know you can talk to me about anything. It's important that we do."

"I guess my days of going out in faded jeans are over," Rosie said.

"It's not all about appearances." Olivia paused. "Well, a lot of it is."

"If there's one thing I've learned during my short twenty-eight years on this planet, it's that we can't look into the future. It's best to take the days as they come, deal with what needs to be dealt with, and get on with things."

"You're wise beyond your twenty-eight years, Rosie Perkins." Olivia stepped closer. "My family could use some of your wisdom."

"I want to be with you," Rosie said. "So I'll focus on the positives of dating a royal." She looked into the distance for a brief moment, letting her mind wander.

The past two days had been a whirlwind of emotions. She'd gone all the way from heartbreak to this madness. When she brought her gaze back to Olivia, whose pretty face she was going to miss — although she'd be seeing her on the evening news, no doubt — she remembered the last time she'd been at the train station.

"Remember when we first met?" Rosie said.

"Of course, at the cafe. You warned me about Connie. I'll never forget." The grin on Olivia's face betrayed that she knew exactly what Rosie was getting at.

"You almost ran me over at this station and I remember thinking you were just another rude Londoner in an expensive jacket, coming down here to annoy us locals."

"I believe I've succeeded in my mission and have sufficiently annoyed you." Olivia kissed Rosie on the nose.

"You just swung by and changed my life in the process." Warmth bloomed in Rosie's chest.

"How do you think of me now?" Olivia asked.

"As a rude, very posh Londoner," Rosie joked. She threw her arms around Olivia. "*My* rude, very posh Londoner."

"What will it take to make you drop the rude?" Olivia whispered in her ear.

"You're calling off a royal wedding," Rosie said. "That should do it." She pushed her nose into Olivia's neck.

They stood in silence for a few beats, then Olivia pulled herself back from their embrace.

"I could also… not call it off," she said.

"What?" Rosie's brow furrowed in alarm.

"I could still get married… but to someone else." Olivia's green eyes sparked with mischief. "Someone I'm madly in love with. Someone who has changed my life as well — for the better." Olivia squared her shoulders and took a deep breath. "I've never wanted the life that was laid out for me. I always thought coming out as a lesbian would be the hardest thing I'd have to do as a member of the royal family, but it was a piece of cake compared to the life my parents have tried to push me into. While I'm so very close to what I really want. A simple life with the woman I love. With you."

Rosie opened her mouth to speak, but nothing came out.

"When we come back from our travels, we can live in the manor house. You can be close to your family and I can be at a comfortable distance from mine." Olivia threw in a smile. Her eyes still shone. Rosie was getting caught up in her enthusiasm.

Butterflies went wild in Rosie's stomach. "Are you sure about this?"

"I've never been more sure of anything in my life." A smile spread over Olivia's face, before she sank down to one knee. "There's a wedding planned in four weeks' time. I love you, Rosie." She swallowed hard. "You would be my perfect bride."

Rosie's jaw slackened. Was this really happening? Was Princess Olivia proposing to her at Otter Bay train station? She looked down at Olivia, whose face was the very image of hope — and perhaps a little anguish.

Rosie's mind raced, but did she really have to think about this? Olivia was the best thing that had happened to her in… her entire life. Rosie loved her and if she'd ever imagined a perfect bride for herself, Olivia would have fit that image like no other.

Rosie started nodding, slowly at first. The intensity of her nodding increased as the smile on her lips spread. She kneeled next to Olivia.

"Yes," she said. "I think you're crazy, but my answer is yes."

Olivia cupped Rosie's face in her palms and kissed her full on the lips. When they broke from their kiss, she said, "I don't have a ring."

"You mean this wasn't planned?" Rosie gazed into Olivia's eyes.

"Nothing about you was ever planned." Olivia kissed her again.

"I do think we should plan to get up now." Rosie held Olivia tight for one more moment. "You don't want to miss that train."

They rose only to fall into each other's arms again. In the distance, Rosie could hear the rumble of the approaching train.

"Here's another unplanned question for you," Olivia said, eyes glinting.

"Be still my quiet Cornish heart." Rosie held on tightly to Olivia's hand.

"How about you get on that train with me and meet your future family-in-law?"

Rosie burst out into a chuckle. "I don't even have a ticket. Or a change of underwear."

"This is where the perks kick in." Olivia winked at her. The train rolled into the station with a loud hiss of brakes. "What do you say?"

"I say yes. Again." Rosie flew into Olivia's arms.

"I'm sure we can rustle you up a clean pair of knickers." Olivia shuddered with giggles as she hugged her firmly.

CHAPTER 33

"Olivia, this way! Rosie, could you turn a little to your left?"

Olivia glanced at Rosie out of the corner of her eye, mouthing "Are you okay?" as she squeezed her hand tight. They were standing in the grounds of her estate, just as she and Jemima had a little over three months ago. Olivia would be lying if she said she wasn't amazed at how much her life had turned around since then, because it had. She remembered that day with Jemima so well: the bright blue skies, her brittle smile, the clouds in her heart. But today, all of that had changed — and that was thanks to Rosie. Her new fiancée — her first proper fiancée as she kept saying — had taken so much onboard since they'd agreed to marry, but this was their first official press conference together. The one where they stood side by side and announced their engagement, officially.

Olivia was beyond proud of how Rosie was coping, and also of how she looked in her sleek, raspberry-coloured dress with cream heels and matching jacket. Rosie had seemed to sense this was needed for today, and she'd gone along with the royal dressers without complaint, accepting their clothing recommendations and sending photos to Paige, who declared her sister 'not half bad — decent, even'. They'd both laughed at that.

But Paige was right, and every time Olivia looked at Rosie, she was wowed all over again. Far from looking like a local from a Cornish village, as Rosie had been worried about, she looked every inch a future royal bride. Olivia couldn't have been prouder to have her by her side.

"Olivia, is it true you sang Lorde's *Royals* on the night you got engaged?"

"Rosie, can you tell us the full story of how Olivia proposed? We've heard it was because you fed her every day at your cafe?"

Rosie appeared steady, but Olivia could feel the tremble in her body as she stood smiling at the cameras. She put a hand on her back to reassure her and took control.

"I think you'll find I did a more than passable karaoke version of that song, but no, I didn't use it to propose — that would be cheesy in the extreme." Olivia paused for maximum effect as the cameras whirred and lenses zoomed in on her. "Don't get me wrong, I can be cheesy — Rosie will tell you that — but not when it comes to proposals. Let's just say, I proposed in Otter Bay, and I hope it's where we're going to set up home eventually, once we're back from our travels."

"Will you be using the same wedding cake you had made for you and Jemima, Olivia?"

Okay, that was a question too far — they'd been told not to bring up Jemima. "This wedding is brand-new, and everything about it will be, too." This time, Olivia's tone held steel. "It's going to be a much smaller affair, so the size of the cake will not be important." With that, she squeezed Rosie's hand and they began walking up the path back towards the estate.

"You okay?" Olivia whispered, putting a guiding hand on Rosie's back. She knew that would be an image pored over in the *Mail On Sunday* this weekend: 'A hand on Rosie's back — we ask our body language expert to reveal its hidden meaning'.

"Just concentrating on not falling over before we get through the gate," Rosie replied, keeping her eyes focussed forward.

"If you fall, I'll catch you," Olivia replied. They reached the black wooden gate and it opened — Olivia's housekeeper, Anna, was waiting for them.

Rosie almost fell through it, before leaning over, hands on thighs like she'd just run a marathon.

Olivia smiled, rubbing her back. She understood, although dealing with the press was second nature for her, seeing as she'd been doing it all her life.

"You poor thing, can I get you something? A glass of water?" Anna was fussing, as Rosie came upright.

"That'd be great, thank you," she replied, as Anna scurried off.

"Your number one fan comes to your rescue," Olivia said, smiling. Ever since they'd got back to London two weeks ago, Anna had been incredible with Rosie, making her feel at home in the estate right away.

"I was hoping you were my number one fan," Rosie replied, cocking her head.

Olivia licked her lips as she wound an arm around Rosie's waist, pulling her close until her lips were in kissing distance. "I am, but I know how to make you feel better without the aid of water," she replied, pressing her lips to Rosie's, kissing her softly. When she pulled back, Olivia shook her head, staring into Rosie's crystal blue eyes. "I don't know what I did to deserve you, but you were amazing out there."

Rosie winced. "Really? I wasn't too stiff? Because it felt like I was." She kissed her again. "I don't know how you do this all the time."

Olivia smiled. "It's what I'm used to — I couldn't run a cafe, but you can, it's what you're used to."

"Not anymore," Rosie replied, untangling herself from Olivia. She frowned before continuing. "Did your mother get back to you on a title, by the way? I still think the Duchess of Bath is a bit much — it's just little old me, I don't really need a city with a massive cathedral. Duchess of Otter Bay would do me fine…" Then she grinned. "Actually, Duchess of Otter Bay would be brilliant, it would piss Amy right off."

Olivia let out a bark of laughter at that. "I thought you and Amy had buried the hatchet and were getting on fine now?"

Rosie shrugged a single shoulder. "We are, but it's still nice to wind her up occasionally." She grinned. "She's been texting me a lot since we announced the engagement, though — I think she's angling for an invite."

"If you want her there, she can come. Just so long as she knows she's not running the karaoke at the reception."

"There's going to be karaoke at the reception?" Rosie's tone was aghast.

Olivia leaned in and put her mouth next to Rosie's ear. "That was a joke."

"Good," Rosie replied, looking relieved. "By the way, I got another text from Aunt Hilary this morning — Connie is offering to give us a discount if we buy our wedding outfits from her boutique. So long as we then let the world know we bought them from her." Rosie was already laughing. "I told Aunt Hilary to let her down gently."

Olivia grinned, glancing at Rosie. Sometimes, she had to stop and remind herself this was really happening, that the world had rolled in her favour for once. Often, though, she still couldn't believe her luck. "You know, if Connie hadn't scared me into running into your cafe, our story might never have happened, so I'll always have a special place in my heart for Connie."

"Enough to buy clothes from her?"

"Let's not take it too far." Olivia shook her head. "I don't much care what we wear for our wedding, so long as we have one." Her words had never been truer as she looked up into the overcast August sky. "Although my mother might throw a hissy fit."

However, even the Queen had come around to the new status quo over these past two weeks, thanks to Alexandra and her grandmother having words, as well as Rosie being charming. Rosie had been so nervous when Olivia had introduced her to her parents, but she'd kept it together and made it through with flying colours — her mother even telling Olivia she could "see the appeal". Olivia had almost fallen over backwards when she'd heard that.

It hadn't surprised her, though. Because having Rosie here these past two weeks had seen Olivia's life fall into place with a satisfying click. With Rosie by her side, there were no ifs, and no buts, there just was. The two of them were made for each other, and when her parents had realised that, they'd come around. Now, far from being the outsider, in just two short weeks Rosie had managed to charm the queen far more than Jemima ever had. And, now that Olivia's mother had been convinced Rosie wasn't an undercover spy sent from Otter Bay to dish the dirt on the royals, she'd begun to relax.

Anna clearing her throat drew Olivia's attention away from Rosie. "Madam, sorry to disturb you." Anna held out a glass of water to Rosie before addressing Olivia. "But your sister's here, and your parents, too. Shall I show them out?"

Olivia frowned. Her sister and her parents? What on earth were they doing here? "Absolutely," she replied.

Rosie gulped the water, then gave it to Olivia, pulling down her dress and brushing down the front of her. "Do I look okay? I'm not sure when I'll ever get over the fact your sister is

Princess Alexandra and your parents are the Queen and Prince Hugo."

"They still have to pee and they both eat marmalade at breakfast — just remember that," Olivia said, taking her hand in hers again.

Feet crunching on gravel made Olivia look up, and sure enough, her parents and her sister were walking towards them, smiles plastered on their faces.

Hang on a minute — was this a moment of family unity? If it was, Olivia wasn't sure she could quite compute it — mainly because she'd never seen one before. Over their shoulder, she saw Anna approaching carrying a tray of champagne.

"What's all this?" Olivia eyed Alexandra.

"Surprise!" her sister replied, hugging first Olivia, then Rosie. "I thought, because this was such an auspicious occasion — your proper engagement and Rosie's first press conference — we should celebrate." She winked. "Anna was in on the surprise, getting the champagne chilled."

A warmth spread through Olivia as she took a glass and passed it to Rosie, before picking one up for herself. "I don't know what to say." And she didn't. Her family normally left her speechless for the wrong reasons, never for the right ones.

"And you did brilliantly, my dear. A natural in front of the cameras," her father told Rosie.

Rosie dipped her chin to her chest, her cheeks turning pink. "I didn't fall over, and that's the main thing."

Olivia put an arm around Rosie's shoulder, raising her glass in the other. "I'd like to propose a toast. To Rosie joining our family, and to us having the best wedding ever." She glanced at Rosie. "I already know it will be, because I've got the perfect woman to be my bride."

"To you and Rosie!" Alexandra chorused.

The Queen raised her glass. "To you both."

Olivia kissed Rosie's cheek. "I'll drink to that."

CLARE'S ACKNOWLEDGMENTS

Comfort zones are strange things, aren't they? I mean, in one way, they're GREAT, because they're dead comfy. But if you never move out of them, you'll never experience anything new, you'll never grow, and you'll never be able to answer the question: what if?

When Harper first contacted me to ask if I fancied co-writing a book, my first thought was, "Are you bonkers? No!" Co-writing was for other authors, and it was *way* outside my comfort zone. However, I didn't hit reply straight away. Instead, I thought about it, and realised this was SO outside my comfort zone, I should do it. So I said yes, with the proviso that I might cry. She told me that she might, too. From that moment on, we were in it together – and I'm so glad we did it!

I loved writing the story of Olivia and Rosie, but most of all, I loved having a partner in crime. Writing is a solitary job, but co-writing turns it into a swashbuckling adventure.

So first up, thanks to Harper for making it so easy. Thanks for cheering me on, for trusting in the story, and for pushing me out of my comfort zone. I jumped with my eyes closed, but the landing was expert! Thanks also to Caroline (her Mrs) for the fab cover and great title; and to Cheyenne for stellar Aussie-flavoured editing.

Gold stars all round to our first readers, Tammara and Sophie, who gave great feedback and assured us we'd written a good book. That was a relief to hear! Also, to my intrepid band of early readers for your enthusiasm and encouragement – you're all fab!

As always, thanks to you for reading – I hope you enjoyed this royal romp! Having you in my corner means the world - so have a virtual hug from me.

Finally, much love to my wife, Yvonne, for being my biggest cheerleader every day – your constant support underpins my success. And it wasn't as painful as you thought in the end, was it?

HARPER'S ACKNOWLEDGMENTS

Whenever I heard authors talk about co-writing, I always automatically dismissed it as 'definitely not suitable for my personality'. Then, also true to character, on a whim I decided to ask Clare Lydon, who I barely knew back then but had always had a good feeling about, how she felt about co-writing. The rest is history. It was a long road, because the idea for co-writing was born more than a year ago, but in the end, it turned out to be one of the best things I've ever done.

Co-writing with the right author creates an addictive bubble of productivity and momentum. Of course, I had rough days, but turns out it's much easier to weather them when your co-author is waiting for your next chapter. I'm very proud to say I didn't miss a single day of scheduled first-draft writing (neither did Clare!), something that has never happened to me before.

I started my writing days of Once Upon a Princess with reading how the story had progressed while I was sleeping--a particularly magical and satisfying experience. Since I started working with my wife years ago, I've been very aware that when it comes to good collaborations, one plus one equals much more than two. Not only did I have double word counts at the end of each day, but there was also the cheerleading, the sharing of writerly woes, and just having a bit of a chat and a laugh.

All of this to thank my co-writer, Clare Lydon, from the bottom of my heart. I was so nervous before I started, you'd think I'd never written a book before in my life. But sharing a first draft with someone I instinctively knew I could trust has changed my process for the better and, perhaps, forever. Thanks for taking the leap with me, Clare!

I also owe a massive thank-you to my wife, Caroline, for being there when the nerves got the better of me and assuring me that I wasn't as shitty as I thought I was during those moments. She also made the most perfect cover, came up with the title and the tagline, and did all the other behind-the-scenes work that mostly goes unnoticed.

Thank you, also, to Cheyenne Blue, our wise-cracking editor extraordinaire, who has worked on so many of my books now, she knows my style better than I do. Cheyenne is always someone I can count on but this time she went the extra mile when she agreed to our crazy schedule to get this book ready for release a few days after the royal wedding.

Thanking Clare and Cheyenne makes me realize how lucky I am to be able to work, almost 100% online, with people I can trust. Writerly camaraderie is not something I'm naturally good at, but they both make it so easy for me.

Thank you to beta-readers Carrie and Sophie. Sending a book off to a first reader (who I'm not married to) is always nerve-wracking, but you made it a joy.

Thank you also to my Launch Team for the continued enthusiasm, the last-minute typo-hunting, and the reviews that help my books so much.

Thank you to our proofreader Claire who has turned into an indispensable part of the intricate publication process puzzle. Thank you for stepping up in those last frantic days before release and making the book shine.

Of course, as always, thank *you*, Dear Reader! It's inevitable that this book is a little different than what you usually read from me, but I hope the joy I experienced while co-writing it leapt off the page. I can already tell you that this will most definitely not be my last co-written book!

ABOUT THE AUTHORS

Clare Lydon is a London-based writer of contemporary lesbian romance. She's a No.1 best-seller on lesbian fiction charts around the globe, and if you're a sucker for romance, prepare to fall head over heels in love.

When she's not writing, Clare enjoys playing the guitar badly, watching far too many home improvement shows and eating Curly Wurlys. In her next life, she'd like to come back as Rayna James. (RIP, sob!)

You can get in touch with her here:

www.clarelydon.co.uk
mail@clarelydon.co.uk

Harper Bliss is the author of the *Pink Bean* series, the *High Rise* series, the *French Kissing* serial and many other lesbian romance titles. She is the co-founder of Ladylit Publishing and My LesFic weekly newsletter.

Harper loves hearing from readers and you can get in touch with her here:

www.harperbliss.com
harperbliss@gmail.com

Ingram Content Group UK Ltd.
Milton Keynes UK
UKHW011255040423
419631UK00001B/155